RACHEL ELLIOTT ~~~~~~~ ~~~~ ~~~~~~ ~~ ~~~~~~ ~~~ough a *Megaphone*, longlisted for the Women's Prize for Fiction 2016. She is also a psychotherapist, and lives in Bath.

Praise for Do Not Feed the Bear

'I was delighted and surprised by this textured, fascinating and most moving book'   CHRIS WARE

'Rachel Elliott is such a beguiling and astute storyteller'
SARAH WINMAN

'An astonishingly good novel about grief and its shadowy partner, guilt. Mysterious, uplifting, and often very funny, it had me totally gripped from start to finish'
DEBORAH MOGGACH

'Beautifully written, Elliott's unique, mesmerising voice effortlessly draws you in'   *Woman & Home*

'Utterly uplifting and a warm reminder that people are here to help'   *Stylist*

'A moving and gently humorous portrait of loss, grief and finding a way through . . . Wonderfully redemptive'
SARAH HAYWOOD, author of *The Cactus*

'[An] ingenious, funny novel . . . Sad, wise and upbeat by turns'
                                                    Daily Mail

'There is love and pain and such humour. The author is a psychotherapist with the key to the human heart'
                                                    Saga Magazine

'A slow-burn, quirky, rewarding story about a group of bereft people (and dogs) who find each other in unexpected ways'
                                                    JULIE COHEN

'A beautifully poignant tale about loss, love, compassion, and being kind to people whose stories and struggles – in the past and present – are overlooked'
                                                    Culturefly

'An uplifting and heart-warming tale about love, loss and moving on, and the importance of being kind to each other – and ourselves'
                                                    Heat

'A perfect read for fans of *Eleanor Oliphant* and *The Trouble With Goats And Sheep*'
                                                    Woman's Way

RACHEL ELLIOTT

DO NOT FEED THE BEAR

TINDER
PRESS

Copyright © 2019 Rachel Elliott

The right of Rachel Elliott to be identified as the Author of
the Work has been asserted by her in accordance with the
Copyright, Designs and Patents Act 1988.

First published in 2019 by Tinder Press
An imprint of HEADLINE PUBLISHING GROUP

First published in paperback in 2020 by Tinder Press
An imprint of HEADLINE PUBLISHING GROUP

1

Apart from any use permitted under UK copyright law, this publication may
only be reproduced, stored, or transmitted, in any form, or by any means,
with prior permission in writing of the publishers or, in the case of
reprographic production, in accordance with the terms of licences
issued by the Copyright Licensing Agency.

All characters in this publication are fictitious and any resemblance
to real persons, living or dead, is purely coincidental.

Cataloguing in Publication Data is available from the British Library

ISBN 978 1 4722 5942 4

Designed and typeset by EM&EN
Printed and bound in Great Britain by Clays Ltd, Elcograf S.p.A.

Headline's policy is to use papers that are natural, renewable and recyclable
products and made from wood grown in well-managed forests and other
controlled sources. The logging and manufacturing processes are expected
to conform to the environmental regulations of the country of origin.

HEADLINE PUBLISHING GROUP
An Hachette UK Company
Carmelite House
50 Victoria Embankment
London EC4Y 0DZ

www.tinderpress.co.uk
www.headline.co.uk
www.hachette.co.uk

For Doris

Contents

Did you never feel like dancing with joy,
like moving where your body wanted to move,
like leaping?

PART ONE

PART ONE

1

Call it what you like, it still stinks

I am eight years old when I see a dead body for the first time. Mum is leading me through Flannery's, the department store we visit every summer. Before we find the dead body, we have to buy Dad a birthday present.

I've got it, Mum says. Driving gloves, she says.

These words set off an intense decision-making process that will last fifty-three minutes.

We stand in front of a long glass counter, staring at five pairs of leather driving gloves, all of which cost more than Mum would like to pay.

Around the block? she says. Which is her secret code for *I think we need a private talk*. In this particular case, it means *let's walk a while so we can discuss our decision*:

black versus brown

stylish versus warm in all temperatures

longevity versus low initial investment

or, shall we just make him an origami owl?

or, shall we just make him a mushroom quiche?

We stroll through a jungle of lingerie, and I listen to all this without interrupting.

We pass the elevator, and a man pops out from nowhere, pointing a bottle of scent in our direction.

Absolutely not, Mum says, holding up her hand.

It's jasmine and iris, the man says.

I doubt that very much, Mum says. It's all artificial, and it probably contains horse's urine.

I'm sure it doesn't, the man says.

It's not your fault. You're just earning a living.

I am deeply embarrassed. This is not the first time she has spoken about horse's urine in public.

Mum? I say.

Sydney, she says.

What does horse's urine actually smell like?

Like jasmine and iris. And I don't want it in your lungs, it may never come out.

I am baffled.

Now we are back at the long glass counter, staring at the gloves.

Hello again, the shop assistant says. Any closer to making a decision?

Mum takes a sharp breath in, as if she's about to speak.

Nothing.

Oh dear, she finally says.

The shop assistant smiles. Her name is Vita, it says so on the name tag pinned to her silk blouse. Vita's hair is deeply perplexing. To me, it looks like a black helmet has fallen from outer space and landed on her head. It's perfectly round, with a straight fringe that dips into her eyes. Blocky, that's the word. I don't know this word yet, but I will use it later when I am remembering the dead body and telling Ruth all about it.

I inspect the helmet for antennae, for alien surveillance technology. No, nothing obvious here. Just immaculate shiny plastic. Disappointing and pleasing, all at once.

You look like one of my Playmobil people, I say. You have the exact same hair.

Is that a good thing or a bad thing? Vita says.

Sensing a loaded question, I look at Mum.

Oh she *loves* Playmobil people, Mum says. She ties string around their waists and makes them abseil down the side of buildings. We're off to look for a cowboy in a minute.

Lovely, Vita says. She looks down at the gloves. So are these for yourself? she asks.

Well no, Mum says. Because they're men's gloves aren't they?

That's right, Vita says, aware that she has swerved off track, deviated from the script.

Okay, Mum says.

She is stressed, which often happens when she is about to spend money. I stand on tiptoe, and all three of us stare at the gloves as if we are waiting for them to do something exciting like shuffle around by themselves.

But Vita is not a magician. Not between nine and five, anyway. What she does when she gets home is anyone's business.

(Little do we know, at this moment, that one thing Vita does is put on a policeman's uniform that she bought from a fancy dress shop and walk through the streets late at night. Later this week, when Mum reads about this in the local paper, she will call it *totally fascinating*.)

Mum finds a lot of things fascinating, and she tries to ignite the same delighted curiosity in my brother and me.

Her, while walking through the woods: Don't you think this leaf is fascinating, Sydney?

Me, looking down: Not really.

I think I'll take these, Mum says to Vita, pointing at pair number three, the gloves in the middle. This is unusual for Mum, who would normally go for the cheapest.

Excellent choice, Vita says.

I bet you'd say that if I chose any of these, Mum says. Then she seems to panic, she starts talking really quickly. That sounded rude, she says. What I meant was, you must have to say nice things all day, reassuring things, it's part of your job really isn't it, to say things like *excellent choice*.

Without speaking, Vita wraps the gloves in tissue paper and puts them in a bag. The bag is stiff and square and the colour of peaches, with the word Flannery's on the side in a flamboyant font. Next week, once we are back from our holiday, Mum will use the bag for storing envelopes, and the tissue paper for wrapping a friend's house-warming gift. This is what's known as being resourceful and creative, or so she will tell Jason and me while we eat our Sugar Puffs and listen to an incredibly long lecture about *our throwaway world*. Mum enjoys giving us lectures. Her favourite topics are wastefulness, commercialism and the importance of boredom for children's brains. She needn't worry about that final

6

topic – mine and Jason's brains are super healthy, mainly thanks to these lectures.

Finally, we're done. Vita's helmet and the cloying smell of her perfume are behind us as we set off for the toy department on the fifth floor. Ahead of us now is a runway, a track, a maze of carpeted lanes. I am moving as fast as I can without breaking into a run, I am speeding along, and Mum is saying slow down, Sydney, take it easy, *slow down*. She knows what's going on, the battle inside me: how I want to cut loose, make a dash for it, my hands reaching for anything I can climb and jump off. Any minute now we will have yet another conversation about safety and etiquette, the things you just don't do unless you are (a) a much younger child in a play area or (b) an athlete performing in the Olympics. I am neither (a) nor (b), so which letter am I? Sometimes (i) for infuriating, (w) for wild, but mainly (n) for naughty. The thing is, I don't understand why people move in the way they do – small steps, robotic. Why aren't they leaping about, exploring all these surfaces, trying out different speeds, making new shapes with their bodies instead of left right, left right, steady and sensible on the ground.

To reach the toys you have to walk through the bed department. My eyes are wide. All these springboards and soft landings. You can keep your sweets, your dolls, your telly. I would swap them all for half an hour by myself on this obstacle course, jumping from mattress to mattress.

But today I am good. I don't test Mum's patience, to use her phrase. I walk properly.

Until I see a man, lying on one of the beds. This man is

propped up on two pillows. I notice him because he is wearing his shoes, and you're not supposed to wear shoes in bed.

How do I know this? I know because Jason got into bed one night wearing his pyjamas and new trainers. An hour earlier, he had worn them in the front garden, where the neighbour's dog had been, and he and his Pumas had run into a pile of dog shit – or *poop*, as we were taught to call it throughout this whole dramatic incident. When Mum came up to say goodnight there were sniffs, quick and shallow, followed by squealing and shouting. She went away and came back, accompanied by Dad, who was wearing rubber gloves and a look of grave seriousness. Jason's sheets and duvet cover were wrapped in three bags and placed in the bin outside, because Dad wasn't sure that any amount of disinfectant would make them hygienic, and they were still quite new, which made Mum cry, drink gin and tonic and listen to Stevie Wonder (Mum is in love with Stevie Wonder). The next day, a woman in a white jumpsuit came to clean the carpets. Her name was Lulu. Is that your real name? Mum said. Is Ila *your* real name? Lulu said. Well yes, Mum said. Lulu's jumpsuit was wipe-clean, like our tablecloth. May I touch it? Mum said. Whatever tickles your fancy, Lulu said. Around her waist was the biggest belt I had ever seen, its golden buckle as wide as my head. I clean up people's shit, she said. In this house we call it *poop*, Mum said. Call it what you like, it still stinks, Lulu said.

I stop to look at the man, the one propped up on two pillows, which makes Mum stop too.

It's rude to stare, she says.

But then she sees what I see.

The man isn't moving.

We are side by side at the foot of a double bed, looking at his open mouth and his open eyes. I reach out to touch his black brogues – super clean, super shiny.

I like his red socks, I say. I'd like some red socks. What's he doing?

Goodness me, Mum says. She moves now, as though she has been startled, squeezes my hand and drags me away, over to the till, where she whispers about a man on a bed who could possibly be dead. It reminds me of the poems Dad has been reading to me at night.

A man on a bed who could possibly be dead
He looks quite ill has he taken a pill?
The bedspread is pink like the soap on our sink
This man needs a doctor not a toy helicopter

Seeing the dead man does not upset me, but Mum expects it to, and this is very useful. To make me feel better, instead of buying a cowboy as promised, she buys me a Playmobil ambulance. I can't believe it. This is the kind of present you get for Christmas, not just on any old day of the week.

Well, Mum says, as we get in the car. That was quite a morning. Are you all right, Sydney?

I'm good, I say, sniffing my ambulance.

Mum opens her handbag, takes out two custard creams wrapped in a tissue and passes one to me.

Shall we listen to some music? she says. It might be good to sing.

Why might it?

It's cathartic.

As she drives us back to the campsite in St Ives, we sing along to 'Matchstalk Men and Matchstalk Cats and Dogs', 'Rivers of Babylon' and 'Take a Chance on Me'.

How do you know all the words? I say.

I have a head for lyrics, Mum says.

We park beside our tent and head straight to the beach to find Dad and Jason.

They are sitting on a blanket, heads down, busy. Jason is dismantling a broken radio that he has saved for this trip.

What's that? he says, looking up.

It's a present, I say, and I hand him the set of mini screwdrivers Mum bought him in Flannery's.

Oh *yes*, he says, because Jason loves tools in the way I love pencils and pens. Weird fact about my brother: sometimes he buries his favourite things in the garden. Yes, like a dog hiding its bone, saving it for later. Except that Jason puts his things in Tupperware to keep them clean. He has been doing this for years, beginning with his Action Man and Lego. Mum and Dad don't know. When we're back home, Mum will ask where the new screwdrivers are. They're in a very safe place, Jason will say, while I eat my alphabet spaghetti and keep quiet. Everyone deserves some privacy, even my weird brother.

Dad is varnishing his latest creation: a wooden box with lots of open compartments inside, each containing a hook.

What *is* that? I say.

Never you mind, he says. Did you buy anything nice?

I tell him about the man on a bed who could possibly be

dead and show him my ambulance. He asks if I need a sweet, sugar for shock, always does the trick. Yes please, I say. He reaches into a cool box and pulls out a tin of powdery boiled sweets.

Thanks. Why were these in the cool box? I say.

Why not? he says.

What else do you have in there? Mum says.

Well, he says, rummaging about.

Sausage rolls, egg sandwiches, cheese-and-onion crisps, Opal Fruits, chocolate teacakes and a bottle of diluted squash.

Not bad, Mum says.

We get comfy, sit in a row, eat our picnic, stare at the sea.

It's a bit cold out here isn't it, Jason says.

All in the mind, Mum says.

I am ten years old when I see a dead body for the second time.

There is nothing cathartic.

There is no singing along to the radio.

2

You could make me hard and delicate and beautiful

I remember you well, Sydney Smith. You squeezed the end of my shoe. I *loved* those Italian brogues, used to polish them all the time. You could almost see your face in my shoes.

Your rhyme made me smile. To be honest though, I think a toy helicopter would have been about as much use to me as a doctor, because I was stone dead, dead as a dodo, dead as a bloke who can't even smoke because his useless body had a stroke. You have to laugh at the timing, Sydney. I was trying out beds for my girlfriend and me, only a week to go until our wedding day.

I'd tried so many beds before I went to Flannery's. I knew this was the one as soon as I sat on it, even before my head fell back onto the pillows. No surface had ever held me like that. My weight sank into it, I was floating, I was happy.

I'm a big reader, Sydney. I love to read in bed. So I wondered what it would be like to sit up against the headboard and read my book in this particular bed. I plumped and readjusted and sat up straight, imagined myself in pyjamas, holding a paperback, saying listen to this sentence, Maria, can I read you this amazing sentence?

And while I was imagining this, it happened.

Somehow, I just died.

Fucking hell, Sydney. What else is there to say but fucking hell?

A girl stood at the end of the bed and squeezed my toes. I could feel that, by the way. The life hadn't left me, not yet. It takes a few days to pass. If only the living knew this. Different kinds of care would be given to the dying, the newly dead and the properly dead. Me? I was newly and improperly dead. And you? You were a sweet thing in dungarees and a stripy top, admiring my red socks.

While you were singing in the car with your mum, a policeman was knocking on Maria's front door. His words would enter her parents' house like a forest fire: impossible flames, rolling through the suburbs from nowhere.

You never know what's around the corner. People say that all the time, don't they? But bloody hell, I feel like slapping them when they say it, or kicking them in the shins, to make them take it seriously, drag it up from platitude to life-altering fact. Because honestly, I'm telling you, it can happen at *any fucking moment*. Don't forget, all right? Don't be so complacent.

I suppose I should thank you, Sydney Smith, for making autobiographical use of me. Your drawing is wonderful. I look like I'm sleeping, I *wish* I was sleeping. I've never been in a graphic memoir before. Never been in a book of any sort. Had I known this when I was alive, that I'd feature in an opening chapter, it would have been cause for great celebration. Thankfully, I got that bit right. I celebrated *everything*. Nothing grand, obviously. You can celebrate in all kinds of ways, can't you? By making bread. By opening all the windows. By telling her she's beautiful.

Her.

Yes.

My God, you've stirred me up, Sydney Smith. So can I ask you a favour, in return? Will you put me in the hands of a woman called Maria Norton? I'd love to be in her hands one more time. I know I'm small and peripheral in the grand scheme of things, in the grand scheme of this story, but maybe you could make me a pebble on a beach? You could make me hard and delicate and beautiful. You could make me soft to touch, bluish white. And a woman called Maria Norton could pick me up and admire me, she could roll me between her fingers and throw me into the sea. I'll make an inaudible splash, then I'll sink.

Put me in her hands, I beg you.

Many thanks in advance, Sydney.

Looking forward to hearing from you.

Kind regards,

Andy

PS I was more than a pebble to Maria. I was the whole damn beach. I was the sand and the sea, the fish and the ocean floor, the clouds, the seagulls, the litter. I don't even know what happened to her. *I don't even know where she is.*

Are you the whole beach to anyone, Sydney?

I hope so. I really hope so.

3

Do not feed the bear

I'm just checking, is there anything you'd like to do on your birthday? Ruth says.

Oh, probably just the usual, Sydney says, as she stands by the cooker, making coffee.

The usual, Ruth says.

If that's all right, Sydney says.

They are silent.

Sydney pours espresso into blue-and-white striped cups, places Ruth's on the table in front of her.

Well, maybe we can go out for some food *after* your birthday, Ruth says. Before you go away?

That sounds great, Sydney says.

She knows that something important just happened: a moment of kindness. Ruth could have vented her frustration, shown her disapproval, and chose not to.

I'm only going for a week though, she says.

I know. Did you book the B&B?

I did it yesterday. Sorry, I forgot to say.

Did you get the one you liked?

All booked.

I think it'll be good for us actually, Ruth says.

Do you?

Ruth nods. It does everyone good doesn't it, a bit of space.

I suppose it does, Sydney says. Well, I'd better get back to work. We can talk about this later if you like. Book a table somewhere?

Fine, Ruth says.

Upstairs, Sydney sits at her desk and sketches Ruth's unhappiness, depicting it as a brown bear with its head low to the floor. This bear is an unspoken creature, but she can sense it padding around the house sometimes, can almost hear its heavy feet on the stairs. To be honest, it will be good to get away from it when she heads down to the coast for a week of freerunning and sketching. Is that an awful thing to think? She adds a sign to her drawing: DO NOT FEED THE BEAR.

She puts the drawing in a wooden box, settles down to work. She looks at the sketch of Vita from Flannery's, creeping through a dark street, dressed in a policeman's uniform. Then the one of Jason, carefully inserting the inner pieces of an old radio into a plastic box, before burying this box in the garden. She places these aside, and focuses on the one she hasn't finished yet, the one of her mother approaching a stranger in a cafe.

Alone in the kitchen, Ruth is swearing under her breath: *For fuck's sake.*

Why must every year be exactly the same? A few days

before Sydney's birthday she will ask the same question, hoping they might go for a long walk, have dinner, drive to a place they haven't been to before. Hoping they might spend it together.

But no.

Sydney will want to do what she always does: run up to a wall, take two steps up it, push off and swing into a backward turn. *That's* how she'll mark her forty-seventh birthday. She'll use a railing as an axis while her body rotates in a 360-degree spin. Not in that skirt and jumper, obviously. She'll change into loose trousers, pull a T-shirt over a long-sleeved top, slip on her beanie and head into the city by herself like a teenage boy. It's a ritual, a thing. Will she still be doing this when she's sixty or seventy? When her bones are more likely to break?

Ruth grits her teeth. Is it wrong to want just a little normality?

Normality: it's in the eye of the beholder, obviously. One person's normal is another person's strange. Yes yes, Ruth gets all that. And freerunning is impressive, of course it is. The endless practice and training, the special diet, the sit-ups and push-ups, the discipline and drive. It takes all kinds of strength, both physical and emotional, not to mention grace. But how would you feel if every time you walked through town with your partner, they launched into some kind of superhero gymnastics routine? It's awesome and tedious. It's amazing and embarrassing. Parkour is the third person in their relationship, and next week, yet again, it will take Sydney out on the town to celebrate her birthday. Déjà vu.

Just once in the fourteen years they've been together, Ruth would like to be the one who takes her out. Just the two of them. No loose trousers, no trainers, and definitely no *back-flips*.

Ruth drinks her coffee, tries to stop herself from seething. *No, it will not be good to go upstairs and shout at Sydney. She's working on her book. It took her ages to get going on this project, to even confront the idea of it. Don't be selfish. Ha! Me, selfish? I'm not the selfish one! Stop it, Ruth. Think of something positive.*

Okay, here's a positive:

Watching Sydney at night, freerunning with the group she belongs to. It's hard not to be moved by this sight. Beneath the street lamps, Ruth sees her softness against the hard geometry of the city. She uses a straight line as a springboard to curve through the air. She is twofold, double, her silhouette dancing across the wall. This could be the silhouette of a girlish boy or a boyish girl, but it isn't. It's the outline of a woman closer to fifty than forty. A cartoonist who spends her working days upstairs in their converted loft, while a fox terrier called Otto snores in the armchair beside her desk. A woman who takes her thirty-five-year-old skateboard to the park every now and then, choosing times when Ruth is out, assuming she doesn't know about these nostalgic outings on worn-out wheels. But more important than any of these things, *a woman who refuses to do anything normal on her birthday.*

Birthdays are a contentious subject. They're a hotspot, a danger zone. Marking the anniversary of Sydney's birth is always discouraged.

18

Why?

Because it's celebrating the fact that she's still alive, and that's uncomfortable territory for Sydney, territory she would rather leap across than land in.

Trouble is, *not* celebrating is uncomfortable for Ruth. It makes her feel excluded, and at the same time, dragged into a past that isn't hers.

Can't I at least make you cake? she said, back in the early days.

I'd rather you didn't, if that's okay, Sydney said. I think birthdays are for children really.

That is *so* depressing, Ruth thought.

And also, she thinks now, this whole thing is counterproductive. If you make a song and dance about not wanting a fuss, what have you effectively done? You've gone and made a fuss, that's what. You've been singing and dancing on your birthday. So we may not be *celebrating* the fact that you've crawled, apologetic and resistant, into another year of your life, but we are definitely underlining this day, making it stand out from the rest with your grumpy refusal to be *normal*.

Not even a fairy cake with one candle? Ruth said.

Not even that, Sydney said.

Fine, I'll do this for now, but it has to change, Ruth said. I'm not doing this for ever, all right? One year, we'll go out for dinner to celebrate. Otherwise I know I'm going to get tired of this.

It's a deal, Sydney said, thirteen years ago.

4

The facts of life

It's day six of our holiday. St Ives for the fifth year running, so to me, this is what *holiday* means: you pick a place and go there every summer. Last year we slept in our tent, and I found a man on a bed who was in fact dead. This year, to quote Dad, *we've gone up in the world*. We've hired a caravan. After stepping inside for the first time, Dad immediately lost 10p to the swear jar. Oh my fucking God, he said, I'll actually be able to stand up while I'm putting on my pants. And where's the fun in that? Mum said.

Tonight, we're having a special dinner. Mum has laid the table in our caravan. Soft cotton tablecloth, blue and yellow checks. Kitchen roll pressed into triangles. Glasses and cutlery and a jug of lemonade.

Tea's ready, she shouts, from the doorway. Come on, you lot, let's be having you.

There is a menu on the table, handwritten by Mum.

STARTER: *Crackers with cheese & pickle*
MAIN: *Haddock in sauce with croquette potatoes,*
   carrots, runner beans & peas
AFTERS: *Angel Delight (Butterscotch)*

We often have boil-in-the-bag fish, but we never have three courses, kitchen roll, a menu and a jug of lemonade.

So this meal, Mum says, as the crackers crunch in our mouths, is going to be the start of a new tradition. When we get home, every Friday night we're going to sit at the table and talk to each other about the past week. We're going to tell each other stories. I think it'll be really good for us.

Dad's brown jumper is already specked with crumbs and cheddar. He always eats like this, like he hasn't had a meal in days, and something gets left behind on his clothes or the table. It's like when Mum eats her cereal in the morning, there is usually a blob of milk on the dimple in her chin.

I don't really want to talk about my week. I'd prefer to eat my tea in front of the telly. That's what we usually do. We have a tray each. Mine is brilliant, it has a boy on it, travelling through outer space in a rocket. I also have a brilliant lunchbox with the Incredible Hulk and Spider-Man on it, yes both of them together, it's one of my favourite things and I plan to keep it for ever. Jason has a *Star Wars* lunchbox and flask with Darth Vader, Luke Skywalker and R2-D2 on them.

Sydney, must you always look so far away? Mum says. When people are talking it's polite to at least *pretend* to listen.

I *was* listening.

So what did I just say? Dad asks.

You said you've had a really relaxing week, and when we get home you plan to fix your bike.

The thing they don't realise about me is I am always

listening. The only time I'm not is when I'm running and climbing. Then it's just me and the surface of things, and my body is so strong, much stronger than in *normal* life. It's like I become an animal, which kind I don't know. A leopard maybe. Or a monkey.

Mum is the last one to talk about her week, and I learn a lot from her story. Turns out we don't have to describe the whole week from start to finish, we can just talk about one thing that happened – one moment. I hadn't thought of doing this. I worked too hard when it was my turn, moving through the days, trying to remember what we had done. But actually, as Mum explains, describing one moment is a way to describe everything. You get the whole story if you look at a series of moments – you don't need to turn them into a story because they *are* the story and everything is already connected.

This is what Mum tells us:

So you know I went off and did some shopping on Tuesday, she says. I went to a gallery, a second-hand bookshop, a couple of charity shops. I was feeling tired, so before I walked back I went to that cafe by the library, the one we'd been to the day before, for coffee and cake. And that's when something important happened. I met a young woman, she says.

Who? I say.

I didn't get her name. She was sitting at a table by herself, and I could see that she was crying. I thought about staying where I was, giving her some privacy. But I also thought about going over and asking if she was all right. The thing is, sometimes people don't like this, they find it intrusive, they want to be left alone. But if you let a person down, a person who needed help, trust me, that kind of moment can haunt you, make you feel really ashamed.

While we listen to this, everyone is still eating apart from me. I am on the edge of my seat. Jason is pushing peas around his plate with a fork, making them swim through a lake of yellow sauce. Dad is eating his fish with a concerned look on his face.

Why can it haunt you? I say.

Well, she could have been feeling completely alone in the world, like no one cared. She might have been on her way to kill herself.

Do you think she *was* going to kill herself? I say.

Ila, Dad says. This is a bit dark. And overdramatic. Why on earth would you think that? All of us cry sometimes, it doesn't mean –

These are the facts of life, Mum says.

You don't cry, Jason says.

Of course I do, Dad says.

When?

I don't know precisely when.

I thought the facts of life were sexual, Jason says, which makes all of us look at him.

There are many facts of life, Mum says. Not everything is sexual.

Dad laughs.

Anyway, Mum says, can we return to the woman in the cafe?

The one about to go off and kill herself, Jason says.

The point I was trying to make, is I didn't want to go home and end up wishing that I'd spoken to her. So I went over. I asked if she was okay, if I could help at all.

And did she tell you why she was crying? I say.

She did, actually. She told me her dog had died.

Why would she cry over a dog? Jason says.

Because the dog was part of her family, Mum says. He got hit by a car and had to be put down. She'd just left him at the vet's and couldn't face going home without him.

Honey, Dad says. I really don't think this is –

No, Mum says. I've given this a lot of thought, and I think they need to hear this kind of thing.

I'm not sure they do.

It's important, Mum says.

Who killed the dog? I say.

Did they go to prison? Jason says.

Did they do it on purpose?

How long do you go to prison for murdering a dog?

Later that evening, we hear their voices coming from the tiny double bedroom. In our caravan, you can hear everything. Honestly, Ila, Dad says, that was completely unnecessary, you'll just make them anxious. I don't agree, Mum says. Children need to learn how to talk about difficult subjects, especially what to do when someone's upset. But death? he says. Yes, she says. It's like when Sydney and I found that dead body last summer, I could have used that experience to teach her something, and instead I brushed it under the carpet. Dead man in the department store? Here, have a toy ambulance and forget all about it. What kind of message was I sending? I still feel awful about that.

Their argument went on for a while, and unusually Dad must have won this time, because we never heard another sad story like that from Mum, and there was no further talk of death.

When the subject came up again, we didn't try to discuss it.

There just didn't seem any point.

5

Date night

He floats on his back in the floodlit pool, looks up at the stars. His face seems younger than usual. There's a boyish lightness, or maybe a light boyishness. She does this to him. His wife, Ila. Even after all these years, she brings out his mischief, his lark, his fool.

He turns over and swims to the edge, where he leans over the side, his chin resting on his arms, his arms resting on a mosaic tile, as he waits.

It's date night. Thursday, once a month, they meet at the lido.

She is slow to join him tonight, but he doesn't mind. She's probably just getting changed, faffing about. She likes to take her time.

He sinks back down into the warm water, goes right under, comes back up.

Howard loves the lido. The best thing about it is the shape of this pool. Unusually, it's circular. There's no length and width to swim, only a circumference, a radius, a diameter. You can also swim an arc or a chord, if you feel like it. You can float around the centre point, knowing that you are

26

as far inside the circle as possible, and every journey you make from here will be equal. Perfect symmetry, inked out beneath him. He would like to see this pool when it's drained, so he could admire the geometric handiwork on its floor, the dots and lines, the measurements and arrows.

Around the pool, a series of concentric circles. First the mosaic tiles, blue and white. Then a yellow path. Then more mosaic tiles, faded orange, leading up some steps to the outer circle of changing booths with wooden doors, like tiny pastel-coloured beach huts.

She is inside one of these booths.

Which door are you behind, love?

Hanging on every other door, chalked onto blackboard, is a drawing entitled *The Properties of a Circle*. At the bottom of each drawing, the words TIME IS AN EXCELLENT EXAMPLE OF A CIRCLE.

He thinks about this while he waits. Until a door swings open.

It's her. Ila, in her polka-dot bikini, stepping out of a changing room.

She sees him grinning.

The lights are on her now as she walks down the steps, crosses the orange tiles, the yellow path, the blue and white tiles.

Now she is right here, at the edge. She prepares to dive, holds the position for longer than necessary, tries not to laugh.

Show-off, he says.

Then she is right above his head. Her belly button, level with his nose.

Now this is what you call perfect symmetry. *This* is the moment to draw, Sydney.

He looks up at those feet, those legs, those outstretched arms.

Then there is a splash, and she is gone.

He spins round, watches her dark shape underwater, sliding away from him.

She is good at this, at holding her breath, disappearing.

And then, as always, her drenched smiling face.

He pushes himself towards her.

She is the one waiting now, treading water.

Hello you, she says, taking his face in her hands and kissing him.

Hello you, he says.

I like your new bathers, she says. Where have you been hiding those?

Who says *bathers*? he says.

I say *bathers*, she says. Bright red, eh? Good for you at your age.

My age?

You're old now, she says. You're my old man.

I bought them in the sale, he says. All the other colours had gone.

Remember when you bought those Speedos? And the very first time you wore them they came off in the sea. We couldn't find them anywhere.

Don't, he says.

That was hilarious, she says.

I seem to remember you taking a long time to bring me a towel.

I don't know what you mean, she says.

That was thirty-eight years ago, he thinks. Which seems ludicrous and impossible, but only if you are naive enough to believe that time equals distance, and the further away you are from a moment, the smaller and less vivid it becomes.

She splashes him.

Oi, he says.

She does it again.

So he does it back.

The water is going everywhere now
neither of them can see a thing
and their hands are stiff rotating paddles
beating the years away
until they are simply a girl and a boy
inside a circle.

6

The point of return

Funny how a place changes and doesn't change at all.

Yesterday, Sydney stepped off the train at St Ives, the town she has been drawing and painting for the past two years. Upstairs in her study, she has recreated these streets, this shoreline, this sea – her own version, all from memory. Now she is actually here, and she has lied to everyone, named a different seaside town, pretended to be somewhere else.

The lie about where she was going had come easy, which surprised her. She always imagined that she would make a terrible liar. This discovery was both freeing and disturbing.

She was glad that she had chosen January. It was cold and quiet, which felt right. Winter or not, the light was one thing that hadn't changed. Her mother always said that the light down here revealed colours the eye couldn't normally see. That's why all the artists come here, she said. And looking at your pictures, I think you'll be coming here too, long after we stop.

Her mother had been wrong about that.

They all stopped coming at exactly the same time, after holiday number six, which ended abruptly.

Did we really come here six times, darling?

We did, Mum.

Blimey. Talk about creatures of habit. We weren't very adventurous, were we?

That's where you're wrong again, Mum. We investigated every corner, don't you remember? We walked for miles along the coast, saw this place from every angle. And we read books, went to galleries, played badminton and tennis. We had three-course meals, picnics, pasties, fish and chips. We went to the cinema, we went fishing, we went to that big town with the department store.

I'm sorry, darling. I didn't realise you were still so attached to this place.

Seriously? Sydney said.

It was a dark attachment. Ambivalent. One she wanted and didn't.

She often wondered what she would say if someone offered to erase her memories of this town, like in that film, *Eternal Sunshine of the Spotless Mind.* Would you let go of memories that were your best and your worst, all at once?

The drawings, the ones for her book, have reached a sticking point.

They go as far as trip number five, then stop.

At the beginning of trip number six, the pen falters, the pencil breaks.

The storyboard is frozen. Her mind won't go there.

Okay, she said to her cluttered desk. What if my feet go

there. What if my body goes there. Is that what it's going to take?

But I don't want to go there, she thought, with a child's stubbornness.

Sydney runs along the sand. She has visited three of the town's beaches so far, and this one is still her favourite. The others are too pretty, too calm. This one sends your hair in all directions. It's harder underfoot, rockier and darker, with waves that could do a person harm.

She stops to watch the dogs, out on their morning walks. Admires how they scamper or leap, explore or stay close, following the scents and distractions before glancing back, looking for their owner, the point of return that must never be lost. Some are muscular and lean, others wobbly and short-legged. There is a curly doting thing, scurrying behind the wellington boots of its keeper, not interested in anything but her. Play bows say come on, you can chase me, or I'll chase you, I don't care, let's do it now just for fun, just because. Dogs don't think about why. They eat because there is food in front of them. They run because their bodies want to.

She misses Otto. Silly really, when she has only been gone a day. She looks at her watch. He'll be out with Ruth now, tumbling through the fields, not thinking of her. Which is how it should be, obviously. The next thought makes her stomach lurch: Ruth, also not thinking of her. She panics. *What if, what if.* What if Ruth moves out while she is here. What if she packs up her things and moves them into a storage facility. What if she moves in with Howard, which isn't as far-fetched as it sounds – he would probably prefer her as his daughter.

The trouble is, Sydney has a hunch. It's a feeling, that's all. A sense that Ruth has been moving further away. A sense that there might be someone out there who could make her happier, and if Ruth hasn't met this person yet, she might be longing for them, or should be. It would be painful and terrible if she left, but also understandable. Sydney feels guilty for holding on to Ruth for so long, and that kind of feeling gets into your bones like damp weather, affects the whole framework of a person. It's affecting her freerunning, this much she knows for sure. She is holding herself tighter than usual. There is a new caution in her muscles.

She sprints up the steps to the gallery, pays the entrance fee, picks up a leaflet. But Sydney isn't here for the art.

I like the shape of this building, she says.

Right, the gallery assistant says.

Artful in itself, in an ugly kind of way, she says.

Hmm, the assistant says, fiddling with the collar of his shirt. This topic is outside his remit. He's not here to talk about the building itself. He's here to talk opening times and closing times, temporary exhibitions and permanent pieces. He looks down at the keyboard, hoping this woman will move on.

Sydney moves faster now. Her body is ready to go. It is *always* ready. She was born that way, wriggling from the start, climbing out of her cot, and later, running along the dining table and jumping onto the work surface. From the work surface to the stool. From the stool to the settee in the corner of the kitchen. Excellent squishy landing, then a forward roll, just because. Cartwheel across the rug, run through the hallway, climb up the banister, slide back down. All these bruises and scrapes but they feel so good. The world is hers for the taking, every surface hers for the making. This will be a slide and this will be a springboard and this will be a running track and –

Sydney Oriel Smith, her mother once said, while applying Savlon cream and a plaster. Why can't you watch more TV like other children? What about Sooty? Do you still like Sooty?

I've *never* liked Sooty, Sydney said, hitching her white socks up to her knees and wrapping her father's scarf around her neck.

Why are you wearing Dad's scarf?

I just like it.

Isn't it dangerously long for a girl who likes to climb up the banister and slide back down?

That's a very clever observation, Sydney said.

Why thank you, dear, her mother said.

When she was a child, there were few words for what she loved to do. There was *acrobatic, lively, dangerous*. There was *hyperactive, fearless, precise*.

Later, when she became an adult, the language changed. She learned the origins, the technical terms, the concepts that made sense of who she was.

And she heard people use the word *flow*. They were referring to total immersion, losing yourself in an enjoyable activity, having no awareness of the passing of time.

She spoke to a friend of hers about this once, a freestyle solo rock climber.

Is it just me, she said, or do you feel like someone else when you climb?

I don't even feel like a person, he said.

She had heard other people say the same thing – how the conscious mind disengages and thinking stops. The world around you becomes vivid and slow, and your body moves with animalistic accuracy. The higher the risk, the quieter the mind. There's no anxiety, no worry, no thinking back or thinking forward. Only this lifting of the leg. Only this reaching of the arm.

It's the purest kind of freedom Sydney has ever known.

She moves through the gallery, pausing to glance at paintings, woodcuts and screen prints, just a quick glance, before heading up the staircase and going her own way, doing her own thing, making use of a toilet, a window frame, a fire escape and scaffolding to reach the gallery's highest point: a semicircular ledge, roof on a roof painted white. Private. No entry. An illegal high.

She sits cross-legged, takes off her rucksack and pulls out a sandwich, a bottle of water, two Jammie Dodgers wrapped in kitchen roll and a packet of Quavers. This is the perfect place for lunch, with no one to bother her and nothing to obscure her view of sea, sand and cliffs.

Sometimes, an art gallery is not an art gallery. It's a climbing frame, a watchtower, a lighthouse.

From up here, instead of small details, her eye catches patterns and sequences of movement. Children and teenagers, learning to surf: a cluster of wetsuits at first, then erratic black dots, bobbing into the blue. Adults advancing in diagonal lines like figures in a board game, dogs drawing figures of eight around their legs.

She takes out her sketchbook.

Thinking clearly has always been easiest when she is up high, away from the throb and tempo of other people's lives, the rhythms that seem to overpower her own. Up on this roof, or any roof, moments will simply replay without effort. Like the time her mother made a herd of pink rabbits out of raspberry jelly. Like the time she cycled up and down their street, hands in the air, because she had lost a bet to Jason. Like the time she got drunk on ginger wine and made them all sing 'You're the One That I Want' from *Grease*.

Sydney sketches a cartoon version of Ila Smith, holding the TV remote up to her mouth, pretending it's a microphone. She draws a rabbit jelly, a woman on a boy's bike.

Enough remembering. Enough of the comic book family.

She eats her lunch and leans over the edge. Somehow, this feels like the safest of places. She leans further, looks down at the street below. Then she freezes.

Someone is watching her, through binoculars. A woman.

How long has she been there? Nothing to see here, madam, she thinks.

Now the woman is shouting something. Are you about to jump? she shouts.

Sydney has been in this town for less than twenty-four hours and one person already cares whether she lives or dies. That's good going, don't you think?

No, definitely not. But thank you! she shouts back.

What?

Just having my lunch!

What?

Just sitting!

Are you all right? the woman yells. Can you confirm that you're all right?

What a kind woman, Sydney thinks, but would I really have brought my lunch if I was planning to jump? Actually, erase that, it makes no sense. What's lunch got to do with suicidal intent? Just because you fancy one last packet of crisps doesn't mean you don't want to leave this mortal coil. In fact, it might be quite fitting to eat a Quaver while you jump. Then you're eating a coil while leaving a coil.

She looks down at the woman, pulls her mobile phone from her rucksack, flicks to the camera, holds it up and zooms in to the small details of the woman's head, her binoculars, her sheepskin coat.

I can see you properly now, Sydney shouts.

She holds up her thumb, which the woman sees, and she returns the gesture, which feels mysterious and comforting to both of them.

Then Sydney shuffles backwards, out of view, in case the woman calls someone or attracts attention. She draws a quick sketch of what has just happened.

Maria Norton lowers her binoculars and stares at the empty space where a stranger had been sitting, just a curve on the roof before she looked through these magnifying lenses, a curve with a dark body and a flaxen tip, like a bracket dipped in gold, like dolled-up punctuation, like something to stop and look at, like someone giving her a thumbs up instead of a thumbs down, which is what life usually feels like, it feels like a relentless song of disapproval, playing in every cell of her body, but just then, for a few seconds, someone gave her a sign that said *you are okay* and *I am okay* and *what is happening in this moment is okay*.

7

I ♥ otters

Jon Schaefer is listening to Maria's story, the one about a woman on a roof, a woman with blond hair, black and grey clothes. Listening to his wife with this degree of attentiveness requires considerable effort and he's pleased with how well he's doing. He performs a range of expressions and sounds, perfectly timed, orchestrating his responses, ushering the story along, hoping it will soon peak and lose energy. Jon assumes that everyone puts this much work into listening to their partners, it's just the natural way of things, all over the world, like having a second job, right?

How did you see the woman so clearly? he says.

I had your binoculars, Maria says.

My binoculars? Why? You hate my binoculars.

I thought I'd see what all the fuss was about.

What fuss.

The fuss you make about those bloody binoculars.

Jon sighs. He puts down his paintbrush. This isn't going to be quick, is it? Just her head around the door at first, not her whole body, but now the rest of her has followed, her neck, torso, arms, legs and feet, the whole woman, but most of all her *voice*, always her voice, when he is trying to paint the sea. He glances at the large circular window beside his desk, his favourite part of this room – looking through it makes his life feel shipshape – then he turns back to his wife. She is talking about a stranger. Someone she'll probably never see again. That's what this town is like. Locals, of course, but all the passing through, all the apartments, cottages, B&Bs. So someone got up on a roof. Drunk, probably. So what? Trivial. She'll be safely down by now, drinking peppermint tea for three quid a cup or buying a box of fudge. Maybe she's looking at one of his paintings in a gallery, thinking it would look good in her living room, wondering whether to treat herself.

They hear the front door open and close. Footsteps, heavy on the stairs. It's Stuart, their Irish wolfhound, announcing his presence after a walk, coming into the room for a pat, a ruffle, then he's back downstairs for his dinner.

They didn't choose Stuart, or so the story goes, and like all stories, this one changes depending on who is telling it.

He was on the beach, patchy and thin, with a name tag that simply said STUART. Maria was out walking by herself. She was frightened at first of this creature in the distance, tall and slow, creeping towards her. He was purplish grey with flecks of black, big sad eyes, a face that seemed to be smiling softly. She held out a limp hand. He stepped closer, ignored the hand and pushed his head against her stomach. She put her arms around his back, wondering if all gigantic dogs do this, wondering if he might be cold or in pain, wondering if he was capable of killing her.

So this is what I find on the beach, she thought. Not a rare coin, a message in a bottle, wreckage from an old ship. But *this*. A dog with such a physical presence, and yet he seemed ethereal, almost mythical.

She took him to the vets. No microchip I'm afraid, Maria. And no phone number on his ID tag, which is highly neglectful.

Terrible, she said.

Stuart trotted beside her as she headed home. It felt like they had walked this way together a hundred times before.

I'm not sending him away, Maria said. Definitely not. He *chose* me.

Well to be fair, Jon said, you just collided. It was random. You could have been anyone, to be honest. And he's *massive*. I mean for goodness' sake, Maria, it's like having a pony in the house. Feeding him will cost us a fortune.

Like all your canvases and your paint, she thought. Like all these brushes and sketchbooks.

Maria wasn't one to get angry, but his suggestion that she and Stuart weren't connected by anything other than coincidence made her furious. The voice that came out of her mouth was so loud it shocked her. Afterwards, it made her smile. The following day, she bought a supersize dog bed for the kitchen, fleece-lined, blue tweed.

Jon picks up his paintbrush. He has heard enough of this story about a woman on a roof. Good good, he says.

Maria hates it when he does that. When he says *good good* for no reason. When there is nothing good at all, let alone worthy of *good good*. And when basically he means

41

that's enough, off you go, on your way now, leave me in peace.

+

Belle Schaefer walks past the beach cafe, takes the little path up to the house, the one she still lives in with her parents.

Shame on you, Belle. This wasn't the plan, was it? Still living at home at the age of twenty-nine. Her jailer is indecision, a jazzy little fellow, zippily dressed, clicking his fingers, saying you could go here or you could go there, you could do this or you could do that, well you could do anything, Belle, just *look* at all these options in the ever-changing world. The music of indecision is pure jazz, plinkety-plonk frenetic, sometimes so fast and wild that Belle can't even think. Where are you gonna go, Belle? How will you decide? Stick a pin on a map, maybe? I'm the pianist in the foyer of every moment, Belle. Come and sit with me, let's sing a song of possibility, let's look at Instagram, let's see what everyone else is doing, why are you covering your ears?

Indecision is addictive. You get to travel across the board without making a move. You get to live in every city without packing a bag. Belle has a notebook full of life's possibilities, and flicking through the book is so musical and tiring that she really doesn't have time for anything else.

No, let's get this right. Her jailer *used* to be indecision. Her brain *used* to be jazzed up and freaked out, back when she was a teenager, too sensible and sexless for this bizarre stage of life, her hormones failing to make anything happen – no lust, no lie-ins, no posters on the wall. Why were her

42

friends suddenly obsessed with Blu-Tacking photographs of complete strangers to the back of their bedroom doors? What the hell was going on around her? The commotion, the eyeliner, the dry humping. The buying of magazines instead of comics, even though they were far less entertaining. The *have you done this?* and *have you done that?* When did someone fire a starting pistol? When did everyone go mad? One minute we were happy playing Lego and staring into rock pools, now we want everything at once and if we can't have it we're going to kill ourselves.

As a girl, Belle liked reading books and helping her mother in the garden. She collected shells from the beach and asked the fishermen about hooks and bait. She had seven T-shirts that said I ♥ OTTERS, a different colour for each day of the week, and she slipped a clean version on every morning with her jeans or cords. (She's rather *uninspired*, her father said. Just let her be herself, her mother said.) Life was good and straightforward.

Then adolescence came. *Chaos*. Girls painted and in a flap. Boys sulky and overheated, always chewing jokes. Everyone smells different and complicated, not of washing powder any more. And the worst thing of all: it is no longer acceptable to wear T-shirts from the otter sanctuary gift shop.

BELLE: I'd like to skip this stage, please.

LIFE: It doesn't work like that, dear. Just keep your head down and see what happens.

BELLE: But it's bedlam out there. A right and a wrong way to look and behave. Even right and wrong music. Things got sharp and mean.

LIFE: As I said, just keep your head down. You can still listen to Elvis if you like.

BELLE: I like his voice. But no one else listens to him.

LIFE: They do, dear. Older people. Elsewhere in the world.

Finally the din stopped and the sky cleared. Her friends left for university and she sat on the beach with a sore throat and frizzy hair.

BELLE: Am I allowed to love otters again now? Is it over?

LIFE: Yes, Belle. It's over. Just one more hurdle.

BELLE: What?

LIFE: They are waiting for you at home, in the kitchen.

Maria and Jon were drinking tea and looking at the clock.

You've been gone a long time, Jon said, eyeing his daughter's saggy chinos, which were an inch too long.

Has something happened? she said.

No, not at all, Maria said. We just wanted to have a little chat with you.

Ugh.

What about?

About your life.

My life.

Yes.

What about my life.

Well, to be specific, your education.

Your career.

What career?

Precisely.

Sorry?

Darling, are you *sure* you don't want to do a degree?

Not this again.

But sweetheart.

Look, I'm fine as I am. I'd rather die than be dropped into one of those holding pens.

What?

Holding pens?

I don't want to go.

But Belle.

It'll cost a fortune and there's no guarantee of a job at the end of it. Anyway, I already have a job that I like. I want to carry on working in the bookshop. Can't I just stay?

You really want to stay with us?

Unbelievable, I know. But yes, for now.

Maria and Jon look at each other.

I have no idea what she is feeling right now, Jon thinks, as he inspects his wife's face, but I hope she shares my disappointment. Our daughter is clearly stunted.

Yippee yippee, Maria thinks.

Belle is now the youngest person in this town to have an allotment. Last year, she won Best Marrow, Biggest Carrot and Most Sublime Sloe Gin. She drinks ale in the Black Hole with her friends, most of whom are aged sixty or over. She volunteers at the otter sanctuary. She sleeps in the annexe, the extension. No front door of her own but you can't have everything, right?

———

This evening, Belle puts her key in the door and unclips Stuart's lead from his collar. The smell of baking, the whiff of oil paint, the sound of Classic FM, on at low volume all day long. She heads for the kitchen and fills Stuart's bowl with kibble.

Look at him, watching her. Who could possibly leave him behind? What kind of life would be better than living with Stuart?

Her mother walks into the kitchen, wearing red pyjamas.

Wow, those are bright, Belle says. New purchase?

I've had these for years, her mother says. I just never wear them.

Did you hear about the woman on the roof of the White Room? Belle says.

I did.

Almost jumped, apparently.

Maria shakes her head. She was eating a sandwich, she says. But she *might* have been planning to jump. Who knows?

You saw her?

I did.

Oh.

Hmm.

Can I have one of these? Belle says, sniffing the tray of blueberry muffins.

Two women, two generations. One is wearing silk night-wear, in an effort to cheer herself up. The other is in oversized trousers and a purple checked shirt. They sit and drink tea and talk about the woman who may or may not have been planning to jump. They ask what would make someone want to do a thing like that – take their own life, risk permanent injury. Belle thinks she sees a look on her mother's face, an expression she doesn't recognise because she has been looking at it all her life.

Have you ever? Belle says.

Have I ever what? her mother says.

I don't know, Belle says, taking a bite of muffin.

They sit in silence.

Two sheep, perfectly still, standing in a field on a frosty morning. That's the image in Belle's mind right now. Weird, she thinks. She can never picture sheep when she wants to, when she's lying awake in bed, but this evening, in the kitchen, there are definitely two sheep and she has the feeling that she's one of them.

She looks into her mother's eyes. You all right, Mum? she says.

Of course, darling, her mother says. You know I'm always all right.

+

Belle walked me today. Said she was off sick from work. Something about a cold she couldn't shake off. It sounded like an excuse, but who am I to argue with hugs in bed and an extra walk?

It's winter here, but there's an ice cream van on the beach. People are walking along the sand, eating wafer cones full of vanilla, chocolate chip, peanut butter or toffee, collars upturned, scarves blowing in the wind. I find it a romantic sight, I don't know why. Belle has gone for vanilla and rasp-berry sauce. In a few minutes' time she will give me the end of her cone. I'm staying close, keeping my eye on her, in case she forgets.

I could tell you a thing or two about my family, the things I've heard, seen and smelled. I'm not sure this would be the *loyal* thing to do, though, and loyalty is in my bones. How does a canine narrator betray his nature to overcome this ethical dilemma? It's not easy, I can tell you that. But I've been persuaded into it. Promised a box of Bonios by a cartoonist called Sydney Smith, who is penning me as we speak, drawing the first time we meet – you'll see her in a minute, when she puts herself in the picture, when she comes running towards Belle and me.

My name is Stuart. I get letters addressed to me from the vet:

> *Dear Stuart,*
>
> *I hope you are keeping well. This postcard is to let you know that your vaccination is due very soon, so please call us, or if you can't be bothered with the telephone, do get your owners to call us. See you soon!*
> *Best wishes,*
> *Pete Armstrong, your friendly vet*
> *PS Pop in any time you're passing by for a quick hello and a salmon flapjack – we don't want you to be scared of coming in!*

Sweet isn't it? And also quite wonderful. I would love to keep these letters in a pretty wooden box, but I have no way of communicating this, so they go straight in the recycling after my appointment has been made.

I receive post because I am no longer lost. Maria found me and took me home. I liked her straight away – that sheepskin coat, slightly seedy and too big; her messy hair, wayward as my own. When we met, the first thing I did was push my head against her stomach. I'm not sure why I did that.

Belle takes after her mother, but she would hate me pointing this out. The judgemental sighs, indiscernible to most ears but not to mine. The endless walking, the pausing at night to look through other people's windows. Are all human beings this curious, this nosy? They both seem sad when they look, as if everything they see through those windows is something they have lost. If I knew what it was, I would sniff it out and fetch it. Belle's parents think she is contentment personified, because that's what they want to see, it ring-fences their self-obsession.

Which brings me to Jon. Don't get me started on Jon. This growl, rising. These hackles, these teeth. Jon is one of life's bastards.

But I was telling you about winter, wasn't I? The ice cream van on the beach. People with upturned collars. Belle about to give me the end of her cone. Which she does, of course. She's a kind person, everyone says so, not just me. She helps around the house, takes me for walks and regularly pig-sits for Winnie next door, a lonely TV producer who bought herself a pot-bellied pig on a whim and is rarely home to look after him. Timothy joins us on our walks, pottering along at the end of his red diamanté lead. At first we attracted attention, but people are used to us now – this young woman in a green mac, taking wide strides with a hound, a pig, a hip flask full of home-made sloe gin.

The piece of cone is tasteless but the vanilla ice cream is good. Wish I could eat a whole one. Probably never will, unless I pinch one from the hand of a small child, and I'm not that kind of dog. We walk a bit further, then Belle takes out her tennis ball on a stick and throws it. Can't say I'm a huge fan of running after her ball, I must be honest, but I humour her and bring it back so she can launch it into the air all over again. At least it keeps her busy, stops her shop-lifting. Yes, *shoplifting*. Every now and then, she sneaks an eyeliner up her sleeve or a magazine inside a paper she is buying. Don't ask me why she does it, I really don't know. It's not as if she's broke. But that's our secret, all right?

I have just retrieved the ball after a rather awkward throw, when I smell something unusual.

It's a woman, running along the beach. Short jacket, yellow hair, big blue headphones. I can't give you better information than that, because my vision is limited when it comes to colour, but she smells different somehow, different to other people I have smelled. And I have lifted my nose to *a lot* of people, some I wished I hadn't, with all manner of substances under their fingernails. Dog owners already know that we can tell what kind of mood you're in, but what no one seems to realise is how specific we are. Some of us, the more *advanced* members of the species, know *exactly* what you're feeling – the nuances, the variations. Every emotion seeps through your pores. It's all over you, to be honest, and most of the time it's rank. Hate to say it, but there it is. You're a stinky lot, you humans.

And this woman, running towards Belle and me, pausing beside us. It's like she has just stepped through rain but there has been no rain today. She is wearing so much weather. Her own climate, dark and damp. I sniff her jacket – it's dry. She smells of fog, moss, wet concrete and petrol. She smells of rivers and weeds and burnt rhubarb. Here is the freshness of clear water. Here is rot and salt, treacle and pondweed.

I stare at her. She smiles at me. I want to lick her hand, see what it tastes of.

Quite a beast, she says to Belle.

He's a complete softy, Belle says, and I notice how the smell of her skin changes when she says this, how there is woodsmoke and vanilla.

There is so much guilt on this person, Belle. If I could tell you, I would. Be careful, it's overwhelming. I may be quite a beast, but she could knock me right over with this guilt.

What has she done, Belle? What on earth has this woman done?

8

Mark Rothko

Asleep in the B&B, it happens to Sydney for the first time in years. She has the nightmare. The one she used to have, intermittently, between the ages of ten and thirty-three. After she met Ruth she slept deeply, and dreamed mainly of other things, some of them frightening but never as frightening as this.

The details of this nightmare change but the story is always the same.

This time she is in the gallery, the White Room.

The room is long and narrow with a sea view.

Sometimes, the waves lash against the window.

The walls are covered in Rothko.

Every painting is black and red.

She sits on a long bench: black leather.

In this dream, she is wearing red trousers, a maroon T-shirt and black gloves.

She has bare feet.

She looks up at the painting in front of her, an expansive wash of pain. Infinite.

This painting has no beginning or end.

She walks up to it, touches it with her gloved hands.

This painting knows her, intimately. It knows

what she cannot draw.

It knows what she did, and what she lost, and why the innocence of unfettered joy is too painful for her to watch.

It knows why she always turns away from the sight of children playing happily.

Yes, Mark Rothko understands, and there is comfort in this. More comfort than she can say with words. So she sticks out her arms, as wide as she can, like a barefooted fisherman miming the size of his catch, like a girl saying I love you this much.

Thank you, Rothko says. Pleased to have been of assistance.

Now she hears a woman's voice.

It can't be, the voice says.

Is it? the voice says. Is it really you?

Sydney turns round.

There is no door to this room, just an opening, a rectangle, an empty door frame.

Her mother is inside this frame.

Behind her, Sydney can hear the steely cold swish of waves, the steely cold swish of Rothko's paintbrush.

Fancy seeing you here, her mother says, impossibly light.

Mum? Sydney says.

Come over here and give me a hug.

Mum?

Yes, darling.

What are you doing here?

I live here.

What do you mean, you live here?

I live just along the beach. I have a lovely apartment, small, but big enough for me. Why haven't you been to visit? I kept thinking you would come.

What?

Why didn't you look for me, Sydney? Why did you just give up?

What do you mean, Sydney says. What are you saying.

It's so good to see you, darling. I can't tell you how good it is to see you.

Mum, I really don't –

Look at how grown up you are. How old are you now?

Why would Dad lie, why would he.

It's all right, sweetheart. We're together now.

You didn't die, Sydney says.

I didn't die, her mother says.

9

Snowwoman

It's the Saturday before Christmas, and they have just finished watching *The Little and Large Show* and *Dallas* on TV.
It's getting late but no one seems to have noticed. They are
all in pyjamas, eating peanuts and crisps, Howard in one
armchair, Sydney in the other, Jason taking up the entire sofa
as usual.

This morning they decorated the tree.

They hung baubles and tinsel for the first time without
her.

No, Jason said, you're supposed to do the lights first,
then the tinsel, *then* the baubles.

Sorry, Howard said.

It's all right, Jason said.

Where are the chocolate Santas wrapped in foil? Sydney
said.

What?

The chocolate Santas, she said.

I don't think I bought any of those, but I can pick some
up on Monday.

I'll put them on the list, Jason said.

What list?

The Christmas shopping list. We told you about it last week, it's on the noticeboard.

Of course, Howard said.

They draped lights over branches, switched them on, checked all the bulbs were working. They wound tinsel from top to bottom. Jason sat on the floor, divided the jumble of decorations into groups, unravelled their strings. Now we can make sure they're evenly spaced out, he said, so we don't get lots of the same type together.

They all agreed that this was important.

They were careful, meticulous.

No one mentioned the Christmas tape, the one she used to make them listen to while decorating the tree, the one they'd moaned about, called cheesy, said please not that again, and now they ached to hear it, and they were frightened of having to hear it, and this was just one of many confusions.

What do you smell of? Jason said.

What do you mean? Howard said.

You smell weird.

It's probably mouthwash, he said.

Sydney and Jason looked at each other. Since when was whisky classed as mouthwash?

It was snowing outside.

Salt falling from the sky into open wounds.

Their mother loved snow. She loved sledging, snowballs, being stupid in the snow.

Yesterday, Sydney and Jason built a snowman in the

front garden and put her pink woolly hat on its head. When their father came out to see, to clear the drive with a shovel, the look on his face made them feel ashamed.

Where did you get that? he said.

What? Jason said.

The bobble hat, Howard said.

I took it from Mum's wardrobe, Sydney said, as frozen as the snowman behind her, its carrot nose, its button eyes.

Howard gritted his teeth.

I am useless, I am cruel, I am out of my depth.

When he spoke again, his tone of voice was different. Not better or worse, softer or harder, just different.

It looks good, he said. I mean, that was a nice idea, to put a hat on your snowman.

Sydney's fear turned to anger, as it often did. Why was he lying, pretending to like what they had done? His voice was odd and mechanical, one step removed, like an uncle's voice. Also, it wasn't *a* hat, it was *her* hat. It belonged to their mother and he had just erased her. He had the power to do this now. He could make them talk about her when he felt they should, stop when he couldn't bear it. He could bring her closer, move her even further away. As the adult, he got to decide how much of Ila Smith was still here, and with no awareness of doing so, his children hated him for this.

Now, in the front garden, Sydney wanted to remove the snowman's head and throw it at her dad.

She wanted to run super fast and knock him over with the furious weight of her body.

But she also wanted him to scoop her up. To place his big

hand on top of her head and ruffle her hair like he used to. He looked like a lumberjack, standing there in his red checked shirt with the shovel resting on his shoulder. A man who could chop wood and make a fire and thaw them all out.

That night, when the children were asleep, Howard crept out into the garden and pulled Ila's bobble hat off the snowman's head, just in case someone stole it. His plan was to put it back the next morning, before they noticed.

But he didn't put it back.

He got up, drank coffee, made scrambled eggs.

It's gone, Jason said, rushing into the kitchen. Mum's hat, it's gone.

Sydney hid in her bedroom, terrified. It was all her fault. She had stolen it from her mother's wardrobe, stuck it on a heap of snow and now it was gone.

And this wasn't even the worst of it.

The hat on a snowman's head, just the tip of an iceberg.

Everything was her fault. What was happening to them now, every minute and every hour, all of it, her fault.

What to do, Howard thought, as he looked at his son.

This was the thought that lived in his mind most of the time now.

What the bloody fuck to do?

It's all right, he said, calm down. It was me.

You? Jason said. You took it?

I put it on the radiator to dry overnight, Howard said, trying to remember where it was. Mostly he remembered whisky, and stepping into the snow without his shoes on, and burying his face in a soggy bobble hat, and punching the snowman in the stomach, and having to fill the dent with more snow.

Jason glared. Why had he taken the hat, interfered with *their* snowman, their gift for their mum, which they hoped she would see from wherever she was, hoped she would know was for her.

Syd, it's drying on the radiator, he yelled as he ran upstairs.

He was running to make her all right, leaping up two stairs at once to protect her. And yet sometimes he wanted to destroy her. Last week, he had taken a felt-tip pen and scribbled all over one of her drawings of a spaceship. He pushed hard with the pen, went right through the paper, onto the kitchen table. The stain wouldn't come off. The table was inked with rage, which he minded at first, felt bad about, then didn't. Don't blame your sister for what happened to Mum, his father had said. So he tried hard not to. And most of the time, he needed her more than he wanted to push her away. For now, at least.

Her bedroom door opened, and the two of them ran around the house, searching for the hat.

LIAR!

I'll sort this out, Jason said, you stay up here.

Okay, Sydney said.

In the kitchen, their father was still making breakfast, buttering toast.

Where is it? Jason said. It's not on any of the radiators, so where is it? Was it actually stolen? What have you done with it?

Calm down, Jase, Howard said.

I won't calm down.

Then Sydney walked in. It's okay I found it, she said, out of breath.

Oh well done, Howard said. Where had I left it?

It was on your bed, she said, leaving out the part about *where* on the bed, how she had found it on his pillow.

Dallas was excellent. This is something they agree on, how excellent *Dallas* is every week without fail.

It's getting late but no one is tired. They are too exhausted to be tired. The lights are low and the tree is bright and Howard is drinking sherry. Christmas is almost here and no one wants it. This is an unspoken truth, garish as a bauble. And tonight, Ila's snowman is not only wearing her bobble hat, it's also wearing one of her cardigans. This was their father's idea, after decorating the tree this morning. Let's just go for it, dress the bloody thing up, he said, because the atmosphere was so revolting he had to do something. He smiled as he said this, and it wasn't fake or awful like so many of his smiles, so they trusted it, followed him upstairs to her wardrobe, then out into the garden.

The snowman was much rounder, much tubbier than Ila. Her clothes were too small to fit. So they put him on a high-speed diet, and shrinking him was easy, and it was nice for something to be easy for a change.

Really, this he is a she, Jason said.

She is a snowwoman, Sydney said.

That's very true, Howard said.

Something easy, something true.

They patted her all over, took chips off the cold block.

That should do it, that should be enough, Howard said.

Not yet, she's still too big, Jason said.

No, she's spot on.

Howard was right. The T-shirt slipped over Snowwoman's head. The cardigan went round her and was buttoned up to the top. A scarf went on last, pink to match the hat, then she was finished.

All three of them stepped backwards.

Howard waited.

What had they done? Was this good, or was this awful? If a person has a kind of barometer for such things, his no longer worked.

They stood in silence, staring at a lump of snow dressed in a dead woman's clothes.

The weirdness of this, somehow it made them feel better.

They went inside and ate sausages, spaghetti hoops, potato waffles.

They got into their pyjamas, watched telly until midnight.

10

It is good to hear the sea at night

If Jon Schaefer's parenting skills were magically distilled into a handbook, it would be called *How to Mess Up Your Child By Ignoring Your Family and Mainly Talking About Art*. It would be a slim volume with a long title, symbolic of Jon as a man – all pronouncement and little substance. Maria Norton's handbook would be called *How to Use Your Sadness to Keep Your Child Living at Home*.

Yes, her parents were partly responsible for Belle's lack of desire to leave the house she grew up in, but there is a statute of limitations when it comes to blaming other people for who you are. Belle now has reasons of her own for staying put.

I can't possibly leave, she thinks. Not that I want to. Fact is, I'm too *important* to move away. There's looking after Stuart and Timothy for a start, not to mention my lonely mother. Who else would play Scrabble with her at the kitchen table? Who else would help her perfect her latest muffin recipe? The bookshop would suffer without my attention to detail, my flair for running events. Plus I'm busy with my allotment, my box sets, my playlist of TED talks, books on animal psychology and novels about misfits and outsiders. How does anyone ever get bored or have time for a relationship? There are a hundred things I could be doing at any moment. So no, Dad, I'm *not* going to apply for an art degree. You only want me to do what you never did yourself. And no, Dad, it won't make me live an *authentic* life, whatever that means, it will just land me in debt and misery, so get over yourself.

Get over yourself is Belle's favourite retort. Nine times out of ten, it makes people just stand there in silence for a few seconds, totally perplexed. Because what does it actually mean? She likes to count the seconds as they pass – seven is the longest so far, which doesn't sound like much, but insert seven seconds of silence into a feisty dialogue and you'll see what a mighty pause it is. If someone told Belle to get over herself, she would say *wake up and smell the coffee,* because that one is even more confusing. Try it and see.

This evening, Belle is lying on the sofa, the one in the snug, the small dark room at the end of the hall with aubergine walls, a wood burner, a lamp and a narrow bookcase. There's a tatty rug, a huge floor cushion for Stuart. Close the door and nothing else exists. Apart from these cobwebs on the window. This dust on the shelves. This carbon monoxide detector, once white now grey, no batteries inside. Two Christmas cards left over from last year, both featuring festive hounds. Can hounds be festive? Oh you'd be surprised. Stuart wore tinsel for the occasion, along with a Santa-and-his-sleigh neckerchief.

Belle brought a boy back once, only once, to sit with her in this snug. They drank ginger beer and talked about school. The boy wanted to be an anthropologist. He was wearing a Fair Isle jumper and brown jeans. I like your jumper, Belle said. My auntie knitted it, he said. She's amazing, you name it she knits it, she's quite famous actually, not for her knitting, she designs boats, these amazing boats. Wow she sounds amazing, Belle said, wishing she could have substituted *amazing* for something else, like fantastic or talented, but hey, she wasn't experienced at this, and probably never would be. Frankly, even now, she can't be bothered. And it doesn't feel like a problem, not any more. Fact is, she's happy cuddling up to Stuart, the crazy way in which they manage to fit together on this sofa, curled and overlapping, it makes her mother laugh when she walks in, she says surely that can't be comfortable? And Belle says it is actually it's really relaxing, we've been watching TED talks on my laptop haven't we, Stu? Just saw a good one about the importance of being vulnerable. That sounds interesting, her mother says. Can I borrow Stuart? I need some fresh air. Fancy a walk, Stuart?

Alone now, Belle puts on her headphones and listens to Elvis. She wonders what happened to that boy, whether he ever became an anthropologist.

(He didn't, Belle. He's an electrician now. Married to a poet, living in Manchester, daughter aged three. Here's what you could've won, if you were actually playing the game. Best not to think about it. Listen to your music. That's it, just relax. Check the homepage of the local news site to see if anything exciting or terrible has happened.)

There's a new headline on the website: SUICIDAL WOMAN IN TOWN.

Belle reads the article, then scrolls down to the bottom of the page to the comments.

6.06pm	I saw a woman on the roof of Tesco – she jumped across to the off-licence. If this trespasser is the one this article refers to, she didn't look suicidal to me. She's probably just a stunt performer in training. They have to train somewhere, right?
6.38pm	I saw a woman running along the wall around the park.
7.02pm	Is this really news?
7.03pm	What if she's spying on us?
7.14pm	If she was spying on us, I don't think she'd be drawing attention to herself by leaping around. And if you were going to spy, why come to a boring seaside town? The last dramatic thing that happened here was Mark Bellini sawing his finger off with a chainsaw.
7.18pm	I imagine there are hundreds of suicidal people already living in this town, just as there are in most towns. Suicide is now one of the leading

causes of death. This is terrible reporting. Is it even legal to run about on other people's rooftops?

7.24pm She's obviously just a traceur, a freerunner.

7.25pm I'm quite turned on by the sight of Mark Bellini now.

7.26pm Parkour isn't a crime, it actually *reduces* crime. I read about a pilot scheme in London where they taught freerunning in a few secondary schools, and youth crime fell dramatically (no pun intended).

7.30pm Mental health is in crisis. Depression has reached epidemic levels and suicidal urges are commonplace. Why doesn't this article suggest avenues of support for those who need it, instead of drawing our attention to one woman? And what if she does jump? Aren't we all a little responsible for that?

7.42pm How are *we* responsible? At the end of the day, her hobby is risk-taking.

7.59pm Hey, this is Bellini, wanna meet? I still have my chainsaw.

8.11pm   She's a hooligan.

8.17pm   I think I saw her in Gregg's buying a yum yum.

—+—

Maria puts on her sheepskin coat and her navy scarf. She clips Stuart's reflective night-time lead to his collar and sets off.

Evening walks are the part of the day she looks forward to the most, especially in winter, when she can wander early through dark streets, gazing into lit-up galleries and artists' studios. Tubes of paint left on streaked tables. Stools and chairs abandoned in the middle of the room. The day's activity is still here, vibrant and discarded, and she likes to imagine the people inside, working all day, thinking their thoughts while they paint, listen to music and drink tea.

Her husband's studio isn't like this – it's not a *real* studio. It's just a man cave, a hiding place. He paints the same thing over and over instead of being with his family. Cares about little else.

She walks towards the church, glancing down the dark lane leading to the dark sea before turning left. She walks slowly, pausing to look inside brightly lit shops, most of them full of trinkets and knick-knacks aimed at tourists: tiny wooden lighthouses, seagull fridge magnets, puffin tote bags, lamps made of driftwood, decorative pebbles. Not that Maria is knocking any of this. It makes the world go round, the buying and selling of pretty things, and let's not forget that her husband sells his little paintings to these shops, so she should be grateful for how the world turns, for how *her* world turns.

Except she isn't.

She stops to look inside the bookshop. A poster in the window lists upcoming events and tomorrow night it's Alexandra Orzabal, who is launching her new book about how to achieve a state of inner calm. To Maria, this seems like a strange thing to write a whole book about, when there are so many other emotional states you could be striving for, like ecstasy, desire or euphoria. You could miss the crux of life while you're sitting there being calm. The most wonderful thing could whirl past, like a wild wind that you were supposed to step into, if only you weren't so busy with the adult colouring book your husband gave you for your birthday, if only you had allowed yourself to get pulled into a vital storm.

(Blow me away
rip my clothes and mess up my hair
leave me dishevelled and unruly
make me feel alive.)

Oh, a colouring book, she had said, on her birthday, as she sat in bed with Jon.

They're all the rage, he said.

They certainly are, she said.

There were no other gifts. Not a story to throw herself into. Not a poem to make her sigh. Not a scarf, a bracelet, any fucking thing that meant he knew her and had given this some thought, instead of wandering into a shop and grabbing the first object from the first table.

You absolute prick!

Thank you, she said.

Not even a storm in a teacup here. Life so pedestrian, polite. Apart from when Jon was angry, obviously. And those moments weren't about passion, they were his attempts to manage her, make her less annoying, silence her protests.

Maria used to be good at protesting. She used to go on marches with her boyfriend before Jon – no, her *fiancé*; do people even use that word these days? – a builder called Andy who read left-wing journals in bed. He was an active member of the Labour Party. He planted trees in the back garden, polished his shoes more than was necessary and got a new tattoo every year on his birthday. My inky boy, she said. I bought you more tulips, he said. And this book about economics. And this heart on a string from a girl at the market. And this marmalade from the new deli, because I know you really like marmalade. Maybe I'll have your name tattooed on my fingers and my thumb, he said, drawing the letters on his hand with a biro: M A R I A.

She used to love marching beside him. They had a shared purpose, they were part of something important. Stomping his way towards a revolution, he had leather patches on his brown cardigan, his eyes were sparkly, greenish grey.

She walks on past the post office, the bank, the old-fashioned liquor store. Past the shop selling nothing but lights and the shop selling sweets and fudge. Down the high street, the backstreets, all the holiday cottages adorned with name plaques and bunting. Finally she comes to the studio, the one she likes to look in at night, and presses her face to the glass.

She sees the tiny plastic kettle. The blue mug half covered in white paint. The tubes, pots, brushes and pencils, left alone until morning.

She never looks inside during opening hours. That would spoil the mystery. The people who work here all day are perfect and unflawed. Their absence is beautiful, she doesn't know why, but it's the kind of beauty she feels in her body and she needs it. Sometimes she imagines herself at one of the easels, painting something abstract with overlapping shapes, a curve astride a hard line, a quick dancing figure. Silly really, to think this way, to put herself inside this room – as if *she* could produce anything of artistic merit. Laughable, she thinks, as she pictures herself paint-splattered and busy. In this picture, she is wearing a loose blue shirt, its sleeves rolled up to her elbows. My arms look stronger than usual, she thinks, leaning in closer to herself, to the other Maria, the one she glimpses sometimes and wonders who that is. Those rolled-up sleeves: why does the sight of them fixate her so much? She watches the other Maria pick up a large mug and sip from it. Watches her walk over to the phone, dial a number, begin to speak. She is laughing now, nodding by herself in this empty studio that doesn't seem empty at all.

Evening, Maria, a voice says.

It's Tony, the butcher, being pulled along the street by Milly, his golden cockapoo. Milly stops to sniff Stuart's bottom, but she is too small, and has to keep hopping up and down behind him, her front paws held up as if she is performing a trick.

Stuart ignores such buffoonery. He is too busy trying to work out why this evening he has two owners, the Maria beside him and the one inside the studio. They smell completely different, but his nose would still pick them out in a crowd as the same person, his *favourite* person. The one inside is sweatier, that's for sure. The one out here smells of lavender, a scent that humans tend to find comforting, which is curious really, when there is lavender in most types of sadness.

You keeping well? Tony says.

Oh not too bad, Maria says. And you?

Oh you know, he says.

Stuart inhales Tony's wrist: the bitter cologne of animal flesh. He growls.

Why does he always do that? Tony says.

Oh he's a funny old thing, Maria says.

So far, they have said nothing of any real significance, and yet they have revealed something deeply personal to each other: the fact of their ongoing loneliness. To others, this may have been hidden inside a sing-song voice or an upright posture. Perhaps this is what happens when you buy meat from the same person for years, when you have passed dead body parts to each other, time and time again. A unique kind of intimacy.

You thinking of signing up? Tony says.

Sorry?

To one of their classes, he says, nodding towards the studio.

Oh no, she says. I just like having a nose through the window.

Don't fancy a bit of life drawing then, he says, then wishes he hadn't. It sounds like a sleazy invitation, in his mind at least.

But not to Maria. All she hears is a man who can imagine her opening this door, stepping inside and sitting down with a pencil to draw. *Astounding*.

I'm more of an amateur baker, as you know, she says, then wishes she hadn't. Talk about having tickets on yourself.

Tony pats his belly. Well as you can see, he says, cake is my weakness.

Not meat? she says.

Meat? he says.

I just thought –

Can I let you into a little secret, he says, shuffling closer, dragging a reluctant Milly with him.

Go on.

I dabbled with flexitarianism.

Did you? Maria says. She has no idea what this means. Something to do with yoga, perhaps.

I did. And last year I went the whole hog, turned *vegan*. Tony grimaces at his choice of words.

You did not, Maria says.

I did. I'm entirely plant-based.

Jesus Christ.

I don't do things by halves, he says. But don't tell anyone will you, it's bad for business.

But why? she says.

Can't stomach it any more, goes right through me. But give me a lentil daal.

Well I never, Maria says. So *that's* why you started stocking Anne's veggie pies.

Funny how our tastes change isn't it, he says.

It certainly is, she says. Which reminds me, I haven't seen you strutting your stuff lately.

He looks confused.

Morris dancing, she says.

Oh, he says.

Your midlife passion.

Maria, I'm fifty-nine, hardly midlife any more is it?

You're only a year older than me, and I'm definitely middle aged, she says.

You're fifty-eight? No way. You're just a whippersnapper of a thing.

You're hilarious, she says. It's dark out here, Tony. Catch me in full daylight . . .

No honestly, he says, you have a real youthfulness about you. Belle is the opposite, she always looked like an old soul, even as a toddler.

Maria is embarrassed. She hadn't expected him, or anyone for that matter, to have looked at her so closely, paid real attention. And he was right about Belle, if not about her. So will I see you dancing in the street any time soon? she says.

This Saturday. We'll be doing our thing, with bells on.

Excellent, she says. So you're a vegan morris-dancing butcher, fancy that.

We all have our secrets, he says.

We do, she says.

My ex-wife wouldn't believe it if you told her. She might've stuck around if I'd made her a lentil daal and danced with her. She loved to dance.

I'm sorry, Maria says.

Don't be, he says. It was years ago wasn't it.

Doesn't always make any difference, she says.

No, he says.

He studies her hair, and she sees him looking, and wonders if something has landed on her head, something disgusting.

What's interesting about her hair, he thinks, is how it's many things at once. It's wispy and loose in the wind, but thick-looking too. It's light brown, with blond and silver streaks, all of it natural, an exuberance of shade and texture that he could look at all day. He wonders how the colours change, depending on the light and how close you are. He wonders what her hair smells of. Coconut, perhaps. Oranges. Sandalwood and honey. The great outdoors. Rain.

Milly is chewing her lead, spinning in circles, bouncing about impatiently.

She's a live wire that one, Maria says.

It's why I like her, Tony says.

You like a live wire do you.

Apparently so, he says, smiling.

She notices how this smile is so different to Jon's. Everyone has many smiles, of course, but Jon's is often derisive, smug and thin. This smile on Tony's face is warm and open.

Earthy, she thinks. And his thick lively eyebrows, they make him look surprised and attentive. She glances at his shirt, the bright blueness of it.

Now she pictures him sitting at the back of a dark concert hall, listening to a woman playing the cello.

What an odd thing to picture. And who is the woman?

Her mind is busy now, picturing this and that, and it makes her feel less damaged, less like one of life's scavengers.

Anyway, better keep moving or she'll eat her lead, Tony says.

Righteo, Maria says.

See you on Saturday?

Absolutely. And your secret is safe with me.

Pleased and disappointed to be alone again, she moves back to the window.

The woman inside has disappeared. Gone home, probably. And Maria would give anything to see where she lives, meet her friends, watch how she spends her time when she is not working. What kind of lover has she chosen, if any? A man, a woman? Does she wear dresses or men's shirts? Does she play the cello, the piano, the guitar? I want to know everything about you, she thinks.

She walks down to the harbour, where she lets Stuart off the lead so he can sniff around the sand. She leans against the railings, listens to the waves.

It is good to hear the sea at night.

All is not lost, it whispers.

It's bright out here, and Stuart has noticed the full moon, become fixated by it. What does a magnificent dog see when he looks at a magnificent moon? Perhaps just a giant ball, a plaything, radiant and untouchable.

The route home takes them past the fish and chip shop, the pasty shop, the Italian diner. Stuart stops outside each one, ever the optimist. Then the pub with all the benches outside, looking out to sea. Now the backstreets again, and the shops.

That's when Maria sees her, up on the roof of the cinema.

How on earth did she get up there?

She is standing close to the edge, her arms outstretched.

She looks like an angel, Maria thinks. An angel on a rooftop.

But then –

Oh no.

She is way too close now, like she's about to –

Hello again, Maria shouts.

The angel waves.

Oh *God*. The weight of this, the responsibility. Maria feels sick.

She should stop this happening, but what's the right thing to do? Who knows what this woman has been through. People often say that life is short, but this isn't how Maria sees it. Life is a long dark tunnel. Perhaps this woman is ready for the light and who is she to interfere? Everyone has the right to take their own life. She believes in the ethics of this, but now, when the decision is right in front of her, when it's not her *own* life –

Please don't do it, she shouts.

She hadn't expected to say that.

The woman looks down at Maria.

Maria looks up at the woman.

I can help you, Maria shouts, if you'll just come down. There must be a BETTER OPTION.

The woman steps backwards, away from the edge. Maria does the same. She crosses the road, tries to keep the angel in full view. That's better, she can see her now, but she's walking towards the edge again, she's going to –

No no no, Maria yells. We can find you a NEW life, all right?

THERE HAS TO BE MORE LIFE.

11

Barry the ferret

Tonight, Howard has tried all kinds of things. A long bath. A pot of sleepy tea containing chamomile, valerian, lavender and spearmint. An episode of *Sherlock*. A documentary about the history of Ordnance Survey maps. Playing his highly unique cover version of 'You Can't Always Get What You Want' on the ukulele, quietly so as not to wake the neighbours. Flicking through his own vast collection of Ordnance Survey maps. Another pot of tea, sweet orange this time. And before all of this some channel hopping, but it's all just rubbish, talent shows, people eating insects. A long phone call with Ruth, who sounded fed up. A video chat with Jason, who always shouts on Skype, gives him a headache. Then three glasses of brandy, one after the other. There is no comfort to be had. Because. It's their wedding anniversary. Because. Ila has forgotten again. Good excuse, being dead. But still. He puts on his pyjamas. Thinks about killing himself. This always helps. Soothing. Not morbid, not dramatic, but you would only know this if you had such thoughts yourself on a regular basis. They offer an exit sign, that's all. A small window at the top of a cell. A fantasy that fills the lungs with breath and water at the same time. How would he do it? The Woolfian way of course. Only fitting. But sea, not river. Rocks in his pocket. Caught between a rock and a hard place, that's about right. So here I go, striding right in, trousers flapping underwater. Oh yes, such sweet and cold relief. Deeper now, you can do it. Don't think about Jason and Sydney. Don't think about lovely Ruth. Let's not tarnish this daydream with guilt. They would understand. They know how you've tried. All these years. Deeper now, come on, that's good. Freezing, yes. I'm coming, Ila. What the hell? Don't even believe in that. Afterlife, religion, etc. But Ila, I am coming. Can you see me? It's just me and my ukulele, darling. You didn't think I'd leave my ukulele behind? Just my head to go under now, then a salty mouthful or two. It's me, Ila. It's your husband and I'm here.

He remembers that scene from *The Hours*, with Laura Brown (Julianne Moore) lying in a hotel room that begins to flood. He's not the only person who dreams of suicide, see. Not that Laura Brown is real, of course. And another thing: Virginia Woolf's suicide note is online for anyone to read. Not just the text, but a photo of the real thing. He finds this disturbing.

Dear Virginia,

One day, long after your death, people will spend most of their time plugged into a global digital network, which they will access via all manner of technological devices with screens and keyboards. And this note you have just written, the note announcing your intention to

die and leave those you love behind, will be available to
anyone who writes your name using one of their
devices. Privacy will explode, not loud and fast like
those wartime bombs, but slowly, silently. Anyone in
the entire world will be able to see this note, Virginia.
No, I'm not lying. It sounds fanciful and far-fetched, I
know. I've just come to warn you, that's all. I feel close
to you tonight. I've taken The Waves *down from the*
shelf to read again. Thank you for your books, I have
found them deeply consoling. I am sorry you
experienced so much pain.

With warmest wishes and my deepest appreciation,
Howard Smith

Cruel joke: not another woman since Ila. Well sex, obviously. A few dates, one-night stands. And there was Gwen, who lasted five months, but only because she was in Canada for three of them. Gwen was on *Britain's Got Talent* once, and when Howard confessed that he had never watched it, she looked at him like he was the most boring man on earth, for which he found himself apologising. It's not your fault, she said. What isn't? he said. Well, you know, she said. Actually I don't, he said. This went on for a few minutes, until Gwen finally told him that he didn't watch enough TV to be interesting and also, she thought he might be gay. Why do you think I'm gay? he said. You dress well and you never want to sleep with me, she said. Two excellent observations, he said, which confused and appeased her. Oh, and you play your little instrument too much, she said. My what? he said, smiling. Your fucking ukulele, she said. Oh that, he said, well it's my lifeline isn't it, I *love* my little ukulele. Well perhaps you and your little ukulele should go fuck yourselves, she said. Which made him laugh harder than he had laughed in years. It was the highlight of their five-month relationship. And the end of it.

Howard slips his cardigan over his pyjamas, puts on a pair of walking socks. He goes downstairs, makes a cup of oolong tea and takes it into the lounge, where he lies on the sofa.

Howard will not die tonight, accidentally or on purpose. Why not? Because he is working on the food tills in M&S tomorrow, and he quite likes his part-time job, likes the company. He used to be the manager of Bloom's Fine Stationery, worked there so long it almost felt like his own business. But it wasn't. He came up with the idea of bespoke stationery, hand-lettering workshops, calligraphy courses. All of which caught the attention of a local businesswoman. You've been here for so many years, I know, the owner said. You're like family to us. But this offer is too good to refuse. When the business became Bloom's Design & Letterpress Studio, Howard was made redundant, which he labelled *retirement*, which came to mean *loneliness*.

So tomorrow, he will work in M&S. And Ruth will come over to watch a film in the evening. And he has promised to walk Otto this week, while Ruth is at work and Sydney is away. These things matter, they are written on his kitchen calendar. They catch him, break his fall. The devil is in the details, which means it's the devil that keeps him alive. The *bastard*.

He puts a cushion beneath his head, closes his eyes.

This summer, it will be fifty-two years since we met, he thinks. And that number, *fifty-two*, it will deceive people when he says it, throw the day they met so far into the distance. See it go, quick as a javelin? *No. 52 what an excellent throw!* A number can do that. Make things seem further away than they are.

But it could've been last year, easy. And he never expected this to be part of getting older. The vividness of then, the murkiness of now.

They met in a marquee, in a field, in the middle of summer. A one-day folk festival.

The trouble was, whoever organised this festival wasn't what you'd call *skilled* at such things. A folk festival should be about music, and while there were a few bands, scheduled throughout the day, the rest of the affair resembled a village fete with bric-a-brac stalls, home-made cakes, kegs of beer and bunting. There was duck herding, hook a duck, dog agility and best in show. There was a coconut shy, tug of war, maypole dancing. A few people arrived in tiger costumes, no one knew why or who they were.

Howard was standing beneath a sign that said CAN YOU GUESS THE WEIGHT OF BARRY THE FERRET? He handed over his money, wrote 3lb 5oz and his name on a ticket, popped it into a rotating drum.

If you don't mind me saying, I think you've seriously underestimated Barry's tubbiness, a woman said.

That's cheating, he said, turning round. You're not supposed to look at what I wrote.

It's only cheating if I copy you, and you've got it wrong. He's got to be well over four pounds, that guy.

Expert in ferrets, are you?

She smiled, filled out her ticket. We'll see who's right later shall we?

You're on, he said. In the meantime, I'm going for a beer.

Sounds good, she said, just standing there, hands in her pockets, an expectant look on her face.

Oh, would you, would you like one? he said.

Mine's a cider, she said.

They were side by side on bales of straw, both of them holding a pint. He sipped, she swigged. He tried to take a good look at her without making it obvious. She was pretty, in a tomboyish way. She told him she worked in the farm shop for now, left school at sixteen like him, would love to do something better but didn't know what, not yet.

What about you? she said.

He told her he was eighteen, worked for a stationer in town, enjoyed handling the fountain pens.

She raised her eyebrows and laughed at that. Fetish? she said.

Never you mind, he said.

I have a lovely mechanical pencil at home that you might like, she said.

How forward of you, he said, but to be honest I prefer the feel of a real pencil to a mechanical one.

She was eyeing him over the top of her glass, grinning as she finished her cider.

You seem to find me very amusing, he said.

I do, don't I.

And you drink very quickly.

This is good cider, she said.

He drank some of his beer, tried to keep up.

So, are you a big fan of fetes? she said.

Well, he said. You do know this was supposed to be a folk festival? I was expecting ballads and poetic lyrics, not dog agility and maypole dancing.

I know, it's brilliant, she said. Best folk festival I've ever been to, to be honest.

They were both wrong about Barry the ferret. Five pounds and seven ounces. Loved his food, did Barry.

Ha! she said. Told you he was a chunky monkey.

Yes but you were *also* wrong, he said. Which means you have to buy me another beer.

Oh do I.

Yes you do.

I don't remember promising that.

You definitely did. You also promised to be my dancing partner at the barn dance later, where I'll be playing the ukulele. Why are you laughing again?

Sorry, she said. You just crack me up.

That's charming.

In a good way, she said, in a good way.

———

As their relationship began, he didn't know that it would last fifteen years and a lifetime. That he would be a boyfriend, a husband, a father of two and a widower, all by the time he was thirty-three.

A friend once asked him a question: If you could go back in time, knowing that you'd only have Ila for fifteen years, would you choose someone else instead, with better life expectancy?

That's a disgusting thing to say, Howard said. So disrespectful.

What?

I should punch your stupid face.

Howard, it's a –

Fuck you.

Jesus, it was only a question, a reasonable one I think.

Howard thought about grabbing him by the collar of his coat and throwing him across the room. He thought about smashing his head against the wall, over and over. The violence coursing through him felt disturbing and good. He felt alive for the first time since Ila had died. And maybe this was how it started, how people began to live through their fists, thriving on a rush of insults that turned into brawls and awarded them bruises. He imagined hitting his friend and being hit back. Taking a good battering. Walking home with cuts and gashes, rips and tears. The outside of him would make sense then, it would match the inside, convey an honest message about the life he had lived and the things he had felt, instead of this incongruous body as he stood here now, looking so outrageously unharmed. In a way, getting drunk and beaten up would be an authentic response. It would be showing Ila's memory some respect. I'm fucked up for you, Ila. He worried that he and the kids were going slowly mad, holding it in, hiding the truth of the matter, the vile and disgusting truth that daily life was now unbearable. And he was teaching them to behave as if nothing had happened. Was this the right thing to do, or should they be smashing up the house, screaming at the top of their voices, expressing themselves?

It hadn't occurred to Howard at this point, unaccustomed as he was to losing a wife and being left with two children, unaccustomed as he was to being around people who spoke openly about their suffering, that there might be a middle ground, an alternative to silence or acting out: namely, just talking. And the prospect of talking about his loss, let alone the children's, was terrifying, like opening a box of rattlesnakes and leaving them to wind their way from room to room.

That folk festival, fete, barn dance. The fact of it being more than half a century ago. And yet it's as vivid as this sofa he is lying on now, this blanket that Ruth and Sydney gave him for his sixtieth birthday, along with some books and records, the face cream he likes, a teapot, some tea, a cardigan *and* a pair of walking boots. They had been far too generous. That was almost ten years ago. He'll be seventy this summer. *Seventy*. And yet he still feels like the guy at the fete. He has always been the guy at the fete.

———

There are knuckles in his face. That sound, what. Not the doorbell, no. Knuckles on the front door.

Shit, he says, sitting up, nauseous. It's quarter past nine and he's still in his pyjamas.

He opens the door to the postwoman, who eyes him up and down.

All right for some, she says, and hands him a parcel.

I have a doorbell, if that's easier next time, he says.

I don't care much for doorbells, she says. I don't trust them.

Dear Dad,

I've spent the afternoon sketching on the beach. Won't be beaten by the weather! Hands frozen and stiff now. Anyway, I found this book about the history of the ukulele in a second-hand bookshop and thought you might like it. I've also enclosed a sketch I did of Mum, when she got us all to sing songs from Grease, do you remember? I hope it's not too weird to receive, just wondered if you might like it, thought it might bring back a nice memory.

Speak soon, Dad.

Love Sydney xx

He opens the book and looks at the sketch. The likeness is excellent. How has Sydney achieved this level of detail? She must have copied a photo, this can't be from memory. She was just a young girl when she last saw her mother. He has always assumed that her memories would be hazy by now, that his children can't possibly carry Ila in the way he does.

Looking at the drawing is uncomfortable.

He feels sorry for Sydney.

He also feels angry and envious.

He puts it in a drawer, along with the note and the book.

I already know the history of the ukulele, he says, as he heads upstairs to get dressed.

12

I like you

Belle Schaefer is trying to make an author comfortable, which is not an easy thing to do. In fact, it's a task that should only be given to someone like Belle – a woman of great patience and stamina. The author's name is Lily Whippet, writer of *The Man Who Jumped Out of a Helicopter and Only Broke His Toe*, a contemporary novel about sex and death, according to the blurb on the back.

She hopes tonight is more successful than last night's event – Alexandra Orzabal's book launch. Alexandra's paperback on achieving a state of inner calm was clearly produced by a ghostwriter, because the author seemed to know nothing about her own subject. She was the most hyperactive stressball Belle had ever met. The speed at which she spoke, breathless as if she were running on the spot, combined with her ill-fitting decision to wear ill-fitting white trousers, created a sense of tension so palpable, so unpleasant, she was excruciating to watch. The trousers were like a second skin, zipped on. Her voice was as relaxing as a puppy nibbling your toe.

You don't find these events calming, do you? Belle said to her, smiling.

What on earth do you mean by that? Alexandra said. What are you implying?

Gosh, I'm sorry, Belle said, I didn't mean to be rude. It must be tough, that's all, trying to summarise a hundred and forty pages in one reading.

(But not as tough as getting into those trousers.)

Not at all, Alexandra said. What's tough, between you and me, is making these arseholes understand it.

Oh, Belle said.

I mean really, is it that hard to be calm? Alexandra said. She glanced at her watch, the clock, her mobile phone, the door.

Nice trousers, Belle said, because she was staring, and hoped she might be able to stop if she actually mentioned the offending item, the *offensive* item.

Thank you, Alexandra said. You won't believe this, but I haven't worn these for twenty years.

Really? Belle said.

Yes. I found them at the weekend and thought hey, I can still get into these. It was like linking right up to my thirty-year-old self. Such a *boost*. Maybe we should all try on our old clothes more often, what do you think?

All my clothes are old, Belle said. So I think I've got that covered.

Deliberately? Alexandra said. How intriguing. Is that a lifestyle choice?

I've never really thought about it, Belle said. The look on Alexandra's face made her feel like she had just announced that she had never read a book or been to school.

Have you ever thought of exploring your self-image? Alexandra said.

Well no, because I'm way too busy for such navel-gazing bullshit, Belle thought.

Interesting notion, she said. Which is a phrase she often rolls out with writers.

It can be quite illuminating, Alexandra said. Do you have any cookies in here? I normally get cookies.

This evening, the floor will belong to Lily Whippet. Well perhaps not the whole floor, just a tiny corner of the bookshop and a wobbly stool.

Three hours before her event is due to start, Lily calls in to take a look and say hello. I'm here to get my bearings, she says.

Good idea, Belle says.

I like to inhabit a space before I'm properly in it.

Do you, Belle says.

I do, Lily says.

Belle gives her a tour, moving from bookcase to bookcase, describing each section. Lily would have preferred to wander around by herself, but never mind.

I *love* your name, Belle says. I love how it sounds like a dirty command.

Lily Whippet laughs. What a cheeky young woman, she thinks. She almost says this aloud, but she is too nervous about this evening's reading to speak unless it is completely necessary.

Are you all right? Belle says.

I just need a little drink, Lily says.

Sparkling water? Coffee? Earl grey tea? Belle says.

I was thinking specifically of gin, Lily says. (She is often thinking specifically of gin.) Is there a decent pub close by?

Oh, Belle says. Well, I could take you if you like?

That's so kind, Lily says, but I'm really happy to make my own way. You must be very busy.

No, not at all, Belle says. She pops into a back room to speak to the owner, Yvonne Partridge, whispers something about Lily Whippet looking unwell and needing some gin. That's fine, Belle, Yvonne says, we all know what these writers are like, go and pour some gin down her throat, that's a good girl.

Yvonne often calls her a *good girl*. Belle likes it, but doesn't think she should, it feels a bit wrong, and lovely, and patronising, and comforting.

Great thing to get paid for, Belle thinks, as she leads Lily Whippet out of the shop and down the street towards the Black Hole.

Can we pause to look at the sea? Lily says.

Of course, Belle says. So have you done many of these events? I loved your novel, it was pure grit. Are you writing anything new?

Oh dear God. Stop babbling, Belle. Can't you see that Lily Whippet is trying to steady herself?

Lily isn't listening. All she can think of is the reading tonight, the way her mouth clicks when she speaks in public, the way she sweats uncontrollably when she looks up from her book and sees the faces of complete strangers, non-plussed and unamused. Why must authors be forced to take off their dressing gowns, put on outside clothes and speak to people? It's *repulsive*. And she's rubbish at it. Without gin, that is. And *after* the gin, Lily? Oh life after gin is another matter entirely – another territory, quite frankly. That toothy smile, those smutty jokes: a whole new personality. What if she had never discovered this wonderful liquor? Her career would have floundered as soon as she completed her first public event.

They pause outside Munro's Burgers and look at the sea. The air is cold and smoky. Lily turns to see where the smell is coming from. Munro's is jam-packed with customers, sitting at long benches, stuffing locally sourced chicken, beef or bean burgers into their mouths.

People can certainly eat here, Lily says.

Don't you eat? Belle says.

Once a day, Lily says, otherwise I get lethargic. Is this pub quiet?

Not exactly.

I think I need somewhere quiet.

Belle thinks it over. Do you like muffins? she says.

I'm sorry?

Do you like muffins?

Sometimes.

Why don't you come back to mine? I'll feed you gin and muffins and you can relax before tonight.

Lily moans. It's the sound she makes when something feels good, but all Belle hears is discomfort. That's the trouble with the wordless moan, it's so hit-and-miss, so hard to decipher. All the possible variations of tone, from short and squeaky to long, deep and sleazy. And it's never the sound you intend to make. Lily is trying to convey delight, but the moan itself is such an act of pleasure at the back of her throat that she lets it go on for too long, and it slinks along the tonal scale into sultry and provocative.

The air has changed. Still cold and smoky, it's now thick with mixed signals and the smell of fried onions.

Does something hurt? Belle says.

You're so perceptive, Lily says. She is suddenly in awe of this bookseller, who makes her feel seen and cared for. Do take me somewhere quiet, she says, noticing Belle's dark curly hair, her ruddy skin.

Unnerved, Belle leads the wiry author through town, along the path that runs above the beach, until they come to a white house.

Here we are, Belle says.

I can't believe you live this close to the beach, Lily says. I might have to move in with you.

Come through to the kitchen, Lily Whippet, Belle says, as she lets herself in. She is irritated with herself for using Lily's full name, but she just can't help it. The word *Lily* won't come out by itself, it feels too informal, too intimate. Some people must be kept at a distance.

Lily is disappointed to find another person in the kitchen. This is *not* her definition of quiet.

Mum, this is Lily Whippet, author of *The Man Who Jumped Out of a Helicopter and Only Broke His Toe*. This is my mother, Maria.

Nice to meet you.

You too.

A novelist in my kitchen, well I never. Can I make you some tea, Ms Whippet? Maria says.

She wants gin, Belle says.

Maria glances at the clock. I see, she says.

She has an event tonight.

Ah, Maria says.

Lily grimaces.

Don't worry, Maria says. I know *exactly* what to do with you.

Do you? Lily says. Oh the joy of being around masterful people, she thinks.

You need a Calming Cake, Maria says. You might want to eat two, actually.

I'm sorry, but I don't do drugs before a reading, Lily says. Afterwards, I'm all yours.

Maria laughs, assuming this is a joke. A plate appears under Lily's nose with two muffins on it. Belle leaves the room and returns with a bottle of gin and three glasses.

Apparently we're joining in, Maria says, how decadent.

Lily listens to the women talk about small things. The small things are interesting and she wants to write them down. She sips her gin and takes a bite of the muffin, then another. Wow, she says.

I know, Belle says. Mum has cured actual illnesses with her muffins. They're *amazing*. People call round and order them. One woman said they got her through a messy divorce.

Really? Lily says.

She's exaggerating, Maria says. It's what she does.

I've never tasted anything like it, Lily says. Do you sell them anywhere? I mean, is this what you do?

Oh no, I'm a dental hygienist, Maria says.

How fascinating. And you don't mind making cakes, even though they rot people's teeth? I mean, ethically speaking, you don't have an issue with that.

It's not something I've ever considered, Maria says. I hardly think making some muffins is unethical. And anyway, it's not about what you eat, it's about what you do with your mouth afterwards.

You are so right, Lily says.

Do you floss? Maria says, then wishes she hadn't, but she wants to assert control, stand firm in Lily's company.

What? Lily says.

Do you floss or use interdental brushes?

I hate flossing, it really hurts. I do have some interdental brushes, but to be honest I never use them. Having them in my cabinet makes me feel virtuous, though.

I hear that a lot, Maria says. From people with gum disease.

Mum, Belle says. She pours Lily more gin by way of an apology.

I like you, Maria, Lily says. Are you coming to my event this evening? You should definitely come. It would help to see a friendly face.

Maria gets up, edges away, heads towards the sink. She puts on a pair of Marigolds. I suppose I could come, she says, as if it's nothing, as if she doesn't really care, as if someone saying they like her – even someone acerbic and slightly annoying, with terrible dental hygiene – doesn't feel wonderful.

Ten minutes before the reading is due to begin, the three women speed-walk through town.

We are *so* late, Belle says.

I know, Lily says, hoping one of them will fall over and break a bone so that she doesn't have to read.

They pass two men in overalls, leaning against a van, smoking.

I told her I didn't want to do it, one of the men says.

Well you shouldn't have fuckingwell done it then should you? the other says.

Lily stops walking. She wants to know what the *thing* was. She stares at the men, tries to commit the details of their appearance to memory. She could certainly write a scene about this – a woman who forces her boyfriend into a regrettable action.

Want a picture, love? the man says, the one who did something he shouldn't have fuckingwell done.

I think you've pulled, the other man says.

Actually, I would like a picture, Lily says. She opens her satchel and pulls out her phone.

Gin-fuelled mouthy author seeks men to write about. WLTM men full of regret. Dirty clothes preferred.

Want me to take off these overalls? the first man says.

Maria flinches. How common, how uncouth!

Oh no, I'm *loving* the overalls, Lily says. She takes three pictures, posts them on Twitter with the message: *The inspiration for my next short story!*

Belle is furious. Lily Whippet, your event is due to start in *three minutes*, she says, thinking of the five members of the public who will already be sitting and waiting for their favourite author to appear. Well, perhaps not their *favourite* author. Just an author they have heard of. Maybe. Or been persuaded to meet by Yvonne Partridge.

Now they are outside the supermarket, where a small crowd is blocking the pathway. Necks bent, eyes looking up.

What's going on? Lily says.

We need to keep moving, Belle says.

But Lily has stopped again. She is looking up at the roof.

It's her, Maria says.

Who? Lily says.

I keep seeing her, Maria says.

We have to *go*, Belle says. Right now. *Seriously.*

Up on the roof of the supermarket, a woman is running and leaping and turning head over heels. One sideways somersault, then another. She steps onto a wall, sprints along it and jumps across to the next building.

The crowd gasps.

Bloody hell, she's really something, Lily says.

Isn't she, Maria says.

Belle isn't looking. She really doesn't care about some woman on the roof of the Co-op. She is too busy cursing Lily Whippet and worrying about losing her job. Yvonne Partridge isn't the most patient of women, and she certainly won't appreciate Belle turning up late with a drunken author. Dexter, another bookseller, tall and long-bearded, nickname Furry, *he'll* be put in charge of looking after delicate writers from now on if she messes this up. Fucking Dexter, fucking Furry, with his degree in fine art, his MA in modernist literature, his sloppy knitwear and his skinny grey jeans.

For God's sake, Belle shouts. I implore you to get moving. This is highly unprofessional, Lily Whippet.

Lily laughs. The word *implore* sounds funny coming from Belle. And why does she keep using her full name? She's so sweet, so formal. This place is fantastic, she says, slipping her arm through Maria's and trudging towards the bookshop, where twenty-six readers are happily drinking wine and listening to Dexter, who has decided to manage Lily's late arrival by playing his violin.

When Lily appears, and sees not five but twenty-six members of the public, she asks Dexter if he might carry on playing while she reads from her book. She can't handle this alone, she needs support. And while this dark-eyed young man looks like he might smell of clothes that haven't dried properly, he will make an interesting accompaniment.

I'd be honoured, Dexter says. Your writing is inspirational, Lily. It's so primal, you know? And the way you use hardly any punctuation. The sheer force of one sentence that goes on and on, refuses to be stopped, that's powerful, especially with the violence and the obsession.

Lily is looking at him blankly.

Fuck off fuck off fuck off, Belle thinks. And do you know what's also annoying? If *she* put on the jumper that Dexter is wearing now, she would look like she had let herself go, like she had slept in her clothes last night, like there was nothing decent in her wardrobe, nothing she had purchased within the past three years, which would be true, of course, but on Dexter it looks arty and cool. Loathsome man-boy. Makes her feel frumpy and unscholarly. Which she is, obviously. But that's not the point.

During the reading, Maria wonders who actually buys Lily's books. The violence seems random, the storyline repugnant. Also, where is the man who jumped out of a helicopter and only broke his toe? He hasn't appeared so far. Is he even *in* the book? False advertising, that's what this is. Disgraceful.

That was wonderful, Maria says to Lily, as she waits for her to sign the book that Belle pressed into her hands.

Did you enjoy it? Lily says.

Oh yes. A little more violent than the books I usually read.

Excellent, Lily says.

And I was hoping to hear about the man who jumped out of a helicopter.

I'm sure, Lily says. Everyone says that. I'll let you into a little secret. There *is* no man who jumped out of a helicopter. My book forces people to imagine him themselves. The ultimate act of creativity, wouldn't you say?

Maria opens her mouth, says nothing.

On her way home, she hears it again and again:

I like you, Maria.

This statement has unsettled her.

When you feel deeply unlikeable, a moment like this causes chaos.

First there is joy, innocent, almost childlike. Then the wet blanket of shame. The distrust and humiliation. *She was taking the piss, Maria. My God you're so desperate.*

This has happened before, and it's the main reason why she has failed to make good friends. A lunch invite from a woman she met at an exercise class made her blush with confusion: what on earth would she say over lunch? She would rather not risk being a disappointment. There was also the woman she met in the library, who invited her to a book group. And the woman from Dark & Sweet Sourdough class, who suggested they make sourdough starter together on a Saturday morning.

Without realising, Maria had become an expert in rejecting people. She inflicted her own wounds on potential friends, made them feel dull, uninteresting.

In the hallway, before she has even taken off her coat, Stuart runs up to her. He sniffs her hands, pushes his face against her stomach. She bends down to kiss his head. He smells of coconut, from the shampoo she used on him yesterday, which cost twice as much as her own shampoo, but not as much as his toothpaste. Yes, like so many dogs in the modern world, Stuart has his own toothpaste. It's poultry-flavoured. Belle tried it once, an experiment she immediately regretted. Not like any poultry I've ever eaten, she said, her skin paling with nausea.

Jon, Maria says. Jon are you still awake?

I am now, he says, turning over in bed to face her.

I need to ask you something.

What.

Do you think I have low self-esteem?

He sniffs. Have you been drinking? he says.

I had some gin earlier this evening, and some wine in the bookshop. Belle brought an author round. She writes best-sellers, it was quite exciting really. She invited me to her reading.

This is met by raised eyebrows and a smirk. You'd better get some water, Jon says.

I'm not drunk.

Of course not.

Jon, she says, do you like me?

They both freeze.

Sometimes, he says.

Don't go overboard will you.

No one likes another person all the time, he says.

I'm not just another person though am I.

Well technically speaking, you are another person.

You know what I mean, she says.

And the dance goes on. The stripped-naked dance he makes her do for a compliment or reassurance. Exposed and cold, she dances on the shards of his words. He finds it disgusting, how hard she tries. She finds it disgusting, how hard she tries.

Then she goes too far.

Why haven't you ever painted me? she says.

What?

I just –

Why ask me that?

Don't shout, Jon.

Why all these questions when you know I need my sleep?

No need to get so cross.

You come home pissed, have a go at me. I was *asleep*, Maria. Couldn't you have waited until morning?

The moment would have passed, she says.

Well maybe it *should* have passed.

I can't always get the timing right. Sometimes you just need to say something.

That's so selfish. And anyway, what I paint is nothing to do with you.

Ouch, she says.

Well, he says.

That's really hurtful, Jon.

Bollocks is it hurtful. You're being really aggressive. You have no idea how aggressive you're being.

I don't think I'm –

You never think you're wrong. You can't see yourself. You think you're so sweet, so mild.

I don't think I'm sweet.

You push me, all the time you push me. You never let anything go.

I'm sorry, she says.

You're always sorry, he says. No wonder I don't paint you. I see you all the time, why do I need to paint you?

She wants to mention the ocean, there all the time, and yet he paints it *all the time*. But she knows the look on him now. Her body knows it, and recoils.

Sensing retreat, he plumps up his pillow, lies back down and turns to face the wall.

Maria sits and waits. For what, exactly? Without hope or expectation, the wait feels silly and depressing. It feels like sitting in the dark on the edge of a bed, listening to the heavy breaths of a man who doesn't like her. The breathing is louder and more evenly paced than when he is asleep. In other words, he's faking it.

She is annoyed with herself now. She hadn't planned to say any of those things. Why couldn't she have got into bed quietly, respected his need for sleep?

Yes, waking someone up with a needy question is an aggressive act.

Of course it is.

13

Apocalypse

Dear Mum,

It's surprisingly upsetting to write the words Dear Mum.

I'm here again, Mum. I can't quite believe I'm here. It's a little shocking to be honest.

While I'm here, I thought it might be helpful to write you a letter. To write the very first thing I think of and leave it at that. So here we go.

Temperature, that's what comes to mind. How during the first few weeks, people were not warm, as you'd expect them to be. They were hot, so hot. And then they were cold. They were too much at first, always knocking and ringing, driving us mad: If there's anything we can do, anything at all, you know where we are all right?

Earlier today I drew them as a choir, singing that line at our front door all day and all night. I drew Dad, throwing a bucket of water through the bedroom window, and you laughing in bed while he did it, saying honestly that's terrible, they're only trying to help. And

Jason, sitting up in bed, saying did you hear that Syd did you hear it, I could've sworn I heard Mum just then.

Dad said it was peculiar how everyone now expected us to know their whereabouts, as if death had implanted special trackers inside them.

Can you think of something we need? he said.

We thought really hard, then our heads hurt.

We couldn't think of a single thing, except maybe for them to stop knocking and ringing, and they must have read our minds, because that's what they did a few weeks later.

Where's everyone gone? Dad said. It's like the fucking apocalypse, he said.

In the past, hearing him swear would have made us laugh, but now it was disturbing.

One last thing. My name. Sydney Oriel Smith, as in SOS, as in distress signal, as in dot dot dot, dash dash dash, dot dot dot. That's my code: save our souls, save our ship, or something. It's like a sick joke and it haunts me.

Well, that's about it, Mum.

All my love,

Sydney

xx

14

On the rocks

They are sitting at the table in his kitchen, drinking tea and eating toast. His house is a project, a work in progress, a two-bed terrace in a dingy part of town. They love this place. She has taken photos of the launderette sign (a 1950s design classic, or so she tells him), the town hall, the library and the market. She is nineteen, he is twenty-five. She lives with her parents but those days are numbered, she is counting them down, counting down the days to when they will stand in a registry office – *Do you, Maria Norton. Do you, Andrew Hearne* – before going for lunch with their parents and a couple of friends, then saying goodbye and taking a bottle of fizzy wine on a long walk up a steep hill, where they will sit by themselves at the top, swigging from the bottle and saying can you believe we're married now, it feels really weird doesn't it, *Mrs Hearne*, and what shall we have for tea, I can't believe I'm peckish already after that massive lunch. Maria wants to be an artist, but it won't earn her a living, that's what everyone says, so she is studying science while working at the bakery, the one Andy loves, because they deliver unsold produce to the homeless shelter instead of throwing it away. Andy is neither artistic nor scientific, but he is a thing of beauty, a miracle of the natural world. Right now, he is reading her lines from a tatty copy of *Animal Farm* while she finishes her toast. He is wearing a burgundy jumper and worn-out jeans. There is nothing extraordinary about this dream, apart from the fact that Maria never dreams of Andy, not any more. She is saying Andy, can I ask you something? He lowers the book, looks at her over the top of his tortoiseshell glasses. Do you think I have low self-esteem? she says. Why would you, he says. You're fantastic, he says. Then time speeds up and Andy has gone to work and she is just sitting there looking at his reading glasses, left behind on the table, and thinking about how the sight of them when he is not here always moves her, as does the sight of his watch on the bathroom sink. Some objects, especially those kept on a person for a long time, seem to hold something of their owner, conveying his or her presence even when they have been discarded. Something like osmosis, she thinks. Or maybe the word is assimilation. Who is the keeper now? If you wear someone else's watch, you are keeping their time as well as your own. In this dream, she puts on Andy's glasses and picks up *Animal Farm*. The text is blurred. Now she is walking to college by herself, but when she enters the building she is back in Andy's house again, soon to be her house, and they are eating fish and chips on the settee, watching *On the Rocks* on BBC2, a programme about the geology of Britain. You feeling a bit low, love? he says. I am, she says. Well why don't we go to the pictures tomorrow night, he says. She tells him that might be nice. She stays the night, something her parents are fine with now. It took a while for them to come round to their daughter dating a man six years older, but they've grown to like him, they've had three years to adjust, and besides, if they don't approve she'll do it anyway, she's that kind of girl, has a wilful streak, rebellious like her mother, and they secretly admire this, believe it will stand her in good stead, this is what they say to each other one evening over a melon boat, steak and chips and Black Forest gateau at the Berni Inn, before coming home drunk and waking her up. She tells them off, says look at the state of you both, giggling and burping like overfed children, which makes them laugh and try to hug her, she looks so sweet and sleepy and cross, and she dreams of this moment now, how she made her parents black coffee and called them embarrassing. Then Maria is back with Andy again, he is holding her in bed, holding her tight while she dreams of an angel on a rooftop, then a giant hound on a sandy beach, walking towards her, a dog that looks unlike any animal she has ever seen, so regal and gentle and powerful. She wakes up and tells him about the beautiful hound. Well maybe we should get a dog, he says, maybe that's what the dream means, we're bound to get one eventually, why not now? I don't think so, she says, we've got to buy a new bed remember, this old one of yours is just awful, there's plenty of time for a dog.

Maria wakes up, turns over and sees a man lying beside her who isn't called Andy.

What's in a name?
Everything, of course.
Everything.

15

Henry Moore

Howard is lying on the sofa, eating salt-and-vinegar Chip-sticks, watching a documentary about Henry Moore. He has tucked his pyjamas into his new walking socks, then sealed the arrangement with the ankle clips he wears for cycling. Something about this feels deeply satisfying, and satisfaction is hard to come by, so he appreciates every second of this moment – the crisps dissolving in his mouth, these beautiful bronze shapes on his TV screen.

Now they are showing Henry Moore's drawings of his hands, the ones the artist made when he was eighty-one. They are describing how hands express emotion. Howard puts down his mug of ginger tea and looks at his own hands, wonders what they say about how he feels. His neat nails, his wedding ring. He curses himself for never taking a close-up photo of Ila's hands. Maybe all couples should attempt to draw each other's hands. Trouble is, Howard can't draw. Trouble is, his wife's hands are no longer avail-able. He looks down at his stupid ankles and his stupid feet. I look like a complete fool in these bicycle clips, he thinks.

He opens a cupboard, pulls out a cardboard box and empties it onto the floor.

He spreads the photos out, sifts through them.

In this moment, it's imperative that he finds her hands.

He just has to.

Then, finally, look:

she is laughing, and covering her mouth with her hand, in the way you do when you think you shouldn't be laughing.

The laughter is all in her eyes.

He gets out his magnifying glass.

Just as he thought:

her hands were small, pale and chubby.

He hasn't forgotten.

The following morning, Henry Moore's hands are everywhere.

Here they are beside him on the kitchen table as he eats his muesli.

Here they are in the washing-up bowl, swishing about.

Here they are in the dining room, wrapping a parcel with brown tape.

Drawings, only drawings, and yet they are so real and alive.

Has Sydney ever tried drawing hands in such detail? He wouldn't know, but he thinks she would probably be good at it.

He finds one of the sketches online, prints it out, pins it to the noticeboard. For the next few days, he will step into his kitchen each morning and hold his right hand up to the one in the drawing, a hand so open and interested in the world. He can tell, just by looking at these lines, that Henry Moore would have made a very good friend. *High five, Mr Moore.* All the people who have come and gone that he will never meet. Instead he stands alone in his kitchen, touching a print of a print, not even the real lithograph of the real hand.

When this sketch eventually comes down, it will be replaced by something else.

A photograph of his daughter.

The first photo he has taken of Sydney since she was ten years old.

16

It might be overwhelming

This room, Ila says, laughing.

I know, Sydney says. It's a bit over the top isn't it.

Ila glances at the anchors on the duvet cover, the drift-wood mirror, the ships on the wall, the watercolour paintings of the sea. That's putting it mildly, she says. This B&B is nautical in the extreme.

I know, Sydney says. Anyway, what do you think of these?

Ila walks over to the little desk in the corner, and they both stand there, looking down at the shapes Sydney has made on paper:

– Jason, holding his cassette recorder up to the radio.

– Their hallway, piled high with suitcases, bags, duvets, board games, buckets and spades.

Something is beginning to take shape, Ila says.

I wouldn't go that far. They're only rough sketches.

A rough passage, Ila says.

A rough sea.

Rough and tumble.

Rough and ready.

I used to love playing that game with you, Ila says. You were always good with words.

Not these days, Sydney says. Not with Ruth. Not with Dad. And not with this bloody book.

Let me help you, Ila says.

How.

Tell me how it begins, she says.

What?

You know what.

I can't.

Of course you can, why else have you drawn our things piled up in the hallway? Let's lie quietly on the bed, and when you picture it in your mind, I'll be with you.

I don't know, Sydney says.

Come on, Ila says, taking her daughter's hand. You're all so stuck, I can't bear how stuck you are.

Do you think Dad is stuck? I mean, do you have much awareness of Dad?

Ila laughs. I am aware of your father, she says.

✝

Can you hear the sea? Sydney says, looking up at the ceiling.

Shh, Ila says. Concentrate. Try to remember how excited we were.

I don't want to.

And yet you just did.

✝

We are stupidly excited.

We have never been this excited about a holiday before. Why? Because this one is going to be different.

The journey is long but we really don't care. We have crisps, a Thermos, giant rolls full of ham and pickle, bottles of pop and the radio. Jason has recorded some of our favourite songs especially for the trip. He held his tape player up to the radio, made us a compilation.

This summer, we are not in agreement about music, not at all. Our tastes have diverged more than ever, especially since Jason developed a crush on Olivia Newton-John. He is deeply serious about Olivia and won't hear a word against her. Dad had to have a little talk with him about this in the privacy of the garage, after he threw a chocolate bar at my head. Your sister is entitled to her opinion, he said. Not everyone has to like 'Xanadu'. I love 'Xanadu', Jason said. Yes, we're all very aware of that, Dad said, and that's not the issue. The issue is how you behave when someone *doesn't* like it. You have to develop a little tolerance, all right?

When 'Xanadu' comes on in the car, Dad turns to look at me, just for a second. I know what this look means. It means please, for the sake of a quiet life, do not criticise Olivia Newton-John. So I don't. Instead I sing along. Jason doesn't like this either, he thinks I'm taking the mickey and ruining his listening experience. Sometimes I can't win.

Near the end of the song, Jason can't contain his emotions any longer. He starts punching the air with an intense look on his face. I find this so funny I almost wet myself.

Sydney, stop it, Mum says.

Dad looks at me again in the rear-view mirror. He winks.

Mum's favourite track this summer is 'Everybody's Got to Learn Sometime' by the Korgis. When this comes on, the mood in the car changes. We all go quiet.

What's this song about? I ask.

What, Sydney? Mum says.

It's really sad, but I don't know why it's so sad, I say.

Me neither, Jason says. And what has everybody got to learn sometime?

Mum doesn't answer. She unwraps two ham rolls and passes them to us in the back seat while the song finishes and the next one starts. This one is 'Could You Be Loved' by Bob Marley. We eat our rolls and wriggle, because you can't help but wriggle when this song comes on. This is why I think it's brilliant.

You lot have no idea about music, Dad says. When's my song coming on?

Soon, Jason says. Because he knows his compilation tape off by heart.

Dad's favourite – 'Love Will Tear Us Apart' by Joy Division – is just as sad as Mum's, but in a different way.

I really think Olivia Newton-John is much better than this, Jason says.

We play this tape over and over, until the sea comes into view.

I fucking love holidays, Jason says.

Excuse me? Mum says.

Sorry, he says.

There's no parking at the cottage, Dad says, so I'll pull up outside to unload, then I'll drive to the car park.

Yes, you heard that right. He did say *cottage*. This is why we are stupidly excited. We've slept in tents, we've hired a caravan, but we have *never* stayed in a cottage.

It used to belong to a fisherman, Mum says. Then it belonged to a sculptor.

Jason and I don't really care who owned it before. What we care about is the toilet, the fact that it has one. Last year's caravan was great, and so much better than a tent, but it didn't have a shower or a toilet. The cottage has both, *and* it has a big TV, *and* it's right in the middle of town, so we can go out by ourselves to look in the bookshop or, in Jason's case, the hardware shop. He is obsessed with the hardware shop.

Actually, we have a bit of a surprise for you, Jason, Dad says.

Jason looks frightened.

You know Mr Trent, who owns the hardware store?

Yes.

Well I spoke to him last week, Dad says.

Why did you.

I called him.

Why did you.

To ask if he needed any help in the shop this week. Last year, you said you'd like to work in there, remember?

What did Mr Trent say?

He said he'd love some help, if you were still interested.

Seriously? Jason says.

Yes. He can't pay you, but if you'd like to help him keep the place tidy for a couple of hours this week, you can take something away with you afterwards. As long as it's not massively expensive, obviously.

Jason looks nervous and happy. I can tell that he wants to accept this offer, but doesn't know if he is capable.

It might be overwhelming, he says. This is one of his phrases.

You could wear your headphones the whole time, like I do, I say. No one will speak to you then. You'd have time to look at everything properly.

That's true, he says.

The car pulls into a narrow lane.

Blimey, this is a bit tight, Mum says.

Don't panic, Dad says.

We turn a corner, enter another narrow lane, then stop.

Here we go, Dad says. Your abode for the next week. Do feel free to use and admire the bathroom facilities immediately.

He wrestles with the front door, can't get it to unlock.

Let me try, Mum says, there might be a knack to it.

She waggles the key about, and grins.

Dad tuts.

And we tumble in.

Jason and I run upstairs, fling open every door, poke our heads into every corner of the place.

There's a bath *and* a shower, Jason shouts.

There's a cupboard with fishing nets, I shout.

There's an ironing board, Jason shouts.

Mum and Dad aren't listening. Much to our disgust, they are in the kitchen, kissing.

Gross, Jason says, I feel sick.

Go and unload the car, Mum says. Everything apart from the suitcases. We'll make it worth your while.

How will you?

50p each.

A pound.

Fine.

+

And this is how it begins.

It begins with us carrying board games and duvets into a tiny fisherman's cottage.

It begins with Jason crying because he has forgotten his headphones, and me saying he can borrow mine if he likes, if he promises not to play 'Xanadu' all week.

He tells me to get stuffed, and we argue.

We argue as we carry things upstairs.

We argue in the bedroom about who will sleep in which bed.

We argue because we are tired and hungry.

We argue because it hasn't happened yet.

17

A jar of flowers

A jar of flowers has caused all this trouble.

Dutch tulips, magenta and white.

Maria bought two bunches from the market this morning. On the way home, she kept thinking how perfect they were. She spread them out, put some in a jug, a vase and a jar.

Now she carries the jar up to his studio.

I bought you some flowers, she says.

Jon is sitting in an armchair, reading. He looks up.

I thought you might like to paint them, she says, putting the jar on his desk.

I'd appreciate it if you didn't tell me what to paint, he says.

It was a suggestion, not an order, she says.

You want me to paint flowers, I know you do. You're always saying it.

I'm sorry, I didn't realise.

You may love flowers, but not everyone does.

I'll take them away, she says.

Good, he says.

Then she stops. She imagines someone watching them from the doorway. Another woman.

You bought them as a gift, the woman says. Leave them where they are. He's an ungrateful moody bastard.

Maria looks at this woman, then back at Jon. He is reading again now, ignoring her.

You're right, she says. I do love flowers.

He grunts.

And you've never bought me any, not even once, she says.

He closes his book. He turns it over, seems to be inspecting the back cover now, but he is not inspecting the cover. His rage is upon him, mawkish and familiar. Anger disturbs Jon – not the feeling itself as such, but its tone, its character, the way it grips his imagination as well as his mood. Were he to paint this anger, it would be a sick old man, anaemic, lymphatic, a bilious figure with dry skin and brittle nails, clamped on to his shoulders.

Maria, why must you always do this?

He can feel the warmth of her body now, beneath him on his desk.

Her lovely warm arm, twisted.

He remembers what a Chinese burn feels like.

So he lets go. Staggers backwards.

She doesn't move. He stares at her, slumped over his desk. My God he wants to paint her now, just like this. She is perfect.

Still she doesn't move. The sight of her heats him to the bone.

Maria, he says.

Her arm is still burning.

He touches her back, taps it three times with the ends of his fingers.

She shivers.

I'm so sorry, Maria, he says.

Somehow, then, she is in his armchair. He has helped her across the room as if she is a hundred years old, and he is kneeling at her feet, his hands on her knees. His love shows only in remorse – this is when she sees it, when he adores her, when he runs his hands through her hair and kisses every part of her face. He is saying that she needs too much from him. She has a problem, and it's obvious, and he'll try to cope better with how stressful it is to love a woman with this problem. Her neediness makes him feel bullied. Why must you bully me, darling, he says. You're always pushing me. She wipes his tears away. She seems gentle, sad. He pulls a tulip from a jar and places it on her lap, rests his head beside it.

Today had started so well, full of good intentions. She had bought flowers from the market. She had bought bread and cheese and olives.

He follows her downstairs, watches her as she makes them a pot of tea.

All day he follows her, stays close. She has craved this intimacy, and now hates it.

Eventually, his head sore from what he has done, a soreness of flashing lights, he falls into bed, asks her to bring a cold flannel from the bathroom.

She stands in the bathroom for half an hour. Tugs the string that hangs from the mirror, makes the light switch off and on, off and on.

She picks up the flannel, puts it down again, leaves it by the sink.

Then she goes into his studio, sits at his desk. She sits here for a long time, looking out of the window, watching the world from her husband's vantage point.

I must have loved him once, she thinks.

The love is hard to recall. What she does remember is drifting about in a state of grief and shock, and Jon calling it a tragedy, what had happened, her fiancé dying of a stroke at the age of twenty-five, dying on a bed in a department store, I mean how can that even happen, he said. Jon was simply there, Maria kept bumping into him, and his paintings were quite good back then, full of promise. She loved looking at all the jam jars full of coloured water, the brushes, paints and palette knives, the paraphernalia of a creative life.

He's a good father to Belle, she thinks now.

Then something catches her eye, down on the beach.

There is a woman, taking off her wellington boots and stepping into shallow water. She begins to dance. She sings to the sea.

Everyone in town knows this woman, without knowing her at all. She had an operation once, or so someone said, and disappeared for weeks. To their surprise, people began to miss her. Has anyone seen the dancer? they said. The beach looks a bit empty without her. When she returned, full-voiced and singing, people smirked and rolled their eyes but they also felt relieved. The sight of her is like the sight of the harbour, the town hall, the galleries and the market. She makes them feel at home. No one has ever told her this, she has spent her whole life without this knowledge. Because it exists and should be hers, a sensation of emptiness often passes through her. I feel like I haven't eaten for hours, she thinks, reaching for the Maltesers. And maybe I need a pet. Or maybe I should learn a language. Maybe I should do the lottery. Maybe I should join an evening class. She writes these things down, full of anxiety and hope and emptiness.

Sometimes, this is what neglect looks like.

A list in a brand-new notebook.

A solitary tulip on a grey carpet.

A woman, dancing in front of the sea.

A woman, watching through a window.

18

Kangaroo

They are two hoodies on the beach.

One hood is up, the other is down.

They have their backs to the land, their fronts to the sea.

Life should always be like this: sea-facing.

They watch the waves and chat. Mother and daughter.

Mum, look over there, Sydney says.

A woman in a long Puffa jacket and wellies has walked across the sand, up to the water's edge. She kicks off her boots and begins to dance.

What a lovely sight, Ila says. A free spirit, like you.

Ha, Sydney says, I don't think so.

Well sort of, Ila says.

Sydney tells her she has seen this woman many times this week, says she finds her quite charming somehow, and might speak to her later, ask if she'd mind being sketched, if she'd mind appearing in a book.

Talking of which, Ila says.

Hmm, Sydney says.

This book.

What about it.

You need to get on with it.

I am getting on with it, that's why I'm here.

I know, but you've been procrastinating lately. You can't waste your talents.

Sydney sighs. It just feels a bit fanciful, that's all, she says.

What does?

Me, writing a memoir.

How can telling your own story be fanciful?

Well I don't have much to tell, not really.

Of course you do. Anyway, it's all about your take on things isn't it, your personality and style, not actual events. Every moment in a person's life is interesting if you find out how they see it.

Sydney puts both hands inside the kangaroo pocket at the front of her top. She pushes the material as far out as it will go, doesn't realise she's doing it.

Do you remember those special dinners, she says, when you made us describe one moment from our week?

Ila laughs. That family tradition didn't last very long, she says.

No, but it stuck with me.

It what? Ila says, peering out from inside her hood.

I said it stuck with me, Sydney says, louder now. I ran a workshop a few years ago, called How to Write a Graphic Novel, and I talked about those dinners. I said they launched my career.

Really? Ila says.

Sydney nods. I told them what you said, about how describing one moment is a way to describe everything.

Well I never, Ila says. What else did you tell them?

Sydney takes her hands out of her pockets. I talked about how graphic novels are a showcase of moments. How they're life, emotion and dialogue, distilled into an image, and every image expresses many things, it has its own surface story but it's also truly open, rich with ambiguity, the story is always multiple.

Ila's eyes are bright. I've never heard you talk like that, she says.

And Sydney shrugs it off, says well, it was a workshop wasn't it, you have to say something.

I'm excited, Ila says.

Excited? Sydney says.

Yes. I love your graphic novels, I can't wait for another. The first one's my favourite though, it's so melancholy and beautiful and weird.

You've read my books.

What kind of mother doesn't read her daughter's books?

The kind of mother who's dead, Sydney almost says.

I'm not surprised you won that first book award, Ila says. That was such an achievement, it really was.

Thanks, Sydney says, quietly. Then her voice changes, goes sing-song. Downhill from there, she says.

What? Ila says, moving closer.

Mum, you can't hear me properly with your hood up.

Yes I can.

What did I say then?

Something sarcastic, Ila says.

Sydney rolls her eyes at her mother's stubbornness. She looks down at herself.

Do you remember when you bought us matching tops from the surf shop, she says. We looked ridiculous, all four of us in blue hoodies.

We looked fantastic and highly amusing, Ila says. Anyway, don't change the subject. And by the way, are you aware that *graphic memoir* sounds like a book full of explicit sex? It sounds like the story of a *life* full of sex. Just saying.

Sydney smiles.

Seriously, Ila says. I do think it's exciting, your work in progress.

I really wouldn't call it exciting. Especially considering what I'm going through to create the bloody thing.

Yes, but *you* wouldn't call anything exciting, would you?

Sorry?

Darling, you never get excited about anything. Correct me if I'm wrong.

With a childish scrunched-up nose, Sydney thinks this over. Her mind is blank. With her arms by her side, she leans forward, on tiptoe, into the wind.

I'm concerned, sweetheart, that's all, her mother says. It's not how I brought you up, you see. To be so –

They are silent.

They look into each other's eyes.

Then Sydney looks away, puts her hood up.

And now they are simply two hoodies on the beach.

Sea-facing, hand in hand.

19

Running through sprinklers

After their mother died, the house filled to the brim with empty space. Sydney and Jason kept bumping into it. It was like an unseeable balloon, a magic inflatable, hall-shaped, kitchen-shaped, the shape of every environment it snaked its way into.

Concerned about his son and daughter, Howard came up with an idea. He spoke to other parents and decided to fill the house and garden with something else, at least once a fortnight. *Other children.* This was uncomfortable, because Sydney and Jason were attached to the empty space. Their mother had left it behind, which meant that it belonged to her and they must take good care of it.

The other children were strange. They wanted to run through the sprinkler in the back garden, over and over again. As soon as one of them did it, they all wanted to follow. Sydney drew pictures of them as they ran, turning them all into small clowns. Later, when they had gone home, Jason picked the sprinkler up and examined it. He attempted to take it apart and put it back together. Neither of them ran through it. It was water flowing through a pipe and coming out of tiny holes. It was like the shower upstairs, only upside down. So why all the excitement? Did these children get excited about rain and fountains? Why were other children so childish? Some of them were Jason's age, they were twelve years old – he was baffled, embarrassed.

This is so fucking weird, he said. I mean, twelve is pretty much an adult, right?

I know, Sydney said.

So, do you think we should try it? Jason said.

What?

He nodded towards the sprinkler.

Oh, Sydney said. All right.

Afterwards, they were even more bewildered and their clothes were wet.

Running through sprinklers is stupid, Jason said.

It totally is, Sydney said.

I'm going to watch TV.

I'm going to ride my bike.

Fast-forward to university, and a friendly lecturer takes Sydney aside after his seminar. Do you think you might be depressed? he says.

Why would you ask that? she says.

I just wonder if you might benefit from seeing the university counsellor, that's all.

But why? Sydney says.

Well, you just sit there, eating your sandwiches, not saying anything.

What's wrong with that?

Nothing in principle.

What do you mean? she says.

It's the way you do it, he says, as if nothing's going on around you, as if there's no one else in the room.

Fast-forward to Jason's wedding day, and his new wife says honey, today of all days I thought you'd look excited.

But I am excited, he says. Excited in my own way.

That's fine, she says, but let's make sure it's visible in the photographs, yes?

What? he says.

She wonders then if she has made a mistake, for she is not a tolerant woman, and she prefers a man to wear his excitement like an expensive new shirt. She wants it to be obvious to everyone, especially their friends. A relationship should reflect well on a person, surely, or what else is it for? And his gloomy disposition as the months roll by, his head always stuck in non-fiction, happily immersed in ideas, well it's enough to drive her insane.

What about *her* ideas? Isn't she as important as those essayists and historians?

Seven months of cajoling and still no decent results. Tired of being thrown around and egged on by his wife's hyper joviality, Jason spends most of his time at work. So she leaves him for the manager of Debenhams, the guy who sold them suitcases for their honeymoon. He is effusive about clothes, wine, interior design and luggage. He is effusive about *her*. Eventually, when she has become more confident, she will find herself longing for Jason – the peacefulness of his company, the slow warmth of his body. But for now, her ears crave only a rhapsody of approval.

I found her a bit brash, if you don't mind me saying, Sydney says, when Jason comes to stay with their father.

I don't mind, Jason says. To be honest I agree with you.

Me too, their father says, and the three of them settle down in Howard's lounge to watch an old episode of *Cagney & Lacey*. Before the programme starts there is an advert for a local theme park, in which three children squeal in anticipation on the journey towards it.

Why do people get so giddy over stupid things? Jason says. I don't understand it.

I know, it's really weird, Sydney says.

It's usually fake, that's my theory, Howard says.

Then the *Cagney & Lacey* opening credits begin, and the sight of Tyne Daly and Sharon Gless makes them relax down into their seats.

Pure class, Sydney says.

Now *this* is something to get excited about, Howard says.

Absolutely, Jason says.

They sit in silence, staring at the TV, eating salted peanuts from three individual bowls.

Afterwards, Howard makes them a pot of Granny's Garden tea, his latest purchase from the tea emporium in town. He often visits this shop on his way home from work. He likes the big glass jars full of dried fruit and herbs, the loose-leaf concoctions for every possible mood, ailment or stage of life. The smell of the place is soothing. It smells of nature, kindness and patience – only to him, of course, and these things come to mind because they are what he needs.

I think you'll like this one, Howard, the shop assistant said, as she scooped the fruit into a brown paper bag. She always used his name, which brought him more happiness than he felt was reasonable.

Is there such a thing as unreasonable happiness, Howard? she would say if he ever told her this.

Yes, he would say. It's when something small and silly means too much because everything else means so little. There is something sad about that.

I don't agree, she would say. I've lived alone in a friend's shepherd's hut since my partner left me, I listen to the radio half the night because I can't sleep, and I take enormous pleasure in the fact that you come in here twice a week and always ask me how I am. At this time of my life, there is no one else who enquires about my wellbeing as often as you do. In other words, you matter to me, Howard.

Granny's Garden tea is a mix of elderberry, raspberry, beetroot, blackberry leaves, redcurrant, strawberry, apple, hibiscus and chokeberry.

This one's all right, Jason says.

It's not bad is it, Howard says. I might get it again.

I like the colour, Sydney says.

Would you call it scarlet? Jason says.

No, this red's too warm, and there's a lot of purple and black in here. Sydney brings her cup to her nose and inhales. It smells of hope, I think, she says.

Which makes Howard and Jason look up.

Just smells of dark fruit to me, Jason says, tapping his foot in the way he always does when he is frustrated. He has been at his father's for twenty-four hours, and while nothing at all has gone wrong, and everyone has been perfectly nice, he is ready to leave as soon as possible.

Because *nice* is precisely the problem. Why must his father be so bloody nice? And where has being nice got him anyway? Nowhere, bloody nowhere. His loyalty to a dead woman seems so romantic and commendable to outsiders, but actually, it's pathetic. Do you know what it's like, Dad, to have to *pity* your father for your entire adult life? To come back to this house, see those bloody keys hanging in that cabinet with Mum's fucking labels. It's sick, Dad. It's *awful*. Why do you have to remind us all the time? Can't you let us move on? Let *Sydney* move on? If you hadn't been so fussy, if you'd accepted love from one of the many women who offered it to you over the years, we could have known what it was like to have a father who was capable of grasping life, of loving more than one woman, of moving on from a tragedy that has affected us all, not just you. And sometimes, Dad, I fucking *hate* being around your loneliness. Why else do you think I live so far away? The two of you, honestly, I just don't need it.

But Jason doesn't say any of this.

He drinks his tea and looks at Sydney, whose feet are also twitching.

Ha, he thinks. She's frustrated too. She's had to sit still for three hours while we've cooked and eaten and watched

TV, which is virtually unheard of, she must be desperate to put her trainers on and run home. Me, I have to stay the whole pissing weekend.

And he is right. Sydney *is* desperate to leave, but not because she's bored or frustrated or wants to get away from her father.

She is jealous.

Jealous of her dad and Jason, who talk so easily about anything at all, seem so relaxed and close, even though they only see each other a couple of times a year. She is here all the time, sees him at least twice a week, and yet the distance between them never shrinks.

This distance is astronomical.

If not for Ruth, they would probably have drifted further apart by now.

Two planets, for ever misaligned.

20

The answer to every question

Inside the Black Hole, Sydney drinks her fifth whisky.

She is beginning to love this pub. It reminds her of their old local, the one she, Ruth and Otto used to walk to for last orders, before it was turned into a gastropub called the Jumping Fox, where the staff wear black trousers and white shirts, the tables are reserved for diners, and you feel bad if you only go in for a drink. On the wall in the Jumping Fox, there is a sign that says EAT IT AND TWEET IT!

The Black Hole is cramped, shabby, falling apart. If this place had a sign on the wall, it would say TAKE US OR LEAVE US, FRANKLY IT'S UP TO YOU. Tatty velvet seats, navy blue walls, thin candles dripping wax onto wonky tables. The furniture here is distressed, not deliberately, as a fashion statement, but because it's knackered, hanging in there for dear life, longing to collapse into a tired heap of firewood. The snacks are Monster Munch, pork scratchings, mini packets of custard creams. The specials for dinner tonight are chicken in a basket, rice pudding and bourbon biscuit delight.

Why did chicken in a basket ever go out of fashion? And what on earth's a *bourbon biscuit delight*?

Do you remember coming here? Ila says, stirring her gin and tonic.

Sort of, Sydney says. Did we come here a lot?

We did. This pub's been here for ever, hasn't even changed its name. You and Jason always had scampi and chips and a knickerbocker glory. Huge appetites.

Must've been the sea air, Sydney says.

She reaches into her coat pocket, pulls out a tiny fox terrier made of metal and places it on the table.

I bought this earlier, for Ruth, she says. It's from the 1950s. His paint's quite chipped, but she'll like that.

Will she?

Sydney nods. She has a thing for dents and scuffs, she says.

I like her already, Ila says.

Have you heard of kintsugi? Sydney says.

Ila shakes her head.

It's the old Japanese art of repairing broken or chipped pottery. They use layers of lacquer, often with powdered gold. Instead of hiding the damage, it's embraced. It's treated as part of an object's ongoing beauty.

I love that, Ila says.

Well, Ruth goes to kintsugi evening classes, Sydney says. All our crockery was broken at one time or another.

Ila is smiling. She preserves moments in time, Ila says.

I suppose she does. I never thought of it that way.

So where did you find this little fellow? Ila says, as she inspects the fox terrier.

In the second-hand toyshop. I took a photo of the shop window, look.

She holds up her phone, shows her mother the window full of Postman Pats, Mr Plods and Noddies. There's an ALF, a Roland Rat, a Paddington Bear whose sleeves have been torn off, leaving him dressed in a ragged waistcoat. There are dolls with bland circular heads and tubular bodies, dolls in lace dresses, some with eyes and some without. Destroyed by love, now worn-out and discarded, every toy is hoping for a new start.

Mum, Sydney says.

Yes.

That thing you said before, about how I don't get excited about anything.

Hmm.

Well, that's not the only emotion I have trouble with.

Right.

And now I'm worried. I mean, what if I'm some kind of low-grade psychopath or something.

I think that's a bit dramatic, sweetheart. And I'm not sure you can even be a *low-grade* psychopath. I'd have thought someone either is or isn't.

But we both know what I did. We both know I *qualify*.

Stop it, Ila says. I won't let you talk such rubbish.

It's not rubbish, Sydney says.

She looks around the room. If I'm not a psychopath, then what am I? she thinks. The answer comes easily. I'm a woman who has spent her entire life obsessing over her parents, the dead one and the live one, both of them.

In the corner of the pub, an old TV set flickers.

Isn't that our old Philips telly? she says.

The television hisses. Its noise is white, vintage, too much.

It's so cold in here, she says. Are you cold, Mum? They should turn up the radiators, turn down the TV.

She remembers something her counsellor once said, back when she was at university. When you have these flashbacks, shrink the images down and imagine them on a TV screen, then try switching it off. What a ludicrous suggestion. Clearly this man had never ruined a family's life. His *own* family's life.

It's so bright in here, she says. I don't feel so good.

Ila checks her daughter's forehead. I don't think you have a fever, she says. Let's get some air, shall we? I think you need to call Ruth.

On her way out of the pub, Sydney leans across the bar. Excuse me, she says.

Yes my love, the barmaid says.

What's a bourbon biscuit delight?

Now that would be telling.

Yes it would, Sydney says.

It's biscuits, isn't it.

And?

The barmaid rolls her eyes. It's a bowl of ice cream with bashed-up biscuits sprinkled on top, she says. But you can have them mixed in if you want. You look like the sort of person who'd want them mixed in.

What do you mean?

Isn't it obvious?

No, Sydney says, it's really not.

The barmaid shrugs.

It's been raining all day, the air is cold and damp. They sit in the dark, in the middle of the beach, close together for warmth. And Sydney does what she is told. She calls Ruth.

I'm at your dad's, Ruth says. Then she says something else, something strangely ordinary, about a takeaway, a game of Scrabble.

Sounds nice, Sydney says.

She feels betrayed. She knows it's unreasonable to feel this way: jealous of her own partner, jealous of her own dad.

He was a bit down, Ruth says, so I thought I'd keep him company.

Are you trying to make me feel guilty? Sydney says.

Sorry?

Like a crap daughter.

Hold your horses, I was –

There are no horses, Sydney says.

Are you drunk?

I spoke to him earlier, he didn't tell *me* he was down.

Stop, Ruth says. Just stop, all right? You're doing it again.

What.

Having a go at me for something I haven't said. I'm tired of things always becoming so overcomplicated.

Since when have things been overcomplicated? Sydney says.

She waits for an answer.

While she waits, she looks at her mother's feet, those familiar trainers, bright pink.

Tell her you're sorry, Ila whispers.

Why should I? Sydney whispers back.

Because you're no longer a child.

I'm tired, Ruth says.

She says this ever so slowly, in a way that's different somehow. And Sydney wants to know what she means, if there's something in particular she is tired of, but she doesn't ask. Only an idiot would dip their toe in that kind of water. Fast-moving currents, dangerous and deep.

I'm really sorry, she says.

It's all right, Ruth says. I've had a *really* busy day. I just wanted to have a relaxing evening. If you feel guilty about something, that's your problem.

Sydney hears Otto barking in the background. How's my boy? she says.

Oh he's fine. He's just trying to get rid of a pigeon that's sitting on the fence, taunting him.

Is Dad with you now?

He's right here, he says hi.

Put him on if you like.

There is a pause. Actually, I think he just popped into the garden to get some wood, Ruth says.

Oh, never mind.

Sometimes it feels like Ruth would rather spend all her time with Howard. He makes her laugh, plays her songs. This dynamic isn't easy, and Sydney has often wanted to bring it up, to say yes, she's glad that Ruth and her father are so close, of course she is glad, it's obvious that they need each other, but for her, it's difficult and it's painful.

But she has no right to say any of this. To pull them apart.

Are you all right? Ruth says.

I'm fine, Sydney says. Bit tired too, probably. Maybe I'm getting a bit old for all this running about.

Do you think so? Ruth says.

I probably just need to eat more protein.

Ruth sighs.

I need to go and wash up, she says.

Sydney keeps the phone to her ear, even though the call has ended.

Maybe this is it, she thinks.

Maybe she'll do it when I get home, tell me how *profoundly* tired she is.

Of me, of us, of me.

I've never been quite able to give her what she wanted, she says.

To the sea, to a phone, to her mum.

Ruth opens the door and lets Otto back in. She stands in Howard's kitchen, looking at drawings of a man's hands on the noticeboard, flicking through the calendar on the wall.

How's Sydney? Howard says. He steps into the room just as Ruth is inspecting his scribbled plans for the coming month. He likes the sight of her nosing around like this, as though she lives here, as though the events on his calendar belong to someone else too.

I think she's a bit drunk, she says.

This evening, they have eaten Indian food, played Scrabble and looked through his vinyl collection. Soon they will walk Otto before Ruth drives home, and he will point at the bedroom window of a house nearby, its curtains drawn, the light still on inside. The lady who lives there is a retired archivist, he will say. She gets milk delivered in bottles, and sometimes I see her on the doorstep in the mornings, wearing pyjamas with some kind of Japanese print, pale blue with pink flowers. And Ruth will say Howard you're such a sweet old thing, noticing details like that. She'll nudge him with her elbow, say maybe you should ask her out, she sounds right up your street if you'll excuse the pun – old-fashioned and into pyjamas. I think a woman should have more going for her than *that*, he'll say, although I do like the way she sits in a deckchair on her front lawn, reading a hardback, even during the winter months. Oh she sounds great, Ruth will say, I want to meet her myself now. And he'll roll his eyes and say you, my dear, think most things sound great.

Which is true. Where does her cheer, her steadfastness, come from? People who know Ruth's background often ask this question. Her mother walked out when she was three. Her father's favourite words for his daughter when she was a child were *bitch*, *ungrateful* and *little shit*. In other words, she's had her own problems to deal with. In other words, she would do anything for Howard Smith. He's the best thing Sydney ever gave her, no further gifts required.

(If only relationships were that simple.)

Why would I want my biscuits mixed in and not on top? Sydney says.

She looks up at the moon, closes her eyes against the misty rain.

Tell me, she shouts.

She spins round. Mum? she says. Mum, where are you?

Nothing.

And now, as always, she runs.

Running is the answer to every question.

The cinema, yes, that's the place to go. But not to see a film. Its roof is the best this town has to offer: a good clear space with a gritty, non-slip surface, and just enough room to jump safely down onto the roof of the toyshop below.

She begins her ascent.

It's easy if you know how, easy if you've done this before. Up here already, see.

She looks down at a young couple, two umbrellas bobbing about. One of the umbrellas is bright yellow, and watching it accelerate through the streets and turn a corner reminds her of Pac-Man.

Do you remember how we used to play that all the time, Jason? How we used to make Pac-Man escape from his ghosts?

Oh and guess what else, Jason. Below my feet, people are eating popcorn and Revels and watching John Cusack in *Say Anything*. It's 80s night. You loved that film. Me, I can't remember much about it, apart from the bit where John Cusack holds a boom box above his head playing 'In Your Eyes' by Peter Gabriel.

That song is in her head now. She sings it loudly as she stands by the edge.

I miss you, Jason. I had no idea until this week that I miss you. I never miss anyone, you see. Because when I do, I miss *everyone*. And you can't live your life that way.

She can feel vibrations, bass rising up through her feet and legs. It's magical thinking, of course. There is no music, and tonight she has no rhythm, which is why she shouldn't be up here with a whisky-lined mouth. It's careless, irresponsible. And thinking, magical or otherwise, is the antithesis of freerunning. A busy mind, the enemy of instinct.

She scans the streets in the distance. The jumble of homes, hotels and guest houses, a motley collection of two-up two-downs, studios, one-beds, apartments, terraces and semis, tightly packed from the seafront through to the backstreets, the high-rises, the mansions with a view.

And inside that jumble, five streets in from the beach and down a narrow lane, she can see the old fishermen's cottages.

From midwinter, she can see a summer's evening. The tide is out, the air is warm.

There is a ten-year-old girl, slouching over a green stable door, open at the top. She turns back, goes inside to eat pizza and salad with her parents.

Outside, beside the step, there's an orange bucket full of seawater and shrimps. There are two pairs of children's wellies, a bucket and a spade.

In a few minutes' time, a woman will open the door and shake the sand from a towel. She will be wearing flip-flops, shorts, a pink T-shirt.

It's the second evening of her summer holiday.

A girl and a boy will tumble out from behind her with badminton rackets and a tube of shuttlecocks.

These children have no idea that people have been speeding up the passing of time with feathers stuck into cork for at least two thousand years. Theirs are plastic, of course. They play in the street. There's a thwack and a shriek. The girl hits too hard, she's told to slow down. Be gentle, their mother says.

These children have no idea that there are people in the world who have made their shuttlecocks travel faster than 200 miles per hour. This is called a smash, which usually means to shatter into tiny pieces, there is nothing gentle about it.

Sydney looks down at the roof of the toyshop, imagines Paddington Bear in a torn waistcoat, dolls without eyes. There is a person in this world who believes that these toys are worth taking home. Right now, this feels like an important fact.

And here is another:

I killed my mum, she says.

Words let loose like a mob of crows, a gulp of magpies.

———

Yesterday, and the day before that, a sequence of movement took place without any problems at all. Sydney went from here to the ground in four jumps, four landings.

But tonight, she is thinking of the cottage.

Remembering how she and Jason had a room with twin beds.

They took their duvets downstairs in the morning, watched *Huckleberry Finn and His Friends*.

It's midwinter and it's summer.

Her feet are not firmly in one place or another.

Can't be in two places at once, someone said, a long time ago.

They were wrong.

Head full of, sky full of.

Her eyes are wet and the floor is wet,

from the sprinkler, the sprinkler, do you remember the sprinkler?

Other children leaping across it, soaked and squealing.

And the sight of them felt violent,

because it *was* violent. Some things are

and they hide it well:

like the violence of spring, sleep ruptured by light and birdsong

or the lurid dandelion yellow of oilseed rape, in your eyes and your nose and your eyes.

Sydney makes it down to the flat roof of the toyshop.

But not the garage beside the shop, not the wall beside the garage.

She doesn't land with both feet on the ground, not this time.

There is a smash, that's all.

And because she has no feathers
she falls.

And because she is not cork
she breaks.

PART TWO

21

Airborne

Stuart smells it before he sees it. The body on the ground ahead of them. It smells of whisky, wheat, a baby's head. It smells of fresh paint, fire-engine red. It smells of a church bell, a flag, a Nanci Griffith song.

Which Nanci Griffith song, Stuart? Because there has to be a big difference between the odour of something like 'Heaven' and 'Late Night Grande Hotel', right?

Wrong. All her songs smell the same.

Fascinating.

The human body is lying on the floor outside the second-hand toyshop. This shop is one of Stuart's favourite smells. He has only been inside once, when Belle went in to acquire (i.e. steal) a Matchbox toy car for Dexter, the co-worker she despises, the one she moans about night after night over dinner, all the annoying things he says, the way he's read every book anyone mentions, and if he hasn't read it yet he's seen the reviews, knows exactly what it's about.

Imagine the smell of vintage toys to an emotion-detecting wolfhound. That kind of inhalation is a serious trip, like airborne LSD for canines. Each toy carries the scent of when it was bought, received, adored and discarded. It wears the scent of rough love and night-time embrace. Sometimes, desperation. The stressed-out sweat of a child who clings to it while listening to her parents fight. It's all here: on plastic, on tin, on flammable fur, on fake glass eyes and robot feet, on a teddy bear's back, a doll's ear.

Stuart's nose is easily distracted, drawn from one odour to another. Not only can he smell hundreds of things at once, from the vinegar of mistakes to the husk of parting words, he can also sniff out the connections between them.

And right now, he can smell something terribly sad.

It is somehow connected to his owner, and yet entirely remote.

Calm down, boy, Maria says.

He drags her along the street. He is usually careful, never pulls like this.

What's got into you? she says.

And then she sees.

He is right beside her as she crouches down.

It's the angel, she says, to his soft grey head.

22

Groucho

Howard is used to living alone, doesn't usually mind it. And it's hard to even imagine living with anyone else. But Ruth changes the feel of the place, the atmosphere, and every time she leaves he has to readjust, wait for things to settle again. He knows this process by now, how it comes and goes whenever she comes and goes.

This evening is no exception.

She kisses him on the cheek, bundles Otto into the car, drives away.

He goes back inside and closes the door.

He has learned that the best thing to do is busy himself with chores. He tidies his records away, cleans the kitchen, makes a pot of chamomile tea, takes it into the lounge and lies on the sofa.

He opens his laptop and plays a song loudly through his wireless speakers, the ones Sydney set up for him at Christmas: 'Psycho Killer', being performed live by the Ukulele Orchestra of Great Britain. For Howard, this is a work of pure genius, and much better than the original. He picks up his ukulele and plays along.

Now he plays along to their cover of 'Teenage Dirtbag', and by the time this song has finished, the house is his again.

He texts Ruth: *Thanks for a lovely evening, see you soon x*

She replies quickly: *Thanks H, and thanks for the take-away too. Love you, hope you sleep well xxx*

He wishes she would call him Dad. People do that some-times don't they, call their in-laws Mum and Dad. Or maybe that was years ago and he's being old-fashioned. And anyway, H is probably better. You only shorten someone's name to one letter if you like them.

The next track on his playlist begins: Bruce Springsteen, 'Tougher Than the Rest'. He loves this song too, despite the fact that its narrator is the exact opposite of him, or perhaps because of it. Howard is not tougher than the rest when it comes to love. In fact, he'd rather be left alone.

He pulls the blanket from the back of the sofa and drapes it over his legs. Thinks about Nina, his neighbour, wonders if she is in bed yet, if she is wearing those pyjamas with a Japanese-style print, pale blue with pink flowers. He likes those pyjamas, would happily wear them himself. He won-ders if she saw that documentary last night about the French Impressionists, whether she likes watching stuff like that. He never expected to be this kind of man, one who spends his evenings glued to BBC4, and sometimes he feels like he is betraying his past, pretending to be someone else, faking it. He has zero qualifications. He grew up on a diet of tinned meat and sardines, didn't eat out until he was eighteen, didn't go to a theatre until he was twenty-eight, and that was a pantomime with the kids. Everything he knows is self-taught, his general knowledge is appalling, his memory for facts even worse. So if he loiters by Nina's front garden in the morning, tells her about the excellent documentary on BBC4 about the French Impressionists, she'll think he's someone he is not, and any conversation from that point onwards could easily catch him out, disappoint her. She will assume, simply because he watches BBC4, that he's the kind of man who is comfortable in restaurants, who knows about wine, and art in general, not just the French Impressionists; that he has probably lived abroad, speaks more than one language and can tell you the plot of every Shakespeare play. No seriously, women have made these kinds of assumptions before, these kinds of mistakes, all based on what he tells them he watches on TV or listens to on the radio. When actually, he just likes documentaries and going to the lido. He likes ukuleles, herbal tea, making playlists and listening to *The Archers* sometimes. And that's about it. And that's also the problem with dating – every woman who likes him thinks he is someone he is not. *Extrapolation*, that's the word. People are too prone to extrapolation. So dating, it's off the cards.

Ila never did that. She didn't box him in, want him to like certain things, all because it made him seem like the kind of person she thought she would get on with. He was simply Howard Smith, who rode to work on his bike and loved music and stationery. And she was just Ila, who spoke about politics and conservation, but without ever using those terms, because those were subjects that *other people* spoke about, people who knew about history, people who had read the classics, people who ate lunch instead of dinner, supper instead of tea.

What to do tomorrow? he thinks. Clean the Volvo, maybe. It's not the Volvo he bought years ago with Ila, obviously. That one's in the garage under a blue cover. Sometimes he unzips the cover, gets inside and sits in the navy blue darkness. It's like being in a car that has forced its way into a tent, and he likes to imagine this, the wildness of it, the recklessness.

He looks up at the wooden display case, hanging on the lounge wall.

Ila used to collect keys. At first she kept them in an old tin, rectangular and rusty with Scottie dogs in tartan coats, the shortbread all eaten one Christmas and replaced with her pieces of precious metal: keys for front doors, sheds and padlocks, keys for cupboards, jewellery boxes and cars. Symbols of our ins and outs, our openings and closings, the things we try to keep safe. But the ones Ila liked best were the ancient keys, heavy and mysterious, the ones that find us and survive for years because no one can throw them away.

Would you like to be able to *see* your keys? Howard asked her.

I can see them, she said.

What I mean is, would you like them on show? he said.

Oh, she said. I really would, she said.

And so he made a small display cabinet full of squares, varnished it, bought some hooks and thick string. Still on the lounge wall, it evokes the feel of a museum, or the reception area of a strange hotel. Inside it there are eight keys on individual hooks, each with its own label, and in the final compartment there's a tiny silver ferret on a key ring.

no. 1 – our first house
no. 2 – Gran's jewellery box
no. 3 – our Hillman Imp
no. 4 – my old bike lock
no. 5 – writing desk
no. 6 – Grandad's shed
no. 7 – the Volvo
no. 8 – who knows what this unlocks
no. 9 – Barry

You can remove a key if you like, but only if you return it to its rightful place. Otherwise, Howard will lie on the sofa with the wrong key in his hand, one that won't unlock the memory he is seeking, like the time he bought Ila a bike, one he'd seen advertised in the corner shop window. It needs a lot of work but I'll enjoy tidying it up, so don't be put off by the state of it will you? he said. Oh it's much better than a new one, she said, you know I'd hate a new one. Or the time they argued about which car to buy, and Ila said she wanted a Volvo because Volvos last for ever and are built like tanks and she wouldn't have to worry in one of those.

When they sold the Hillman Imp, she refused to part with the second key. It's good to remember the journeys you took, she said, slipping it into her crumby skirt pocket.

———

But the thing is, he thinks now. If we consider the laws of probability, if we look at how easily other people seem to find a prospective partner, someone suitable must have crossed his path since Ila died, someone who wouldn't have expected him to be something he wasn't. So what happened to this person, did she get missed, rejected? Were his own standards too high? Did he give her the brush-off without giving her a chance?

There have been times when he has been open to the idea of meeting someone else. He remembers walking through a park, seeing a couple having a picnic, pouring tea from a flask, and wishing he could be like them. His friends urged him to go online. They told him to write a profile and click a button and see what happened. Life is short, they said, which felt like an insult, because he knew this already in a way they didn't. Be sure to put down that you enjoy mountain biking, they said. But I don't, he said, I just cycle to work. It doesn't matter, they said, you need to list some hobbies so you don't seem boring or depressed. But I *am* boring and depressed, he said, and laughed. They didn't find this amusing. But listing the things I like, what does that actually say about me? he said. Just because a woman likes going to concerts doesn't mean we'll get on. This process of reducing myself to a list is so cold, so abstract. It's like advertising isn't it – identify your unique selling point, Howard! But we just love who we love, don't we? I loved the smell of Ila's skin. The back of her neck, *my God*. I'd give anything to smell her skin again. Oh no, his friends thought. He's off, he's gone, he's with Ila *again*. Quick, bring him back. Look,

Howard, it doesn't really matter what you write, as long as you come across as *dynamic*, they said. Good grief, he said. He looked at the online profiles of single women, then walked away from the computer and went upstairs for a nap. In his absence, nineteen women clicked on him. They scrolled down, zoomed in, felt urgent and competitive. He dreamed that he was stabbing someone to death with a kitchen knife, which he later took to be a sign that looking for a new relationship would only lead to harm. And anyway, the notion of *looking* was ludicrous – who in their right mind would go looking for someone they had never seen before, someone they knew nothing about and couldn't possibly recognise if they found them? That was the definition of insanity.

Also, the few dates he went on were weird. Other women, women who were not Ila, asked him idiotic questions. Instead of Are you a big fan of fetes? and Is this your favourite beer? they said things like What drives you? Where do you want to be in five years' time? What's on your bucket list? What are your hobbies? He felt his chest tighten as he replied:

– A Volvo drives me. Or I drive the Volvo. Good safe car. Amazing safety statistics.

– I imagine that in five years' time my life will look pretty much as it does now. But any of us could die tomorrow. It feels rather presumptuous to be thinking about what you'll be doing in five years' time.

– Bucket lists, I think, are for people who don't appreciate the small details of everyday life. To be honest, the only thing I'd like to do before I die is see my wife again, and that's not going to happen, so I'll carry on eating good food, reading good books, taking walks and playing music. I'm not scared of dying. I'm ready for it, have been for ages. My affairs are in order.

– I don't really have hobbies, as such, I just live my life.

Howard's routines, his pleasures, had deep roots by now. He wasn't sure that any woman could unearth them, or whether he would want her to. The small rituals that got him through life were hard-earned. He didn't want to negotiate, compromise, discuss or disappoint. He didn't want to reorganise the rooms, argue over the merits of butter or margarine, open his kitchen cupboards and see unfamiliar items that he didn't like to eat.

He and Ila had grown up without money. They teamed up against commercialism and insecurity, living frugally, buying in bulk and on offer. They fixed, mended, recycled and swapped, trying to instil the same values in Jason and Sydney. Ila got a better-paid job as a receptionist at the vet's, but she still worked at the farm shop on a Friday, bringing home local meat and veg bought with her staff discount.

Idyllic? Rose-coloured glasses? Definitely not. It was hard work and there was plenty of bickering. Bouts of stress made them reject and wound each other, sending them into cycles of push and pull, chase and withdraw. There was never enough time to just sit in a chair and stare at nothing. They argued about money, not because the other had spent too much, but because they were always scared about money, and fear is like a frightened cat, skittish and lashing out.

Sometimes they understood each other. At other times, they were bewildered by the other's presence, let alone their preferences and moods. *Who is this woman in a nightie, standing in the kitchen, speaking to me as if I were a child for buying the wrong cereal?* All of which was normal, of course. Idyllic marriages only exist on Instagram: this sunny riverbank, this perfect day out, this marvellous B&B we found. What mattered, was they were building something together – messy, tricky, but theirs to lie down in and bash up against.

There was never going to be another Ila. As the circle closed around them, Howard grew fond of the term *widower* – an identity that once repulsed him. He began to use the word with pride and wilfulness. Hello, nice to meet you, I'm Howard Smith, long-time widower. He came to understand that *widower* is a complicated term, meaning something different not only to each person who uses it, but *each time* they use it. Unlike a friend of his from the lido, Howard didn't use it to announce that he had loved and lost and was now available. For him, it was the opposite. He was asserting Ila's absence *and* placing her firmly beside him. Every time he said it, he felt close to her. If it were still acceptable to call himself married he would have preferred this instead, but it led to questions and social awkwardness – so where is your wife? etc.

I am married to a dead woman. Why can't he just say that? It's the truth after all. It's the truth.

And talking of what's socially acceptable, talking of awkwardness. Now we're on the subject, he thinks. Let me tell you something I've noticed about becoming a widower at the age of thirty-three.

For the first few years, people are sorry for your loss. After that, their sympathy is less about your grief, which is supposed to have diminished, and more about your aloneness – the missing new partner. People will advise you to *get back out there*, as if you have merely been hiding indoors, not going out to work and raising two children by yourself. And while you may never have ridden a horse in your entire life, you will be urged to get back on one.

Then things get interesting. Try saying you're a widower ten to fifteen years after your partner's death. There is curiosity now. A *lot* of curiosity. Less grimacing, less *I'm sorry*. Without ever saying it, people will imply that you are lazy, stubborn, not trying.

Now imagine declaring that you've been a widower for over thirty years. Suspicion enters the mix. *Is there something wrong with you? Why haven't you moved on, met someone else?* That's what they're thinking.

Howard has also learned, from talking to other widowers, that things are different if a man's wife or husband dies when he is much older. There is less pressure to move on, to find someone new. Which is insulting to both the younger man and the older one.

He remembers something else now, as he pulls the blanket up to his chest.

A couple of years ago he was shopping in town. He found himself in a gift shop, rifling through a small wicker basket full of badges in the style of those worn at school by prefects, head boy or head girl. But these badges said other things, like BOOKWORM, GENIUS, HEAD GARDENER, BEST MAN, CAPTAIN, GROOM and SEX KITTEN.

Do you have one that says *widower*? he asked. It was his own question, and yet it took him by surprise.

The shop assistant looked flustered, embarrassed. I'm sorry, sir, we don't. We may be able to order one in for you. I'm not sure they make them, though. Um . . .

They should, he said. They *should* make them.

Of course, she said, but she didn't understand, couldn't think of a single reason why this man would want to walk around with that badge on his waterproof jacket. Why draw attention to being a widower? Oh, she thought. He's looking for a new wife. Sad, terribly sad.

He bought a little book for Ruth, which made him laugh: *The Ladybird Book of Mindfulness*. Then he flicked through the Ladybird 'How it Works' series – *The Husband, The Wife, The Mum*, even *The Dog, The Cat* and *The Shed*. Again, what about the widower? He felt invisible, and his anger rose. We are capable of making fun of ourselves you know!

Then he stopped.

Of course there's no Ladybird book about widows or widowers. No one wants to poke fun at them because everyone dreads becoming one.

He wished he hadn't come into this stupid shop.

I'd like to return this book, he said, lighting a match of misdirected anger close to the shop assistant's face.

She recoiled. Already? she said. You only just bought it. I've changed my mind, he said.

We only give credit notes.

Look, you know full well that I haven't read this book, I haven't even left the shop.

Okay, fine, she said, opening the till.

He felt guilty then, as he saw her face redden. I'm sorry, he said.

It's all right, she said.

Then he spotted another bowl full of badges, of mixed shapes and sizes, most of them plastic this time. He looked through them while she counted out his change.

Just when she thought the trouble was over, she heard him tut.

He was holding up a circular badge that said GOLF WIDOW.

This, my dear, is offensive to anyone who has actually been widowed, he said.

Is it? she said.

It is. I hate it when people use that phrase. I want to say really, you're going to make jokes about being a widow are you, when your husband is out there hitting a ball with a stick, not dead in a box underground, not turned into ash and thrown into the winds?

Gosh, I've never thought of it that way, she said. She took the badge from his hand and dropped it into the bin. How's that? she said.

He smiled, asked her name.

I'm Harriet, she said.

Well, Harriet, I'll take this silly book after all, and I'm very sorry for snapping. Most of the time I manage to keep it under wraps, you see, but sometimes it just comes out. I really am sorry.

Harriet was silent for a moment. Then her face altered. She took the bowl of plastic badges and tipped it into the bin. Then she took the small wicker basket full of prefect-style badges, emptied that out too. She pulled a paper bag off the roll, slipped *The Ladybird Book of Mindfulness* inside it.

On the house, she said.

Really? he said.

Yes, she said.

Then she held out her hand, and he shook it.

Do you mind if I ask you a question? she said.

Of course not.

I just wondered if you'd thought about joining a bereavement group.

Pardon?

Are you on Facebook?

I don't have time for Facebook. Too many new songs to learn how to play.

You could join a group for widowers. There are support groups, social groups, even special dating groups. I know because my uncle is a widower. His wife died two years ago.

That's very kind, he said, but my wife, she died more than *thirty years ago*.

And he waited for it to land.

There we go.

The curiosity, the suspicion.

So, he said, I don't think any group would have me as a member, do you? My right to membership probably expired a long time ago. And even if they would have me, *especially* if they would, I have no desire to join one.

How very Groucho Marx of you, she said.

23

Hello you

Stuart sniffs the body. It is dressed in trainers, loose trousers, a waterproof jacket. It has landed on its luggage, a thin rucksack rather like Maria's, with a red dog's paw on the front beside the words *Jack* and *Wolfskin*. But this is not Jack Wolfskin, who presumably is a man. This is a woman. The one he has seen and sniffed several times this week.

And now, instead of salt and treacle and guilt,
she smells of cherry blossom in full bloom,
one of the most emotional flowers,
its petals carrying the lesson
that what is truly beautiful
must also be fleeting,
fly-by-night.

Maria calls 999. As she does this, and is taken through all the questions, it strikes her that she has never had to call 999 before, she has managed to reach the age of fifty-eight without ever having to do this. And it doesn't seem right, it doesn't seem to fit the life she has lived, the sense of crisis held in her stiff shoulders.

She sits beside the hound and waits.

She takes hold of the woman's hand, cups it between her own hands, tries to warm it up.

Then she glances at the rucksack the woman is wearing. She instinctively opens the side pocket, rummages around, finds a phone in an ugly rubbery case.

It isn't broken.

She thinks that maybe she should get one of these cases too. In fact, every phone should come with one, so that something about us, something on us, is always indestructible.

Funny what the mind does at times like this.

She presses a circular button on the phone, places her thumb on the word *Emergency*, then *Medical ID*.

She presses the red telephone icon beside the name *Ruth Hansen*.

Hello you, a woman says.

24

The shipping forecast

And through the night, the wind gets up.

And through the night, they travel south.

And through the night, they fear that they may never have the chance to tell her how irresponsible she is.

They wish they had been better.

They have an acute sense of how fragile everything is, how quick.

And they vow to never forget this – a common vow, impossible to keep.

There is no I spy with my little eye on this car journey. No banter, no music. Ruth is driving. Howard is her passenger. Otto is snoring on the back seat, curled up on his fleecy blanket.

A few hours ago, they were eating Indian food, listening to records, talking about subjects that didn't matter. Like, for example, whether people still buy kitchen calendars when their lives are organised digitally. Like, for example, whether it's safe for dogs to eat garlic naan bread. He's always loved a poppadom, Ruth said, but can dogs stomach garlic, I just don't know. They walked Otto around the block, said good-bye. Howard lay on the sofa after that, drank chamomile tea. And Ruth stood in her kitchen, drinking hot chocolate. She went upstairs and had a shower, let Otto snuggle up on Sydney's pillow instead of making him sleep in his own bed in the corner of the room, and they lay close together, gazing at each other as Ruth stroked his head, and then her mobile rang, and she saw Sydney's face appear on the screen, but it wasn't Sydney calling it was someone using her phone, a complete stranger, saying *is this Ruth Hansen have I come through to Ruth Hansen.*

And now they are inside the darkness of Ruth's car.

The car is jam-packed with things they do not know.

These things press up against them, make them feel sick.

They don't know why she lied, why she told them she was going to a different town. This lie must say a lot, about them as well as her, but they have no idea what it says.

And also, was it an accident.

And also, what damage has been done.

They have never felt as ignorant as they do right now.

I just don't understand, Howard says.

I don't either, Ruth says.

What the hell was she doing in St Ives? I never thought she'd go back there. Has she been there all week?

I don't know.

Why go there alone? Unless she was planning to –

No, it won't be that, Ruth says. She begins to cry. I was grumpy with her, she says. On the phone, I was so grumpy. I wish she'd told me where she was.

She obviously didn't feel able to.

Don't say that. She didn't tell you either did she.

Yes, but she never tells *me* anything.

Stop it, Ruth says.

And through the night, they take it out on each other.

Because they have to do something.

When they are silent, Ruth throws her mind at Sydney like a fire blanket over a burning body.

How could you be so stupid?

What have you done to yourself?

When they are silent, Howard remembers the last time he made this journey.

It's good to remember the journeys you took, Ila says.

No, it really isn't, he says. I wish I'd turned the car around and driven home.

Sydney's antics, he thinks. Her carelessness.

Selfish, he says, loudly.

What? Ruth says.

She's selfish, he says.

Howard, don't, she says. Please don't.

They are full of rage and panic.

There are no words for this, so they speak about other things instead.

Ruth says she needs a strong cup of tea and does he want one.

He says no I don't need one.

She says look, I know it must be awful, where we're going. I can't even.

He says I guess we could stop, just for a few minutes, let Otto stretch his legs.

She says oh God I forgot about Otto, he'll need some water.

At the services she parks badly, across two spaces, and doesn't care.

It is sort of liberating, not to care.

Inside, night-time travellers are dotted about under electric lights, their fingers wrapped around mugs of caffeine. They sit at tables by the window, staring at the drizzle, the car park.

This is all very Edward Hopper isn't it, Ruth says. She wants to say that Sydney would love to sketch this scene. The transience, the loneliness, she would find beauty in this. Instead she asks Howard if he wants herbal or builder's.

Builder's please, he says.

Back outside, they walk around the car park with Otto, clutching paper cups full of tea.

They stop on a patch of grass beside a lamp post, and Ruth looks up at the misty rain, looks up into the light.

She begins to shake.

Let me take that, Howard says, putting both drinks on the floor.

And he holds her.

And her face is against his damp wool coat.

My poor girl, he says, as he rubs her back.

——

And through the night, they are quiet.

They listen to the car radio.

Every half an hour, the news. Each broadcast feels like fresh news, because neither of them has been paying attention.

There is a programme about correcting faulty genes to prevent disease.

Another about animal welfare standards in the wool industry.

And now, the shipping forecast.

Tyne, Dogger, Fisher, German Bight

I love listening to this, Howard says. I find it deeply comforting. If I'm not awake when it's on I always listen on catch-up.

That's funny, Ruth says.

Why is it, he says.

Because Sydney does exactly the same thing.

25

A sugar-free sliver of rebellion

Smells sticky, smells blue, smells old, smells of glue. What this hospital doesn't smell of is good health. Polystyrene, more like. A wipe-clean place mat. The inside of a brand-new shoe.

The main doors open into an airport lounge, but there are no flights from here. There's just a cafe and a gift shop. A random arrangement of faded green chairs, some of them at tables, some of them scattered about.

Welcome to Zone A: you've arrived at the concourse, the portal, the mouth.

In the early hours of this morning, Maria wandered around this space, pausing on one of the hard chairs to eat a KitKat and drink a latte.

Now she is west of here, in Zone D.

She is standing in the toilets, looking in the mirror.

Awful to admit it, but this is the most exciting thing that has happened to her in years; since she found Stuart, in fact. Not these toilets in Zone D – her life may be boring, but it's not *that* boring. No, she means the woman she found on the pavement. The fact that *she* found her. No coincidence, surely. It's deeply meaningful. Not one lost soul, but two. And like Stuart, this soul is her responsibility now.

In a way, Sydney Smith belongs to her.

She is taking this seriously, her sleeves are rolled high, she's chewing gum with a new defiance and she never chews gum. Rots the teeth, ruins the smile, and smiles are Maria's line of business. Gum causes ulcers too, and there's also how it looks, boorish and uncouth. But now it's rolling around her mouth, a sugar-free sliver of rebellion, and she wishes she'd done it years ago, this futile chewing, it puts her at ease, no wonder everyone buys it.

She has an idea: anti-anxiety gum. Slip a little Valium in and Bob's your uncle, he's your mother's minted brother, he's cock-a-hoop, all because he's peddling his brilliant new remedy for stress: *Uncle Bob's Anti-Anxiety Gum.*

Hmm, Maria thinks. I'm liking that. I'm liking what's happening in my brain today. Basically I'm on fire. I could fly a plane, write a book. Why have I been sleeping for eight hours a night when I clearly don't need all that sleep?

She opens her handbag. And by *handbag* she means her super-thin rucksack, a polyester lozenge with a zip. Official term: daypack. She takes this with her everywhere. It's amazing what you can fit inside it. A purse, obviously. Floss, obviously. And tissues. A penknife. A muffin in a freezer bag. Two pages torn from a collection of poems about survival. A notebook with her handwriting on its cover: The Book of Many Silences. Two pairs of gloves. A pair of baby socks, newborn-size. Her passport. A letter inside an envelope. And finally, right at the bottom, the thing she is trying to find: a lipstick. It's four years old, this fat little stick, and only used twice as far as she can remember. It was a birthday present from Belle. Does lipstick go off? Now her lips are bright red, she isn't sure it's appropriate for the occasion, decides to just go with it. She wonders if the other Maria, the one she imagines inside the gallery sometimes, the one with confidence and artistic talent, wears lipstick. She runs her fingers through her hair, pushing it up and flicking it out. Maria's hair is like a wind-beaten tree, obeying the laws of nature, nothing else. It looks much the same as it did before, but she feels more presentable, which is all that matters.

Then she remembers something. A moment from her childhood. There was a *third* soul. Of course there was. *That's* when this started. How can she possibly have forgotten?

There was a kitten in a sack, dumped in a stream.

Maria was six years old, out walking with her dad. What's that? she said, pointing at a large hessian bag moving by itself, neither underwater nor above it. They crouched down, carefully lifted the sack onto the grass, untied its string to reveal a soggy black kitten, white feet and white chest, its small body trembling. Maria began to cry. She cried because she was shocked that anyone could be so cruel. She cried because the sun was on her back, the stream was sparkling, it was clean and warm, full of dancing weeds and tadpoles, and someone had tried to drown a kitten in here, someone she could pass on the street or become friends with one day, without ever knowing it was them. This tiny mouth, this tiny belly, would soon have filled with water. A stream on a summer's day would never look the same to her again. And she cried because she and her father had found a quivering life, a light about to go out. That life belonged to them now. Of course they would keep it. She didn't even need to ask.

Her father removed his Pringle jumper, wrapped the kitten inside it. She's okay now, he said, passing the bundle to his daughter. She's okay.

Is she, are you sure? Maria said.

I'm sure, he said. We were just in time, I think.

They named her Georgie.

Georgie lived for five weeks.

Maria stood clutching her father's unwashed jumper. Why? she kept saying, through her tears. What did I do wrong? I thought we'd saved her. I thought –

These things, they just happen, her mother said. It's no one's fault. We'll wrap her up in a lovely blanket, bury her in the garden, say a proper goodbye.

Years later, when Maria was nineteen, her mother would use the same words at Andy's funeral: *These things, they just happen.*

Maria heads for the gift shop, the one in the main entrance. What to buy a complete stranger? Well for a start, how about this bear in a T-shirt, the one with a string hanging from its back. Pull the string and the bear says *Get well soon!* as quickly as possible in a high-pitched voice. This bear is a battery-operated maniac, but Maria likes it. Also a Snickers bar, a Chomp and a Curly Wurly. Four magazines, best to cover all bases, who knows what she's into: *Livingetc*, *BBC Good Food*, *Simply Knitting* and *Hello!*. And maybe this pencil with a monkey eraser on the top. And this crossword book. And this detective novel. Definitely this pack of cards. Play your cards right, Sydney Smith, and I'll look after you like this for as long as you need.

She hears her husband's voice: Too much, Maria.

Jon often says this, it's one of his catchphrases. You're too much, Maria, pull back a little why don't you, for God's sake settle down.

Other things Jon has said:

Isn't it time for you to take a walk?

For fuck's sake, Maria, just give me a break.

Your hair looks fine, I already told you didn't I.

You see me all the time, what are you talking about?

Do you really think dropping hints about flowers makes me *feel* like buying you flowers?

I don't notice things like new clothes.

Nor do I have a flair for remembering dates, you knew this when you married me.

The woman I married only had one chin.

Oh come on, where's your sense of humour?

If you'd taken my name, if you were *Maria Schaefer*, none of this would be happening.

I did *not* break your wrist. That was your own doing. You brought it on yourself.

Shit, I'd better call him, she thinks, when she has paid for the gifts, left the shop.

Hey, she says.

Maria, he says.

Everything all right?

Of course. You at work?

Well no, I'm still at the hospital. I swapped with Kath.

You're still there?

Yes.

You've been there all night, *and* all day?

That's right. It's a long story. I'm not sure what time I'll be back.

Are you the only one there?

Oh no, her partner's here, lovely woman called Ruth. Her father's here too, but he's a little odd.

In what way?

Well, by the time they arrived this morning, just before six I think, Sydney was in her own room.

Right.

And I was there, sitting by the bed.

Why? he thinks. Why were you even there?

Right, he says.

It's quite a nice room, better than I expected. Big window, plenty of light, with –

The punchline, Maria. (This is another of Jon's phrases.)

Thrown off track, all she can see is Sydney's room, the stiff curtains, the sheets on the bed.

What happened when they arrived? Jon says.

Well instead of coming in, her father just stood in the doorway.

For the whole time?

No, he eventually came in, but only because Ruth told him to. But he carried on being weird. He walked up to the bed, then he just turned and left without saying a word.

Bizarre, Jon says. You're better off out of there. Why don't you come home? Or *go to work*.

I found her, Jon. I have to see this through.

Not this again, Maria. *Honestly*. Her family's there now. Just come home, have a shower.

A shower?

And something to eat.

I've had a bacon sandwich. Did I tell you they have a dog?

What?

Sydney has a dog. It's in the car. Ruth keeps walking it around the car park. I thought I'd bring it home with me.

What?

They'll be in the B&B tonight, where Sydney was staying. There's nowhere to sleep in this hospital, only the waiting rooms. The B&B, Jon, it's not dog-friendly. And you can't leave a dog in a car.

He is silent now. Well almost. She can hear him walking about, breathing heavily. It's the sound of irritation, but she isn't there for the flack, the hassle, so she doesn't care.

And they trust you with their dog, do they?

Of course they do. Why ask me that?

Fine, he says. Guess they can find a dog-friendly hotel tomorrow.

Oh no, Jon, she says.

Sorry?

I won't have it.

What.

Them staying in a hotel when we have plenty of room.

You're not serious, surely.

They need to be with their dog.

And as I said, they can find a dog-friendly hotel. Or a cottage. Everywhere's empty right now.

Exactly. How unwelcoming. And what will they do with the dog when they're at the hospital?

How should I know?

Well it can be with Stuart, can't it. He likes other dogs.

For crying out loud.

I've already insisted, there's no point arguing.

No, Maria.

Jon, I never ask for anything.

Absolutely not. They're *strangers*. We don't know anything about them. Think about Belle's safety.

Belle can look after herself better than any of us.

Look –

They're in crisis, Jon. Wouldn't you like someone to take care of you, and of Stuart, in a crisis?

I think you've gone mad.

Being hospitable is mad? No wonder society is such a mess.

This isn't about *society*.

Of course it is, she says. What else is it about?

Our marriage, for a start, he says.

Well the personal is political.

Oh don't go all radical feminist on me.

What?

You're not a feminist, Maria.

Of course I'm a feminist. What the hell are you saying?

Just because you kept your maiden name, you think it makes you a feminist. Well it doesn't.

Not that again. And it's not my *maiden* name, it's just my name.

Well, you had no right to invite people to stay without asking me first.

It's my house too. Do I need your *permission*?

I wouldn't bring a woman home.

What?

You heard me.

Don't shout at me, Jon. You're overreacting. It's only for a few days, this is important to me.

We don't. Even. Know them.

I found her, Jon. Me. That means something. *It matters.*

For fuck's sake, Maria, just get in the car and come home so we can talk about this properly.

Maria takes the phone away from her ear. She can still hear his voice, smaller now, in her hand. Which reminds her that he is not here, she doesn't have to engage with this, she has the power to –

She does something she has never done before. She cuts him off, ends the call. Without so much as a goodbye, see you later, there's a portion of chilli in the freezer.

Not everything is about you, Jon, she thinks, as she heads through the corridors and up the stairs, swinging her carrier bag full of gifts so hard and fast that somehow it activates the teddy bear inside, makes it say *Get well soon! Get well soon!* in its maniacal way, and she pauses to stop, to make *it* stop, but the toy has gone haywire, it won't shut up. She considers throwing it in the bin, but what if it chants all evening and all night, keeps everyone awake? Putting it in the bin would be passing the buck, passing the bear, refusing to take responsibility for what is hers and what is broken. No, she won't do it. This is *her* duff bear, *her* problem to solve. So she inspects it from all angles, turns it upside down, lifts its T-shirt, looks for the battery compartment, but it's sealed with screws, and while Maria has many useful objects in her daypack she doesn't have a screwdriver. So she does what anyone would do in her situation, in her emotional state. She smashes the bear against the wall. Seven times. Then it stops.

And I thought *I* had problems, Howard says, from behind her.

He walks past, in the direction of his daughter's room. But when he gets there, instead of slowing down he speeds up, keeps on going, all the way to the end of the corridor, then he is gone.

The bear comes back to life in Maria's hand.

Get well soon! Get well soon! Get well soon!

26

Ila's blue parka

He was in his thirties when he last came here. But he didn't walk in through these sliding doors. He didn't step from darkness into a brightly lit reception with a cafe, a gift shop. With Jason right beside him and Sydney trailing behind, he chased two paramedics and a stretcher into the emergency department.

It was like another country. No, another world entirely. A world with its own laws, where time behaved differently.

Everything was too fast and too slow.

The notion that anything could be happening *outside* this world was inconceivable.

No one could possibly be buying milk, playing Scrabble, whistling a silly tune.

Not while this was going on.

The smell of the place hits him now as he walks through the doors of the main entrance. How can it smell the same after all this time?

He takes Ruth's hand.

It's all right, she says.

Sometimes, this is what kindness sounds like. It sounds like words of reassurance, spoken by a woman who is desperate for reassurance.

There is a shoe on the floor, just ahead of him. It's one of Sydney's plimsolls. Yes, he remembers now, how it came off on the race to A&E, how he had to wait for her to put it back on. *For God's sake hurry up*, he yelled. She loved those white and green plimsolls. Never wore them after that. Nor the clothes she had been wearing that day – all of it, straight in the bin. Can I burn them? she said. No, he said.

And over there, draped over the back of an empty chair, that's Ila's blue parka.

Can you see it, Ruth?

Thought I'd put that up in the loft.

He reaches out to grab it as they rush past.

His hand hits the plastic chair.

Ow, he says, stopping to rub his hand.

Ruth keeps going.

Wait, he says. My plimsoll, my coat.

Why remember the coat. She wasn't even wearing it. It was summer, idiot.

She bought it in the sale, typical Ila.

Orange lining fluffy hood.

Hey, I can probably fit three jumpers under here, she said, laughing. You can borrow it if you like, if you're *good*.

And he did. Just once. Two years after she died. When technically, she was no longer its owner. And yet she was.

They were about to go shopping. Jason and Sydney were waiting for him by the front door.

Dad, come on.

He lifted it off the coat stand, slipped it on. Grabbed his wallet and his keys. As if this was simply the natural order of things, his daily routine.

That's Mum's coat, Jason said.

Sydney just stared, as usual.

Yes, he said.

Why are you wearing Mum's coat?

I don't know, he said. I couldn't help it.

You couldn't help it?

No.

What does that mean?

I don't know.

Disturbed and overwhelmed by his father's behaviour, Jason had an asthma attack.

The shopping trip was cancelled.

Sydney went upstairs to draw the complex dashboard of a spaceship.

Jason watched TV under a blanket on the sofa.

And to prevent this incident, this *episode*, from ever happening again, Howard wrapped the parka in a bin bag and put it in the loft.

While he was up there, he found Ila's wedding dress.

FOR FUCKING FUCK'S SAKE, he shouted.

He kicked the boxes full of baby clothes.

Punched a framed photograph of Ila's parents.

Looking at his broken skin, the blood on the back of his hand, was like waiting for a sedative to kick in.

Ah, that's it.

So. Much. Better.

Pain from a clear and obvious source, one he could ramp up or slow down. One he could control.

He punched it again. Then he remembered the kids. How they would be hungry by now. Sometimes it felt like they were always hungry.

After baked beans and fried eggs, everyone felt calmer.

No one mentioned the blue parka again. The fact that Howard had been wearing it. The fact that he now had Mickey Mouse plasters on his knuckles.

How about I take you two out for pizza later, he said. Or burgers, you choose.

Their smiles made his eyes sting.

There is a stranger in Sydney's hospital room. A woman, older than his daughter, younger than him.

He stands by the doorway, listens to their introductions.

He watches Ruth lean in to kiss Sydney's lips, her cheeks, the top of her head.

He watches her brush Sydney's hair away from her face, press her hand flat against her forehead as though she's checking for a fever. She keeps her hand there, doesn't move.

He tries to imagine what it would feel like to have a warm hand on his forehead like that. Where did she learn such tenderness? The sight of it is unbearable, and yet he can't look away.

Thank you for staying with her, Ruth says to the stranger.

Her name is Maria. And no, she doesn't need thanking

for staying with Sydney, definitely not, she has only done what anyone would do.

And Howard can see her glancing at the doorway, looking at him and right through him, for he is transparent, he must be. There is nothing inside him, not now.

And he can see Ruth, giving him a look he hasn't seen on her before. For God's sake, the look says.

He tries to move.

Nothing.

Well this is a first, he thinks.

What the hell *is* this?

In A&E, ten-year-old Sydney went missing. She disappeared, just for fifteen minutes or so, soon after they arrived. While the staff were trying to save her mother – for show, he thinks now; they only did this to show him they had tried – Sydney was hiding. Don't worry, we found your daughter in the cleaning cupboard, a nurse said. She and her brother have been taken for some macaroni cheese. Great, he said, relieved and angry and also not caring at all. In this moment, he had no capacity to care about anything but the sight of people he didn't know, leaning over his wife's body. Why was someone talking to him about macaroni cheese?

And this is how he feels right now. Relieved that someone found his daughter. Completely bloody furious with his daughter. And also, like he doesn't even care, like something is erasing his emotions at the same time as he is having them, like he is tipping into numbness and has no love inside him for any living person.

These emotions don't go together. They are the dark heart of a scream, trapped in his stomach. Will someone please operate on this man, remove the hard screaming stone from his belly?

He wants to throw up.

He wonders why no one says anything.

Hello hello? I'm just standing here, at the door of my daughter's hospital room, I'm not doing this for the joy of it you know, I'm well aware that this isn't *normal*. I just paused at first, who wouldn't pause, but I can't seem to move, I'm sweating, I'm soaked, my tongue is stuck to the roof of my mouth. You were all looking at first, I saw you look, but the longer this goes on, I'm invisible now, is this what asthma feels like Jason, as I wait as I wait for the verdict. *I'm so sorry, Mr Smith* – that's how the verdict began, the doctor spoke so slowly and softly, and I remember thinking later how it was like that Roberta Flack song, 'Killing Me Softly with His Song', except the doctor wasn't singing, he was telling me that my wife was dead.

Are you going to come in? Ruth says.

Must be the tone she uses with her pupils. Must be.

And now he is a red-faced man in a pink shirt, edging towards them.

He shuffles into the room.

This is Howard, Sydney's father, Ruth says.

He shakes Maria's hand, remains silent, moves towards the bed.

And he wants to say that this woman lying so still, she is not his daughter. She doesn't even *look* like his daughter.

You were always running wild, he says to her, in his mind. You were always hiding up a tree or in a cupboard. Even at the funeral you hid in the toilets. Didn't you. *Didn't you.*

He takes a step backwards.

What's wrong with me, he thinks. What kind of man am I. What kind of girl is this.

She's our little mountain goat, a voice says.

Who said that?

He turns round.

Then he leaves.

27

Lego world

Dear Mum,
    I didn't sleep well after writing you that letter.
Did you hear the rain outside last night? I sat by the
window and watched, it was sort of peaceful. And
I wrote your funeral. I wrote it as a list, because lists
impose order on chaos don't they, that's what they're
for, so I thought it might be a good idea to use that
form. And I'll draw us waiting on the path, Dad, Jason
and me. There'll be a close-up of Jason's shoes, how he
positioned the tips of his toes so neatly on the kerb, and
we stood either side of him and copied, and that made
him smile, just for a second. We must have looked a bit
odd, all in a row on the edge like that.
    All my love,
    Sydney
    xxx

1. A black car enters the cul-de-sac, containing a shiny brown box containing Mum. I remember picturing her inside, not how she really was of course, not drained of

blood and fluid, pumped with formaldehyde, her nose and throat stuffed with cotton wool. She was still our mum, in flares and a blue polo neck, about to do a Houdini and burst out of that box. Come on, Mum, you can do it. It's time for your big escape, we're waiting, we're here, Dad, Jason and me, all dressed up in our smart clothes, lined up outside the house as you come towards us. I've never seen a car move as slowly as this. Jason salutes. He is in shock, confused. His hair is full of wax, he looks older and smaller than usual. Someone told Dad we were too young for a funeral. Rubbish, he said. It's their *mother*, he said.

2. Inside the church, 'Morning Has Broken'.

3. Inside the church, Stevie Wonder, 'You Are the Sunshine of My Life'.

4. Outside the church, a hole in the ground, tidy and deep. Once Mum is inside this hole she will have no chance of escaping and I am very worried about this. What if she is only asleep and she wakes up down there? I am so worried and itchy, scratchy and tense.

5. Turns out it doesn't matter if I'm worried or not. Things happen just the same.

6. Now we are in a big lounge in a big hotel.

7. Quiche and mini sandwiches, crustless and triangular.

8. Dad smells of beer.

9. Dad smells of whisky.

10. Jason and I play cards at a table in the corner. We argue about the rules.

11. People look at us weirdly.

12. A drunken uncle lets me drink some of his wine.

13. I go round all the tables, drinking from people's glasses.

14. I am sick in the toilet. A woman called Becky puts her hand on my back, says she's a waitress and did I know the woman whose funeral it was. No, I say. And anyway they've all buried her alive, I say. They are *evil*. Becky doesn't know what to say to this. She leaves me by the sink, goes for help, comes back with Dad. He just stands there, in the doorway of the ladies' toilets, looking at me. I hear you've been sick, he says. Then he turns round and leaves and the door closes with a bang. Oh, Becky says.

15. In the middle of the night, Jason and I get up. We haven't played with Lego for a long time, but now we empty a big box of it onto the floor of the lounge, where we sit opposite each other and concentrate hard on building things. The things we make are complex and impressive. Eventually we go back to bed, and when we return in the morning, one of our aunts has tidied the Lego away. Jason cries. I can't believe it's gone, he says. I fetch a pack of malted milk biscuits from the kitchen cupboard and we eat them really fast, every single one, leaving crumbs all over the carpet where our Lego world had been.

28

Little man

Well what do we have here? This *is* a surprise. Let me sniff
your bottom, your nose, your face, your underbelly, everything. Hmm. Interesting. Who are you, young pup? Oh, not
young. I can smell the years and the years. Eight, almost
nine? You're as still and upright as a stuffed dog as I make
my way around you. Petrified, it seems. I can smell your
stress. I can smell today's hours, you spent them trapped in
a small space, is that right little man, have you been closed
in today, ignored? Today hasn't been one of your best, it's
coming right off you, my word it's strong, you may as well
have rolled in fox shit. I'm sorry you've had such a bad day.
Relax now, I'm not going to hurt you. I don't think so,
anyway. As we both know, a dog can never say never. That's
it, you have a sniff too. Oh, you can't reach, that must be
frustrating. Well take in what you can, try to read me, it'll
settle your nerves. You can sniff my food bowl if you like. I
doubt you'll ever have seen such a large food bowl. And do
help yourself to water. I don't get territorial about water, or
my empty bowl, but I'd rather you didn't eat my food. And
please don't piss in the house, the smell will never go, it'll

drive me insane. Welcome, tiny fox terrier. My name is Stuart, I'm an Irish wolfhound. Ever met one of those? I was lost and now I am found. Did Maria find you too? How have you ended up here this evening? Right, let me take a proper look at you. You are mainly white I see, with an aesthetically pleasing saddle of black. You have brown ears and brown patches on each side of your face. You're wiry and curly, with a rather sweet fluffy chest. You look like a sad old man, an inquisitive puppy. I wonder if you share any of my capabilities? Do you have my sense of smell, by any chance? Hmm, clearly not. This much I can tell by how affectionate you're being with Jon. Bad judge of character, oh well, we can't *all* be advanced canines. So is this a flying visit, are you heading off again soon? Who is your main human, do you have one?

Ah, this woman coming into the kitchen now, you'll like her very much. This is Belle. Good, you like her. I hope you don't like everyone, dear boy – that you possess some power of discrimination? Belle is a superstar, that's what I call her. A truly wonderful human being. I sleep on her bed most nights. We have a deeply physical relationship. Oh no, not in that way, goodness me, how could you even think such a thing?

It's a nice kitchen, isn't it? There was no kitchen in my last home. I use the word *home* loosely. I had never seen a kitchen with a sofa in it until I came here. I often doze on that faded yellow settee.

Oh, I need to stay quiet for a moment. They're talking about you.

So, your name is Otto.

Here for a few days, they expect.

Jon doesn't like you. I'm not telling you this to be mean, I just want you to have your wits about you. Jon is a dangerous man. Don't cower, it's all right, he only hurts Maria. And right now, he wants to hurt her. She knows this. I can smell it on both of them. He's angry that you're here. Angry that your owners have entered our lives.

Sounds like we're in for a treat tonight. Maria is tired, so they're just having pizza and chips, we're bound to get a taste. She's also going to bake some muffins: blue cheese, pear and walnut. They are for someone called Howard, who isn't eating right now, hasn't touched a thing all day. Ah, you love Howard, I see that. Look at your tail wagging at the sound of his name. What a sweetie you are.

Have you been to the beach yet? Belle is going to take us there later, just for a quick stroll she says, so you can stretch your legs. I should warn you now that while we're out with Belle she will probably tie us up outside a shop. Not for long, I assure you. Just long enough for her to steal something. I always know when she's about to do it – there's a surge of adrenaline, you see, which makes me play up. I bark and I howl. What's got into you? she says. I howl the whole time, hoping it will put her off. It never does. This happens a couple of times a week. Nothing big, of course. A packet of sweets up the sleeve, a magazine tucked inside another that she actually pays for – it's an old trick, that one. What about you, do your owners have any illegal pastimes? You don't have to tell me. We've only just met, after all. I'm a bit excitable, aren't I? I do apologise. I don't get many canine visitors. Timothy, yes – the pot-bellied pig who lives next door. But it's not the same.

Oh dear. I'm terribly sorry to hear your news. No wonder you smell so awful, no offence. So one of your owners had an accident. She's concussed, has a broken hip, ouch. They need to operate quickly.

Oh. I'm so slow sometimes. You belong to *her*, don't you? How did I not detect that? You don't smell of her, not at all. That's why I didn't make the link, put two and two together, you and the woman on the ground.

Look, here are your things. Your fleecy blanket, your rabbit. I see that you've given the rabbit's ears a good chew, probably played tug of war with it too. Do you play with it after dinner, is that why it smells so strongly of turkey kibble?

Oh how adorable, you're one of those creatures that turns its head to one side when you hear a certain word. I thought those kinds of dogs only existed on birthday cards. You like the word *Ruth*, do you? The perfume on your neck, is that hers?

I have to say, my main owner, my Maria, she smells most peculiar this evening. She's completely exhausted, which doesn't help. But she smells of burning cloth, and tiny seedlings inching towards light.

Belle has already stolen something today. I've just had a whiff of it. So it looks like our walk will be crime-free tonight after all.

No, is what you're telling me really true? The woman in

hospital, sometimes she holds you in her arms while she rolls along on a skateboard? And you actually enjoy this? You city folk are another breed entirely. I'm envious, I must admit. No one can carry me, let alone on a skateboard. If I want to go anywhere, I must always use my own feet.

Please excuse the noise, Otto. You get used to it in the end. They think we can't hear them if they go upstairs, but of course we can. We hear everything, yes? Your tail is down, you're obviously not used to arguing. It's all right, don't worry. They don't take it out on dogs, only each other. It's Jon, you see. He's a bastard, a cock. He wears her down, until she is half the woman she is capable of being, then he complains, says she is not the woman he married.

It might be a while before we go for our walk. Belle won't leave while they're arguing. See, she's getting comfy on the sofa now, we're not going anywhere, especially now she has put on her glasses and opened her book, the one she's having to read because she lied to Dexter, said *yes of course I've read it*, Dexter being a man she works with at the bookshop who has read everything. It's a novella about a sculptor and a cleaner, that's all I know so far.

Fancy a game with your rabbit, little man?

29

High tide and a red shirt

Evening beardy, she says.

Don't call me beardy, he says, with a sleepy smile.

And why not, when you are, in fact, *beardy*? she says.

Because my grandad used to have a bearded collie called Beardy. And I am not a bearded collie.

You were close to him weren't you, your grandad.

He pretty much brought me up, he says.

Oh, I didn't realise that.

So who's this one, Dexter says, nodding towards the fox terrier. Has Stuart acquired a new friend?

This is Otto, our house guest. It's a long story.

He reaches down and ruffles Otto's curls. Belle watches her colleague's small hands, how he scratches the dog's neck. Otto tilts his head, leans into it.

He likes that, she says.

So what can I do for you? Dexter says.

They are standing at the front door of a narrow house, converted into two flats. It's one of five houses at the edge of this beach, just along from the artists' studios and holiday apartments. Belle doesn't understand how Dexter could have bought this place – how did he afford it?

I'm making deliveries, she says. She leans backwards, lets her gigantic rucksack drop to the floor behind her.

How mysterious. I won't ask about your *deliveries*.

Sorry?

Your secret's safe with me.

What secret.

Drugs, he whispers. Then he laughs. Because he knows full well that Belle is more likely to be distributing aubergines than drugs.

She blushes. I can't find it, she says, elbow-deep in rucksack.

She empties the entire thing onto the floor, and Dexter crouches down, blatantly curious about what she has been carrying on her back. There's a gardening magazine, a pack of seeds. A trowel, dog chews, a roll of poo bags and a pair of knitted rainbow socks. Strands of seaweed, shells, a gust of sand. And finally, seven bags of muffins, wrapped in cellophane and tied with ribbon, a handwritten label tied to each one with brown string.

The dogs move in too, begin to sniff.

The air this evening is salty and sweet. It smells of leather, of hush, of high tide and a red shirt.

Hey no, Belle says, pushing the dogs away.

Did you make all these cakes? Dexter says.

My mum made them, she says. They're medicinal. You know, for people going through hard times.

Really, he says. What sort of thing do they help with?

Oh it can be anything. There's turmeric for inflammation, dried apricot for low iron, banana and dark chocolate for good mood. And some vegan ones with chilli too, but I'm not allowed to say who they're for.

Can I try a vegan one?

No you cannot.

So none of these are for me?

I'm afraid not, she says, unzipping the side pocket of her rucksack. Ah, here we go. Typical. *This* is for you.

He takes a slim paperback from her hand. Why thank you, he says. What did I do to deserve a gift?

Oh it's not a gift, she says, her hands on her hips now as she straightens her back. It's homework from Yvonne. The author's coming in to sign copies and she wants someone to mention its *key themes*. I'm not good enough for this one, apparently. You're the most suited, the most *eloquent*. I did tell her you've read it, but she wanted me to drop it round anyway, just to be safe. You have, haven't you?

He nods. It's not amazing, he says.

You weren't keen then, she says.

Well it's all right. It's about a sculptor and a cleaner.

Yes, I know that. It's a love story.

I hate love stories, Dexter says. He looks up from the book. I'm so sorry, I should've invited you in. Would you like a cup of tea?

Thanks, but I'm in a rush.

Fair enough.

Aren't you cold? she says, looking at his knees. He is wearing loose grey shorts and a scarlet shirt, its buttons half undone.

I don't really feel the cold, he says.

Do you not, she says, her head down as she prepares to set off. She carefully refills her rucksack and pulls it up onto her shoulders with a grunt. Then she glances at the book in his hand. That novel, she says.

It's a novella, I think, he says.

Whatever, she says, talking over him. For me, it's a really powerful study of loss. The old sculptor is trying to recreate his lost love, over and over again. And the friendship he develops with his cleaner is a distraction, she makes him look away, she brings the outside world into his home, she represents life, and yes he moans about how clumsy she is, how she never shuts up, but he also loves that about her, he grows dependent on those things. That's how I see it anyway, she says, all without blinking or looking away. But what do I know? I'm not *eloquent*. See you tomorrow then, cheerio.

She marches along the beach, lets the dogs off their leads. She is seething now.

She is furious with Dexter, and with herself.

Why did she say all those things about the book? What an *idiot*. And why does he always have to laugh at her? He was laughing then, as she walked away, she is sure he was laughing. Every day at work they annoy each other. Because Dexter is posh, educated, he grew up in a big city. He has a long burly beard, a slicked-back pompadour haircut, a tattoo and a unicycle and is fluent in French. Belle is a self-confessed bumpkin with muddy fingernails, one A level (sociology) and a signed photo of David Essex. She is frumpy and uncool and looks baffled when people say things like *joie de vivre* or *amuse-bouche*. Oh, and let's not forget that Dexter has been madly in love *and* desperately hurt, while she has only had sex once and once was enough.

Were Belle and Dexter a type of drink, he would be a single malt whisky and she would be Ribena. Even his presence feels humiliating. And so she is prickly, churlish. And he finds this interesting.

Dexter heads up the stairs to his flat and sets Ben Folds playing again in the living room. He puts the novella on his coffee table beside the pile of orange Penguin paperbacks, the fountain pen, the blood-red notebook with an illustration of a cassette on its cover. He takes off his shoes and sits on the sofa, holding a framed photo of his grandfather.

Dexter loved anything to do with his grandad. He made this patchwork throw, the one draped over the back of the sofa. He was a textile artist, known professionally for his grand-scale political pieces, *The Stitched-Up Working Classes* he called them. And he also made presents for his family. This throw was a gift for Dexter when he left home.

He puts the photo back on the coffee table, thinks about what to do next. He had planned to tidy his flat tonight, but now he has to read this stupid book. So he will ignore the mess, take a shower and get on with it.

Later, he stands in his kitchen, all damp coppery beard and silk dressing gown, opening a bottle of red wine. He runs the little Matchbox car along the windowsill, a 1957 Chevrolet Corvette, metallic blue. It was a present from Belle for his thirtieth birthday. I couldn't think what to get you, you pretty much seem to have everything, she said. The gift suggested that she might be getting to know him, but her words proved otherwise. Dexter does not have everything. He has his flat, of course – his bolthole, his haven, one of the great loves of his life. But apart from his home and his job at the bookshop, there is little else that matters.

He picks up his homework, opens it at chapter one. No, not yet. He's not in the mood. He puts it to one side and opens his laptop. His homepage is set to the local news. He clicks on a headline.

'Catwoman' survives fall from toyshop roof

Yesterday evening, sometime before 11.00pm, Sydney Smith, aged 47 – recently given the nickname 'Catwoman' by locals since her arrival in St Ives last weekend – fell from the roof of Piper's vintage toyshop on Broad Street.

Edward Piper, formerly known to residents as Edward Cock before his substantial Premium Bonds win, said: 'Nothing like this has ever happened outside my toyshop before. I can't believe it.' Sources close to Mr Piper claim that Ms Smith had been drinking in the Black Hole that evening.

Ms Smith was discovered by Maria Norton, who is married to local artist Jon Schaefer. 'I was out with Stuart, my dog,' Ms Norton said. 'He always has a late evening stroll before bed. He pulled me towards her, she was just lying there in the dark. I called 999, waited for the ambulance. Then I ran home, dropped Stuart off and drove straight to the hospital.'

When asked if this was an accident or a failed suicide attempt, Ms Norton said: 'It's not my place to speculate about such matters.'

Sydney Smith has been spotted several times this week, leaping over benches and cartwheeling on the rooftops of local businesses. Residents have been tweeting their photographs with the hashtag #Catwoman. Ms Smith practises the extreme sport known as parkour, which originated in France, but there has been a great deal of speculation about her mental state. Many photographs show her simply standing on rooftops, staring into space.

Pete Winner, manager of the Black Hole, said: 'I've seen her in the pub most evenings this week, and she doesn't look happy. Yes, I suppose she could be depressed, now you mention it.'

Local police are urging youngsters in particular not to imitate Ms Smith's behaviour. Sergeant Anna Rubin said that while freerunning is admirable, the sport should be practised in a safe and legal way. 'Causing damage to property and civil trespassing are both criminal offences and will be taken very seriously,' she said. 'Ms Smith has not been accused of any such offences. However, those who practise freerunning need to make sure they are not engaging in antisocial behaviour or risking serious injury to themselves or others. Rooftops are highly dangerous and can easily be damaged, so we advise members of the public to stay off them. Let this incident be a very sad warning. As the public are well aware, the police have serious crimes to attend to, and I'm sure people don't want us to waste precious time and resources. I wish Ms Smith a speedy recovery.'

Dexter scrolls down the page to the comments. He hates doing this, doesn't want to look, but he can never help himself. Put his fellow residents in an online room, give them a username as a mask and they quickly turn wild. Fascinating, but also disturbing. A sociologist should study this, or maybe a psychoanalyst – how people's behaviour changes according to social context or, even more interesting, virtual context. Dexter has been reading Carl Jung lately – what would Jung make of all this? Perhaps he would see the comments pages of newspapers as a playground for the shadow.

He sips his wine, scratches his beard and reads.

1.03pm   She's a drunk freerunner – why all this talk of suicide? This paper is obsessed with it. Utterly ludicrous and lazy journalism.

1.09pm   Most people just saw her standing on top of buildings, looking like she was about to jump. Just because YOU lack empathy doesn't mean

208

everyone else does. Someone can be a freerunner *and* suicidal. Life is complicated, yes?

1.14pm She's a show-off who did a stupid thing.

1.19pm I hate to say this, but if you prance about on top of buildings . . .

1.23pm Jesus, 1,009 photos! #Catwoman

1.27pm Make that 1,010 ;-)

1.29pm 'As the public are well aware, the police have serious crimes to attend to' – this is very intriguing from Sergeant Rubin. But why on earth should we be well aware? We don't have access to police files, do we? Has something happened?

1.34pm We could hear the ambulance sirens in the cinema.

1.40pm Oh dear, did that disrupt your viewing experience?

1.51pm I wasn't saying it for that reason ****sucker

1.59pm Ha! Not sure why you've used **** when the word cock was in the actual article! Piper's been

---

cleaning his shop windows apparently, making it look nice for reporters – first proper work he's done this year!

2.04pm   This area has a terrible drug problem, for a start. Two girls have been murdered in the past ten years, not to mention all the sexual assaults. Is that enough 'serious crime' for you, or would you like some more?

2.08pm   This is such a shame, as my son has always fancied trying freerunning, and was going to ask her for advice about finding a coach. He's been through a terrible time and this is the first thing he's shown an interest in for ages. He took some great photos of Ms Smith (they are not online – we do not believe in Twitter) and says he might try photography instead. I've tried to explain that if she had been consuming alcohol, sadly she was bound to have an accident. She might have landed on someone and killed them. She has set a bad example for our youngsters, who could have found the presence of a freerunner inspiring. And let's face it, what else is there to do in this town? There's no youth club is there.

2.14pm   Twitter is not something we 'believe in' – it's a social networking service, not a religion.

2.18pm LOL! :-)

2.39pm Hey, let's not tarnish the world of parkour.
I'm a coach and will happily talk to your son.
I had a chat with this woman earlier this week,
she's been freerunning for more than twenty
years, is *very* experienced, attends regular high-
level classes, is part of a long-established group
and has worked with some amazing coaches,
athletes and performers. Freerunning is a sport,
an art form, a serious discipline – it's athletic
and acrobatic and requires a high level of fitness.
It's about self-advancement, not self-destruction,
and I have NEVER known anyone else drink
while they practise. We also try to avoid
rooftops. I can only assume this woman was
having personal problems, so let's not judge her
OK?

2.57pm Why did you feel the need to inform us that
Maria Norton is married to local artist Jon
Schaefer? Does she not exist in her own right?
Maria is my dental hygienist and she does an
excellent job. You might want to train your
writers in misogyny.

3.16pm Do you actually mean 'train your writers in
misogyny'?! Think you might need writing

training too, unless you want the journalists to all be misogynists!

3.20pm Anyone recommend a good dentist? I can't understand a word mine says.

3.31pm OMG, a woman is possibly dying in hospital. Does no one care about what's happening to this woman?

30

Gypsy Creams

I am ten years old when I see a dead body for the second time.

This body belongs to my mother.

We are on holiday by the sea. Mum has been looking forward to this holiday for months and now –

She only gets three days of it.

It rained on one of the days.

She hasn't even had a pasty yet.

Or an ice cream.

There are sirens and a hospital with a cracked blue floor.

A lady buys Jason and me some macaroni cheese in cartons. It doesn't look like any macaroni cheese we've ever seen before, so we don't touch it. We drink the Coke that came with it and wait. I knock mine over. Jason grits his teeth. The lady says never mind, never mind.

The hospital smells of the inside of our Volvo after Mum has shampooed the seats. It also smells of Pritt Stick and felt-tip pens, but not in a good way.

There are framed paintings on the walls of the corridors, and we try to look at them but we are not tall enough.

Our shoes squeak on the floor.

I try not to stare at a man on a trolley with wires coming out of his nose. He waves at me and I wave back.

People are nice in here.

We have no idea where Mum and Dad are, so we don't care about the people being nice.

Today is my first experience of hating myself. At this point, I have no way of knowing that this feeling will always be part of my life, like a kidnapper I forgive and become friends with, then forget that she ever kidnapped me.

But for now, here is Dad.

Just Dad.

We have to go back to the fisherman's cottage. The one with a stable door, the sort a horse would poke its head through. This morning I was draped over it, watching people go by. You're so nosy, Mum said.

Now Dad is holding Mum's walking shoes, her water-proof jacket, her purse, her watch, a set of keys, four Gypsy Creams wrapped in kitchen roll and some sausages from the market that were supposed to be for tea.

Turns out we don't really fancy any tea.

We eat the Gypsy Creams from Mum's coat pocket.

Looking back, I don't know why we did that.

Where are you, Mum?

Dad explains that she won't be returning to our cottage. And someone else will be driving her home.

Who? we ask. Who is this special person who gets to drive her home? She is funny about cars, she worries about staying safe. Is this person a good driver?

Dad seems to mime something in reply. He lifts his right hand, spreads his fingers wide. Is he telling us to stop, stay back?

I want to walk up to him and hold my fingers near his, as if we are separated by glass and all we can do is put our hands together without touching. I saw two people do this on an American TV show. One was in prison, the other was visiting, and they were speaking to each other on special telephones. The visitor shouted and slammed her phone down and then there was only glass.

I go to lift my hand, change my mind.

This moment contains my whole future relationship with Dad. It's all here, right now. This is microcosmic, that's what it is. There will always be something between us, from this day onwards, no matter how close we are or how much time we spend together. And when he holds out his hand, I will never be sure whether he is saying come here or stay back.

In the cottage, we stare at each other.

I know Dad is angry with me and trying not to show it.

We should be eating sausages, playing Connect Four.

Perhaps we should go home, he says. But I don't want to leave your mum here by herself. I don't know what's best.

When he says this, it's as if he is speaking in a foreign language. For a minute he looks like a boy, no older than Jason, and we find this terrifying.

The following morning, he packs our things and throws them into the Volvo. Jason and I get in the back. We whisper to each other, even though there is no one else in the car. I feel sick already, he says. Me too, I say. Dad gets in and shuts the door. He sits there for what feels like a long time. Then he gets out again, stands by the car. We can't see his face, we're not sure what he's doing. When he gets back in, he looks at the empty passenger seat and squeezes the steering wheel so hard that his knuckles turn white. I think of the phrase *white-knuckle ride*, and remember Mum taking us on a roller coaster. It's called a white-knuckle ride, she said, because you have to hold on tight.

I didn't enjoy the roller coaster, not one bit. Jason hated it, but he pretended to be excited for Mum. He carried on making enthusiastic noises, even when the ride had finished, which was embarrassing and peculiar but also sort of normal for Jason, who often reacted to things in the wrong way or at the wrong time – *a little offbeat*, Dad called it. Stop it now, Mum said, stop whooping for goodness' sake. I learned the word *whooping* that day, which was useless, because I never used it again. I am not one of life's whoopers. Actually, a whooper is a type of swan. Interesting fact. Mum likes to tell us interesting facts. She knows all kinds of things, like the names of birds and plants. She knows where the weather comes from and what to do when we are ill. Does Dad know what to do when we are ill? I think about this in the car as he drives us along the motorway, until Jason starts to cry. The crying makes him wheeze, and we have to stop at a service station so he can puff on his inhaler. We get chocolate and comics, not the sort we like, but we smile and say thanks.

I want to cry too, but I don't. I keep quiet. It's the least I can do.

That evening, when we get home, Dad puts three plates of breaded fish, baked beans and chips on the table, then he also starts to cry. I don't even know how to explain what this is like. I've seen Mum cry before, but not Dad. I feel like I am underground, and all of this is happening somewhere above my head.

Jason is wheezing again. He is allergic to many things, and now he has a brand-new allergy: Mum's absence.

Inhalers. Uneaten food. Heaps of an interrupted holiday all over the floor. Buckets and spades. Guess Who?, Monopoly, KerPlunk. My duvet (rockets, UFOs, planets). Jason's duvet (*Star Wars*).

I make myself feel better by closing my eyes and imagining that I'm Spider-Man, shooting webs from my wrists and swinging from one building to another. Then I imagine that I'm James Bond in *Live and Let Die*, using crocodiles as stepping stones to cross a river. James Bond and Spider-Man always survive everything – no obstacle or enemy is too dangerous.

Jason pushes his chair back from the table and stands up. As he does this, I feel like I am watching a boy version of Mum – the thick hair and broad shoulders. Me, I'm tall and wiry like Dad, who is hunting through the piles of holiday, looking for Jason's spacer, the plastic thing he breathes into with his inhaler attached, which always looks empty even when it's full.

Where's your spacer? Dad shouts. Where the hell is it? How should I know, Jason says, then he coughs and cries and turns red in the face, and Dad's voice gets quieter as he empties a bag onto the kitchen floor, says we'll find it, Jase, it has to be here somewhere, I'm sorry I shouted, I'm sorry about that.

Looking for things that are not here is something we do a lot over the next few months.

We listen out for them too.

Mainly we listen for Mum's key in the door.

Eventually we realise that she will never step into the house with her sing-song hello, her stories, her handbag full of tissues, make-up, sweets, old shopping lists and neatly folded receipts.

As soon as we realise this, we forget all over again.

+

Welcome back, a voice says.

Dad?

I'm a nurse, my name is Malcolm. You can see your dad soon. Your surgery went well. Are you cold?

Very cold, Sydney says.

31

Catching a drift

The world is full of spotters. Trains, ghosts, butterflies, dolphins, birds – anything will do. Right now, at this second, millions of people are poised and ready with cameras, notepads, binoculars. This waiting is as crucial as the big reveal. Sometimes, the longer the better: what a rarity, what a find, what a thing to finally set eyes on.

Maria is a spotter, but the object of her fascination cannot be seen with the human eye, only experienced: silence. It's one of her hobbies. Every silence is unique, and she tries to capture its qualities, its texture. She has a notebook, The Book of Many Silences, in which she logs her discoveries. Sometimes, usually while she is gazing into an artist's studio at night, she imagines doing something creative with her observations, bringing them to life in a visual way. She has no idea how she would do this. I'm a dental hygienist, not an artist, she thinks.

Only last week, Maria stumbled upon eleven wonderful examples to add to her collection: stagnant, dreamy, conscientious, communal, excited, desolate, soulful, compliant, malevolent, avoidant, energetic (the work of catching a drift).

And tonight, in this kitchen, here's another. This one is charged with sulkiness. It's a sullen silence, she thinks.

Belle is lying on the small yellow sofa, reading the paper, drinking wine. By her feet, Stuart is asleep on the rug, exhausted from the long walk she gave him and Otto after work. There is no sign of the fox terrier – he's upstairs with Ruth and Howard, who have gone to get showered and changed, to wash the smell of hospital from their skin.

Every time Belle turns a page, she does so quickly, aggressively, flapping the paper about. *Notice me*, the page turning says.

But Maria doesn't notice. She is too busy chopping lettuce, making a salad for her guests to have with the chicken she cooked earlier. She wants this salad to be impressive: finely chopped, pretty, full of fresh herbs.

She spots the silence, labels it as sullen, carries on slicing.

Belle's huffiness subsides, along with her hope of being noticed. Feeling invisible, she drinks more wine.

The sound of footsteps overhead. A woman's voice, perhaps on the phone. A thump on the floor, something falling off a bed or Otto jumping down.

Stuart looks up, listens.

It's all right, boy, Belle says, and the dog lowers his head again, rests it on his paws.

She *speaks*, Maria says.

Sorry?

You've been unusually quiet since you got home from work.

No I haven't.

You have.

Belle lets the paper drop to her lap. Remind me again why they're staying with us, she says.

Her mother stops chopping, turns round. Don't, they'll hear you.

No they won't.

And that's very unlike you. You're usually generous.

Am I?

Of course. You put me to shame, the amount you do for other people.

The difference is, I *know* those people.

So what? Is that a good philosophy, we only help those we know?

Belle shrugs.

Anyway, Maria says. Turn the tables.

What?

Imagine you're away on a trip, and you have an accident, and me and your partner drive all the way there to be with you.

Where's Dad in this picture?

Maria says nothing.

(Interesting silence, Maria. One that erases someone from a picture. Some might call that a *murderous* silence.)

And who's this partner of mine? Belle says.

Well you might have one by then, mightn't you. A boyfriend, or a girlfriend.

I'm not gay, Mum.

Maria looks disappointed. If you are it's fine with us, she

says. I just thought, maybe that's why you don't bring anyone home, because you'd like to bring a girl.

A *girl*?

A woman then, do you want a woman?

Belle laughs. No, I don't want a woman. There's only one lesbian in this house and she is upstairs.

She's nice isn't she. I mean, they both seem like nice people.

Well I only just met them.

Don't be moody.

I'm not, I was just stating a fact.

Are you going to spit it out?

What?

What's wrong with you. Is it Dexter?

Why would it be Dexter?

It usually is.

Belle sighs. I'm fine, she says. How much salad are you making? There are only five of us.

I'm making a dressing.

There's a new bottle in the fridge, I bought it yesterday.

I'd rather make a fresh one. Wasn't it kind of them to bring all those gifts?

Well they *are* staying with us.

Maria glares.

Belle tops up her glass. Do you want some? she says.

Go on then.

She fetches another glass, fills it with wine and stands beside her mother.

So? Maria says.

Oh I don't know, Belle says.

Maria takes a large mouthful of wine. She wipes her hands on a cloth, steps closer to her daughter, places both hands on Belle's head. What's going on in there? she says.

That's the problem, Belle says.

What is?

Nothing's going on in there.

Are we talking about partners again.

No, I don't give a shit about having a bloody partner. Why does everyone keep bringing this up? I'm really not bothered, okay?

All right, no need to snap. You can stay single for your entire life if you want to, if that's what makes you happy.

If you really want the truth, Belle says, I just feel stupid, that's all, okay?

Stupid? Why?

Because I am.

Darling, you're not *at all* stupid. You do so many things, and you're good at all of them.

I do loads of things in an average kind of way. And I didn't even know what homogeneous meant.

Homogeneous?

It means unvarying, uniform.

I know, but –

See, even *you* know what it means.

Who said it?

It doesn't matter who said it.

Of course it does. You obviously felt embarrassed in front of *someone*.

Belle's face flushes. I never know what words like that mean. I feel so thick sometimes.

I had no idea you felt like this.

Well.

Maria thinks for a moment. Look, she says, anyone who uses the word *homogeneous* on a regular basis isn't worth worrying about.

That's a really weird thing to say, Belle says.

Is this why you don't want a partner? Because you think you're too stupid?

Belle's eyebrows shoot up, and Maria wishes she had chosen her words more carefully. This isn't the ideal time for a conversation like this, her mind isn't on the job. Mainly, it's on Howard and Ruth. The first house guests she has had for almost a year, apart from that author, Lily Whippet. Which is a *shocking* realisation. Far more embarrassing than not knowing the meaning of homogeneous.

Look, she says. I know only too well how horrible it is to feel embarrassed and stupid. But trust me, as the years go by, there will be far worse things to feel ashamed of than not being a walking dictionary. What I'm saying is, make the best of this. You might look back on it one day, wish it was still your biggest problem.

This pep talk is met with silence. How would you label this one, Maria? Because this one's on you, you and your big distracted mouth.

I worry about you, Mum, Belle says.

Me? Maria says. Why on earth would you worry about me? To be honest, darling, I really need to get this salad made. Will you give me a hand with this fucking salad?

Mum.

What?

You never swear, Belle says.

Shows what you know, Maria says.

Well as we've already ascertained, I know very little.

Maria shoves a bag of pine nuts into her daughter's hand. Look, just toast these will you? Let's deal with one thing at a time, all right. Tonight, our house guests. Tomorrow, your stupidity, she says, trying to appear light and jokey, but Maria hasn't been light and jokey for a long time, and she resembles someone breaking into a cheeky smile after years in a coma, as if the muscles in her face are too underused to properly engage, her mouth too dry, her whole body creaking with the effort of waking up.

Have another drink, for God's sake, Belle says, as the kitchen door opens and a fox terrier comes running in, followed by a woman with wet hair, who has changed out of the dark clothes she was wearing when she arrived earlier this evening, and is now in a cerise T-shirt, jeans and white trainers. She looks younger, less stern.

Something smells good in here, she says. Can I do anything, can I help?

32

Were you never a boy, Mr Smith

There is a jar of flowers, blue glass, purple bloom. A jug of water. A cereal bar on his pillow. All of this put here today by Maria. He eats the cereal bar, eats it fast. Maybe it will stop him feeling so dizzy, so faint. He sits on the single bed, looks around the room. On the windowsill, there's a row of small needle-felted hares with pricked-up ears, a picture of attentiveness. The hares are listening. What's going on with you, Mr Smith? they say, all at once, an eerie chorus. He walks over, picks one up. Blood orange, he thinks. You, tiny hare, are the colour of a blood orange.

Hey, Blood, he says aloud.

Hey, the hare says. Are you all right? You don't look all right.

I'm strung out. I'm weirded out.

Doesn't get weirder than talking to me, Blood says.

Oh it does.

Tell me everything.

Howard lies down, places Blood on the pillow beside his head. What's the point, he says, what do *you* know about anything?

Well, my parents are Art and Craft, Blood says. I carry their wisdom and resilience.

I see, Howard says.

And I've been needled into existence, so I know about pain.

He holds the hare above his face, gazes into the black dots of its eyes. Well my pain is taboo, he says to the dots. It's the pain that dare not speak its name.

Whisper it into the tallness of my ear, Blood says.

What good will that do?

Just do it, Mr Smith.

And so he does. He says it, as quietly as he can, into the ear of a needle-felted hare, which is as good a place as any: *I hate her.*

Well done, Blood says. Whisper your hatred into me and I'll tell you if it's real. Because sometimes it's not, you know, and all the fuss we made about hate was a fuss about something else. Go on, whisper it again.

I hate her.

And again.

I hate her.

Again, Mr Smith.

I really hate her.

This time it breaks his voice, his thin rustle of a voice, or maybe just his heart.

See, Blood says. See what happens to hate when you whisper it into me? See how it breaks? That's it, have a good cry, let it out. Make space for everything that lives alongside your hate, rubs up against it, sharpens itself. When your hate

227

has gone, everything else will soften. You have broken your own heart, Mr Smith. Day after day, you deprive Sydney and yourself of life. When will you give it up? Accidents happen. Kids run around, follow their yearnings, try to get closer to the sea. Without thinking, parents try to save them, and sometimes they fail.

Shut your mouth, Howard says.

I won't.

I said, shut your mouth.

It was an act of pure love, pure instinct, they were driven by it, full of it, the stupid and reckless love of a mother and daughter. All this love spilling out in front of you – a girl's love of life, a mother's love for a girl who was simply loving the easy days of a summer holiday, her body dancing in the sun, her eyes entranced by the shimmer and flicker of the sea, so much brightness in her eyes as she cartwheeled and jumped. Were you never a boy, Mr Smith? Did you never feel like dancing with joy, like moving where your body wanted to move, like leaping? I, being a hare, am always leaping.

Liar, Howard says. You're made of felt. You just sit there, all day long.

But I'm still a hare, Blood says. The leaps I cannot make in life I make in my dreams. What about you, Mr Smith? Can the same be said about you?

Howard has no idea where he is. As he wakes, he wipes the tears from his face, looks at his watch, then the room. He is on a single bed in a stranger's house. He can smell something cooking downstairs. Shit, he says. He has been asleep for over an hour. Why didn't Ruth wake him? Is she asleep too? Or is she downstairs with Maria and Belle, eating dinner and drinking wine, would they have started without him, would they have done that? He has no idea what they would do, what kind of people they are.

He gets up, looks in the mirror. He is clean, which is something, but his shirt is crumpled and so is his face.

So be it, he thinks, as he tidies his hair, pulls the cuffs of his shirt back down to his wrists, opens the door and goes downstairs.

He pauses for a moment before entering the kitchen. He can hear music, voices, the clink of cutlery. The people behind this door are listening to jazz and eating dinner. He thinks about going back upstairs. Babyish, Howard. And besides, listen to your stomach, you need to eat something.

Maria rises to her feet. You're awake, she says.

Yes, I'm so sorry.

I popped my head around your door, didn't like to wake you, Ruth says. Thought you needed a nap.

He feels awkward, uncomfortable, stepping into this kitchen too late and full of sleep. Their plates are almost empty. And there is a man here now who wasn't here earlier, he's slicing the last bit of meat off a bone, a grumpy-looking man, finally looking up at him now, took him long enough.

Come and sit down, Maria says. Are you hungry? Do you like leg or breast? I put some of both on your plate, here we are, and let's get you some wine, you must be dying for some wine.

I'm Jon, the man says, as Howard approaches the table.

Howard Smith, he says, shaking Jon's hand.

And you've already met Belle, Maria says.

Yes, hi. This looks lovely, thank you.

Oh it's just a salad, Maria says, nothing special.

Howard looks at Ruth, who is shoving bread into her mouth as though she hasn't eaten for a week. She seems like a stranger, sitting here with Maria, Belle and Jon. No, not a stranger, but definitely less familiar than usual. Even Otto, sniffing about on the floor, could be someone else's dog.

Well, he says, squinting. He raises his glass of wine. To your generosity and kindness, he says.

Maria, right beside him, blushes. Her face feels too close, he swears he can feel the heat coming right off it. You're welcome, she says. But really, it's a pleasure. We haven't had guests to stay for ages.

Jon is staring at his wife. He tears a piece of bread in two, dunks it in olive oil, balsamic vinegar, all while staring at his wife.

Apple pie after this, if you can manage it, she says.

Thanks, Howard says. He glances at Jon and Belle, glances at Ruth. He doesn't want to be here, it's too much, the effort of speaking to strangers. Ruth had predicted this, said she wanted to stay at the B&B, but he wouldn't listen. He told her it would be rude to turn Maria down after everything she had done. What was he thinking?

(You weren't thinking, Howard. *That* was the problem. You were spinning on the spot like a boy in a whirlwind.)

As he begins to eat, he does something he hasn't had to do since Sydney and Jason were children. He reminds himself, quietly in his mind, that there is still ground beneath his feet. He places his feet flat on the floor. See, there it is, you can feel it now. The ground, always the ground.

33

Mountain goat

Dad, are you awake? she says.

He doesn't stir.

Daddy? she whispers, to his back.

She reaches out to touch his shoulder, stops herself.

She stands there, perfectly still in the darkness of her parents' bedroom, for five minutes. She watches the minutes change on a digital clock.

06:04

06:05

06:06

Time is blinking. It sees everything.

She walks around the bed, stands at the other side, beside the empty pillow. She can see her dad's face from here. He looks peaceful, happy, like the man inside their photo albums. At first this feels nice, seeing him again, then disturbing, like seeing a dead person.

In her left hand there is a sheet of paper. Last night, she completed one of her best drawings. She knows this, and it makes her feel good. The colouring is neat and the figures are realistic. She has drawn her whole family. *Whole* being the important word. They are standing together on a special planet. A planet where you can arrange visits with dead people. Her dad stands on the left, wearing jeans and a blue hooded top. Jason is next, in grey trousers and one of his beloved smart shirts, buttoned right up – he thinks they make him look clever and old, these shirts, but he already looks clever and old. Beside Jason, their mother. She is wearing cords and a Stevie Wonder T-shirt. Sydney is especially proud of how she has managed to make the face really look like Stevie Wonder – that bit took ages, all afternoon. Finally, at the end, she has drawn herself in a padded space-suit, an oxygen pack strapped to her back, her head enclosed in a circular helmet with a visor that will protect her from absolutely everything: flying objects, weird gases, extreme temperatures, etc. She is a self-sufficient unit, holding on tight to her mother's hand. She isn't sure why she has drawn herself like this, when everyone else is in regular clothes. It's odd, but also cool. It reminds her of the boy in that film, *The Boy in the Plastic Bubble*.

She puts the drawing on the bed and stands with her hands behind her back, in the way people do when they are waiting for someone important to appear. She is silent and upright, a small girlish guard.

The room is so quiet. She closes her eyes, imagines that she is standing at the top of a mountain, looking down at furry white mountain goats. She watched a programme on TV about these goats last month, with their pointed horns and super-thick coats, their cloven hoofs with two toes, feet like brilliant climbing shoes. These kids, nannies and billies, all they need to survive, to move gracefully from one day to the next, one height to another, is the foliage that grows naturally on the side of mountains. Sydney couldn't stop talking about the goats, which, she had decided, were the most amazing animals in the whole wide world – so nimble and surefooted. She drew them balancing on the smallest of rocks. She drew them balancing on the steepest of ledges. When I die and come back again, I most definitely without fail want to be a mountain goat, she said to Jason. Don't say that in front of Dad, he said, which made her feel ashamed, made her screw up her drawings of the goats and push them deep inside the bin.

06:14

She opens her eyes, looks down at her dad's hands. They are dark and rough. She can see his pale green veins sticking out. Why are veins green when blood is red? This is one of many things she doesn't understand.

These are the hands that lifted her out of a tree when she was five, so gently, as if she were a kitten.

These are the hands that held on to her bike, then let go: *You're doing it, it's all you now, that's it keep going that's it.*

These are the hands on the steering wheel of the car, taking them to school, to the shops, to the cinema.

06:16

She looks down at her slippers. They are too small for her now, her toes are poking out.

06:17

There is a spider, crawling down the wall, moving quite fast for a spider. She hopes it doesn't crawl into her room, then into her mouth at night. She has heard that spiders do that.

Her father, he is stirring now. He turns over.

Dad? she says.

He makes a little snorting sound, carries on sleeping.

Maybe it isn't a good idea to give him this picture.

Maybe it will just make him angry or upset.

She tiptoes out of the room, goes downstairs, into the lounge. She pulls a heavy book about astronomy down from the shelf, opens it up, carefully places her drawing inside it. She flicks through its pages, gazing at the stars and the solar system, the pockmarked surface of the moon.

She doesn't draw her mother again for more than three decades. When she does, she sketches her singing into a TV remote, and posts the sketch to her father with a book about ukuleles that she found in a second-hand bookshop.

Afterwards, she wishes she hadn't done this.

She has made herself feel small and vulnerable by posting that parcel. Now all she will do is wait for his response. Even when she is busy with other things, she will be aware that she is waiting. She has been doing this for years. Since her mother died, she has spent so much of her life watching her father's face, studying his responses, looking for the right one, the one she can hold on to as if it were some long-lost treasure, some key to a better life. It's the behaviour of a child, trying to second-guess, appease, make up for, not a forty-seven-year-old woman.

All this talk over the years, all the words in people's mouths about letting go of her mother.

They were the right words, about the wrong parent.

It's her father she needs to let go of.

And the drawing of her mother, she wishes she had kept it for herself.

⊞

Dear Mum,

I've just been to the post office. It was sort of revelatory. I sent Dad a book, and a sketch I did of you messing about. I'd forgotten how daft you were. I shouldn't have forgotten that.

Here are some other things I remember tonight:

You loved crosswords, detective books, The Good Life *and* Rising Damp.

You loved eggy bread, roast chicken, sherry trifle.

And we could make you laugh or cry, really easily. Me, I'm not like that. I rarely cry and I'm not what you'd call giggly. I certainly wouldn't walk into the living room wearing a pair of knickers on my head like you did one Sunday evening, when you were tired of us all being grumpy. I'd never do something as silly as that, but maybe I should, it might make Ruth laugh. You put a colander on your head once too, and I was too moody to even smile, and I wish I hadn't mentioned that now, or remembered it.

All my love,

Sydney

xxx

34

Dusty Springfield

Holy macaroni, Belle says, as she leans too far to the left, wobbles about, regains her balance.

She is at the top of a stepladder in the bookshop window, pinning A5 posters to a noticeboard. The posters are of author headshots and book covers, with details of when each writer will visit the shop to read their work aloud.

Try and make this window display sexy, her boss said, because our mini book festival is sexy, yes? Yvonne Partridge – the kingpin, the big cheese, that's what Dexter calls her – has sex on the brain, and nothing is as sexy to her as books. The trouble is, she reads several a week and expects her staff to do the same. And Belle just can't. She doesn't understand how a person can read so quickly. Yvonne must treat her books like hurdle races, go leaping across whole paragraphs, missing bits out. Belle prefers to go slowly, meandering back and forth, rereading her favourite lines, making connections. She likes to get up close, then step back, grasp the overall shape of a book. Some sentences are so alive it's as if they have a pulse, and she likes to run her finger over these sentences, see what she can feel. But none of this behaviour makes for a well-read bookseller. It's not how you read that matters to Yvonne, it's how much you read. She wants Belle to hurry up, to *absorb core titles, consume more content*. You sound like you want me to eat the bloody things, she said.

Right now, from behind the till, Yvonne is watching her wobble about on the stepladder. Belle smiles, tries to look confident. She is wearing green fingerless gloves, a burgundy polo neck, flared jeans and brown shoes. Dexter is kneeling below the ladder, also in the shop window, wearing a cream Aran jumper, dungarees and walking boots. He is deeply absorbed in his task, enjoying the process of taking books from a pile and placing them here, or there, or maybe over there. Each book has been recently published. There's a new Indian cookbook, an experimental novel, a crime novel, a rebranded historical novel by an author who was about to go out of print, until another author discovered her and mentioned her in the *New Yorker*, and now her books have stepped back from the verge of extinction, been given a good shake, dressed in shiny new jackets. There's a celebrity autobiography, a self-help book about the power of gratitude, a memoir by a sports presenter, reflections on death from a wildlife photographer, and a collection of chickpea recipes for all occasions. Then there is Dexter's favourite new book: *The Early Onset of Love,* a four-hundred-page poem about our seriously fucked-up world.

Dexter read an interview with the author of this poem, in which he explained the book's title. Love only enters the poem near the end, he said, but it wasn't supposed to feature at all. This work was to be purely political, but love barged its way in, made itself at home, in the way that only love does. The blasted thing, the little sneak, the poet said. Love came like a feverish flu. He hunkered down, took vitamins, fish oil, antidepressants, echinacea, prebiotics and probiotics. He had experienced love before, knew that nothing good could ever come of it. Best to let the early stage pass, drink plenty of fluids, flush it out of the system as early as possible, he said.

Dexter was excited by this interview. Finally, here was a person who confirmed his own view of love as something best left to those who were willing to engage in a pursuit so monumental, so dangerous, as if it were as harmless as hanging out the washing. As mad as can be, surely? To him, the Romantic ideal was as ludicrous as extremist religion, so many of us converted and blowing ourselves up, all in the name of love.

Actually, he thought, there's love in every one of these books, even the cookbooks. A biryani cooked for date night, a heart-shaped chickpea fritter for Valentine's Day. Why are we all susceptible to something so pernicious? The gains do not outweigh the losses. The good times do not outweigh the damage.

Yes, you've guessed it: once bitten, as the saying goes. He had moved in with Abbie when he was twenty two, and three years later they were separating their belongings into his and hers but mainly hers. After they moved out of their house, and without telling Abbie, Dexter slept on the floor of their bedroom for a week until their tenancy officially ended, until the letting agent turned up to poke around, to inspect and take photos of the walls, the carpet, the oven, the shower, the sink, the toilet, everything. Looks fine, she said. Looks like you'll be getting your full deposit. Where are you guys moving to, anywhere nice?

He told a story about them moving out of town – more space for your money, even a small garden, he said. It made him feel sick. He described their small house, the dog they would be getting once they were settled. For months the story haunted him, played in his mind like a feel-good movie that made him feel anything but good.

It took him four years to recover, if you can call it that, if *recovered* means patched up and traumatised and settled in a new flat, a home of his own this time, one he has vowed never to share with another person. And to remind him of the risks, he still keeps an empty cardboard box in the corner of his bedroom, left over from the move, her handwriting on the side in felt-tip pen: *D's mugs, tea towels & candles*.

This is one of the reasons why Dexter admires Belle. She seems to possess innate knowledge and wisdom about love, without having gone through hell to obtain it. She is not searching or preening, not swooning over anyone's looks or promises. Nor does she care what people think of her.

Holy macaroni, she says.

Since when is that a phrase? he says.

What?

Holy macaroni.

It's *my* phrase.

He smiles. Do you like Indian food? he says, while flicking through a cookbook.

Of course, she says. I love an onion bhaji.

Sorry?

I said I love an onion bhaji, she says, louder this time, because Yvonne has turned up the music: Dusty Springfield, 'I Close My Eyes and Count to Ten'.

I *love* this song, Dexter says. It's actually the perfect love song, if you really listen to it.

What? she says.

Just listen, Belle.

I would if you ever stopped talking.

The lyrics are full of desire, he says, but the atmosphere of the song itself is malevolent, it seems to spell disaster. I think Dusty knew things that most people don't, and *that's* why she suffered.

What are you banging on about?

She's just brilliant, he says. I mean, 'The Windmills of Your Mind', the way she sings that.

She glances down at him. He looks so serious, earnest, possibly slightly tearful. I don't know that one, she says.

Really? he says.

He starts quoting lyrics, and they sound like a mysterious poem, quite lovely really, but she tries to ignore him. He's being pretentious again, which is what she always thinks when he talks about subjects she knows nothing about.

Dusty Springfield is to music what Patricia Highsmith is to fiction, he says.

She rolls her eyes.

Her voice is so dark, so mysterious, he says.

I wouldn't know, all I can hear is *your* voice, she says, with a quick smile. Then she is stern again, as she comes down from the ladder.

Dexter stands up, starts moaning about his sore knees. Then he makes a sweeping motion with his arm. What do you think? he says.

Of what? she says.

My handiwork, he says, nodding towards the window display.

I think you mean *our* handiwork, she says.

They quietly assess each other's efforts.

Not bad, he says. Even if some of your posters are a little wonky.

They are not.

They are. Just a *bit*.

Well, she says, why are there more copies of *The Early Onset of Love* than anything else?

Because it's truly excellent, he says.

But by having such a huge pile, it makes it seem like his event is a really big deal. Which it isn't, to be honest.

It is to me, he says. I can't wait to meet him. Didn't you enjoy the book?

It only just came out, she says, with a tired sigh.

He must think I'm such a loser, she thinks.

I really like her fingerless gloves, he thinks.

He picks up a copy of *The Early Onset of Love*. Basically, he says, it's about the state of the world. It's about bodies washing up on shores, narcissistic psychopaths who

242

call other people sick, doors closing on a global scale and shutting people out. But then it moves on to love, how love can make us crazy and self-obsessed.

You're very talkative aren't you, she says.

Am I? he says. Does that mean shut up?

She smiles. Maybe, she says.

I just thought you'd like the book.

Why?

I thought you'd appreciate its take on love.

What's love got to do with it? she says.

Tina Turner, he says.

What?

That's the name of a Tina Turner song.

She looks at him blankly.

What's love got to do with what? he says.

The state of the world, she says.

Now there's a question, he says. I got the impression you were anti-love, in a one-to-one context. More into communal living, the neighbourhood.

She has no idea what he's trying to say. What are you saying? she says.

I just mean, he says.

What, exactly? she says.

Well, he says. He thinks carefully for a moment. I'm not sure what you are, he says.

Meaning, she says.

Meaning you're unusual I suppose. You never talk about finding anyone attractive, never mention a partner. It's like that side of life isn't even on your radar. Either that, or you don't like to talk about it.

In her peripheral vision, Belle can see Yvonne rearranging piles of children's books on a nearby table. Trying to eavesdrop, probably. About to tell them off for talking too much. She looks up at the A5 posters, tries to see if Dexter is right, if some of them are wonky. Point taken, she thinks, they're not exactly perfect. Then she turns to face him again, looks him in the eye.

I'm asexual, she says. Is that what you want me to say? You want me to come out of the closet? Well there you go. I'm fucking asexual.

Whoa, he says, to her red face.

Whoa? she says. What are you, eleven?

Fucking asexual, that's oxymoronic, he says.

Oh great, I tell you something really personal and all you do is insult me, she says.

No, it just means contradictory.

Why use a word like that? Why do you always have to use words like that?

Like what?

Words other people don't use. Like *homogeneous*. Who says that in normal life?

I'm sorry, he says. He wants to ask her what *normal life* is, decides it's probably best not to. He feels ashamed, but isn't sure why.

Anyway what are *you*? she says. You're just the same as me, surely?

What?

Asexual.

His nose is twitching now, in a weird way.

Aren't you? she says.

Well, he says.

It's a simple question, yes or no.

Crikey she's a fiery one, he thinks. She looks furious now, and he has never seen fury on her before. It's really quite fascinating.

I think it's bloody brilliant that you're asexual, he says. I bet loads of people are, they just don't come out and say so. I'm celibate, so we're on the same page, sort of.

Really? she says.

Absofuckinglutely, he says.

You two certainly say *fucking* a lot for people who don't do it, Yvonne says, appearing behind them.

Oh *God*, Belle says, so embarrassed she can hardly move. Shame creeps all over her, makes her feel wretched, disgusting.

The only difference between someone who's asexual and someone who's celibate is one of them is a wanker, Yvonne says. Then she bursts out laughing, claps her hands and walks away.

Who gives themselves a round of applause? Dexter says.

Belle's hand is over her mouth. Her eyes are darting about, taking in all of the shop and none of it. She closes her eyes, as if this will solve everything, make Dexter and Yvonne and the world disappear, or maybe just herself.

I'm really sorry, Dexter says. I didn't know she was there. And I shouldn't have pushed you.

Her eyes remain shut.

Belle?

What.

Are you all right?

I'm just taking a moment.

Okay, he says. Very meditative, he says.

I'm not feeling *at all* meditative, she says.

Are you blocking me out?

I'm blocking everything out.

Fair enough, he says.

He watches her. She looks like she is asleep standing up, like one of those living statues on the high street. He listens to Dusty Springfield. Watches her.

This goes on for longer than either of them expect.

Belle is finding this strangely peaceful. She keeps thinking she'll open her eyes, then she doesn't.

Dexter is entranced. There is something Pre-Raphaelite about her. It's like standing in a gallery, looking at a painting, only instead of Elizabeth Siddal or Annie Miller, it's Belle Schaefer, who is curlier than usual today, and has thick eyebrows, he has only just noticed her eyebrows, how they are not plucked into a surprise like Yvonne's.

Can I ask you one more thing if I promise to make us a cup of tea? he says.

No, she says, eyes still closed. Oh go on then. But I want biscuits too. Specifically chocolate Hobnobs.

Okay, he says. So do you mind that you're asexual? I mean, do you care?

Her eyes open now. They look redder than before. Of course I care, she says.

Which isn't true. Thanks to her volunteering, dog walking, pig walking, attending to authors, otters *and* her mother, not to mention all those vegetables at the allotment, the onions and shallots, the sprouts and chard and perpetual spinach, Belle cares about so many things that she can't possibly care about anything deeply. She has spread herself too thin, deliberately filling her time, giving her life so much meaning, there's no space for anything to feel meaningful. You've over-egged your own pudding, her mother once said. And for once, she was right. So the thing about Belle's sexuality, or lack of it, she doesn't care, not really.

Right, he says. Hobnobs it is.

On his way to the staff kitchen, an elderly man in red circular glasses taps him on the shoulder. What classic would you recommend? he says.

Classic? Dexter says.

For my wife, the man says, loud enough for everyone in the shop to hear. He shuffles closer, scrunches up his nose.

What kind of thing does she like?

She likes the juxtaposition of repression and sensuality, the man shouts.

That's very precise, Dexter says.

Quite right, the man says, looking pleased. She recently enjoyed *Lady Chatterley's Lover*. Do you have anything similar?

Has she read *The Rainbow*? Dexter says. Or *Wuthering Heights*, she might like that?

Might she? Very good, he says. And where can I find these books? I'll take both of them. My wife is ill you see, and she's vicious when she's ill.

I'll show you, Dexter says.

As soon as the customer has left the shop, Yvonne calls a staff meeting. I want to talk to you both, right now, she shouts.

The three of them stand by the till, drinking tea and eating biscuits.

So, Yvonne says. That gentleman has confirmed my line of thinking. I'd like to make some changes around here, bring us up to speed.

Ugh, Belle thinks. More *speed*. Why can't they slow down instead? Hasn't Yvonne heard of the slow movement?

He was so pleased with your recommendations just now, Yvonne says.

Thank you, Dexter says.

And that's exactly what people want these days. They want to be told what to do, where to go, what to eat, what to think, what to read. People want reviews and comparisons: if you like this, you'll like that. They also want to comment on *everything*.

Belle cringes.

And that's why I had these made, Yvonne says.

She rummages inside a Books Are My Bag tote bag, then steps forward, pins a badge to Belle's polo neck.

Belle is horrified. She adores this polo neck, which has

served her well for five years without a single sign of wear and tear. How dare Yvonne stick a pin in it, make a hole in it? Talk about crossing a line. For people who love their knitwear, this is basically assault. It's also an issue of power. She would never stick a pin in Yvonne's V-neck – firstly it might deflate all the fakery inside her bra, but secondly, and most importantly, it would be totally disrespectful.

She looks down at the badge, sees Dexter looking too.

PLEASE LET ME KNOW HOW I DID TODAY

No way, he says.

You're kidding me, Belle says.

Now Yvonne is pinning one to Dexter's Aran jumper.

You're not serious, he says.

It's the way of the world, Yvonne says. We need to roll with the times.

Jesus Christ, Dexter says.

It's just change, you'll adjust, Yvonne says. Especially when you receive lots of *wonderful* feedback.

Feedback is a term for unwanted sound distortion, Dexter says.

I'm putting a feedback page on our website, Yvonne says. If customers submit their details, they'll be entered into a prize draw.

What's the prize? Belle says.

I haven't decided yet. It could be a signed first edition, a ticket to an event. Or, something even better: a one-to-one session with the bookseller who receives the highest rating.

Rating? Belle says.

You're pimping us out? Dexter says.

My bookish whores, Yvonne says. She wants to laugh at this remark but it simply isn't funny. In fact, she has made herself feel slightly repulsed. You'll find out what they're into, then give them more of what they like, she says, which does nothing to ease her repulsion.

But we already *do that*, Dexter says. It's our job. People have always recommended books to each other. So why is that a good prize?

Because they'll get your undivided attention for a whole hour, she says. Where else do you get a person's undivided attention for that long?

Therapy, Dexter says.

Precisely, Yvonne says.

I'm happy to talk to anyone about books, Belle says, but why do I have to be given a rating for it? What if they don't like what I suggest? Everything is subjective.

I agree, Dexter says. I don't always suggest something *similar*. Sometimes I might say, if you like this novel about winter, take a look at this collection of paintings of snow.

Yes, Belle says. Or, if you enjoyed this memoir by an artist who lives in a ramshackle house, you might like this book of bohemian interiors.

Or, Dexter says, if you loved this novel set in Paris, you might like this new French cookery book.

Or – Belle says.

Stop it, just stop, Yvonne says. You've gone off-piste. That isn't what customers want. They want more of what they already like. I'm trying to keep this business afloat here, to keep us in paid employment. Your asexual celibate life-styles cost money, you know.

Please don't say that again, Belle says. Can we just erase that whole conversation?

The thing is, Dexter says, we don't always know what we like until we find it, and sometimes it's completely different to anything we've ever experienced.

I echo that, Belle says. Then she flinches. Echo? she thinks. Why the hell did I say *echo*?

Yvonne takes a deep breath. Enough, she shouts. She draws as much breath as she can into her lungs and blows it out in the direction of Belle's face.

The air smells of mothballs, which makes Belle freeze and lean backwards. Today is intoxicating, and not in a good way. First the self-disclosure, which she knows she will pay for later when she is alone, undistracted, horribly embar-rassed. And now *this*.

The room is full of rage.

Yvonne, sick and tired of these neurotic, arrogant, fussy booksellers, would like to take a swing at them both with a baseball bat. Luckily, there is no bat in this shop. Only the rubber winged bat, hanging above the children's books. Her face is tight, her shoulders are back and she has puffed out her chest, pushed her breasts into the room, making them even more prominent than usual. In fact, she has invited her breasts into this impromptu staff meeting, that's what she has done. And yes, her employees have noticed, they are looking right at them, you would too if you were here. Yvonne does this on a regular basis. When she doesn't like how things are going, the breasts come out. Not literally, thank goodness. But it won't work this time, oh no. Dexter and Belle won't be thrown off course by a pair of prosthetic bazookas enlarged to 34E, a bouncy extension on an otherwise ordinary frame, like a giant inflatable bursting through the front windows of a modern nondescript house.

Dexter is seething. I don't wish to be rude, he says, but this badge is incredibly tacky.

Wear it with pride, that's a good boy, Yvonne says. Anyway, it'll be interesting to see which one of you gets the best feedback, won't it?

Ha! Take that, young booksellers, she thinks. Divide and conquer, that's the way to manage a team.

Dexter and Belle look at each other, and for the very first time there is a spark between them.

A spark of outrage.

35

Your fire

She is talking quick and wild, talking fast and loose, loose
with her tongue, fast with her hands, talking about time and
the seasons and the way things are and the way things are
not. She is madly excited to see him. Andy of all people.
Right here on the beach. Sitting on her rock. Her rock, of all
places.

He is laughing.

This is what he does while she rolls words into paper
tubes, snaps words into kindling sticks, chops words into
wooden logs, and uses all of these to make a criss-crossing
fire on the beach to warm his dead hands. While the fire is
getting started she rubs his hands between her hands, blows
warm air onto his fingers.

She paints pictures with words of all the days and months
and years he has missed, all the springs and summers and
autumns and winters. But to be honest, she says, to be really
truthful, I have to admit that sometimes it feels like every
spring is all the springs I have known. Or that every season
is the same season, there are no cycles, there is no real
change, not as time goes by, not as the leaves fall and the

buds push through and everything starts again. Do you get what I'm saying, Andy? she asks him, as the fire spits fire, crackles and doubles in size then doubles again, until it's almost a match for the water, the big old ocean allegedly full of what, of fish and seals and nanosized microbeads of plastic that's what, revoltingly referred to as mermaids' tears, bobbing about in the sea she has thought of wading into, she has imagined this many times, the cold and wet abruptness of this moment, her so-called end, the end of Maria Norton as we know her, end of. Maria Norton has come to a sticky end, a plasticky end.

I have missed you so terribly much, she says. Do you remember how we used to make up our own words for things? Well there are no words for how I've missed you, no words to do it justice, she says.

He smiles.

Look at your fire, he says. You're saying plenty. Your fire speaks volumes.

Yes but I'm an entire library, she says. For you, my dear, I am a library bigger than the Library of Congress, the British Library, the New York Public Library.

Good to see you haven't lost your spark, he says.

Well that's where you're wrong, she says. My spark has been split and torn and dragged around like a bird in a cat's mouth, half drowned in the bottom of a stream, tied to the back of a car like a washed-out empty can on a pair of newly-weds. My spark has been pressed inside the pages of someone else's story. But it's never been with me.

He is laughing again.

Offensive, she says.

I'm sorry, he says, but what you just said reminds me of a song.

What song?

He begins to hum a tune.

'I've Never Been to Me', she says, rolling her eyes. How do you even know that song? I'm sure you were gone when it came out.

I don't know, he says. Maybe it's because you know it.

Anyway, we digress, she says. My spark, now that you mention it, now that you bring it out into the open, has been like a firefly trapped behind glass. I've spotted it sometimes, behind the glass of a gallery window at night.

Why didn't you go in, try to catch it? he says.

That would be breaking and entering, she says. The last thing I need is to spend my life in a second kind of prison. And anyway, she says, why do I keep dreaming about you like this? Tell me, Andy.

Well, he says, getting up off the rock, standing up straight, rubbing his back as if it hurts to stand like a regular person, a living person. He stops to think. I think maybe you are reconnecting with the woman who once loved me, he says.

What do you mean? she says.

From what I've learned while I've been dead, I think there comes a time when this happens, he says.

When what happens? she says, touching his arms, his shoulders, his face, patting him all over to check he's really here.

He feels like he's being frisked, inspected, body-searched,

and he is. He feels like he's being measured by a tailor for a brand-new suit fit for a brand-new life, and he is, if a dream is a kind of coming alive, which it is.

When the trajectory of a person changes course, swings full circle, he says. Yes, that's it. It's not that the person travels backwards, not at all, because there is no such thing as backwards. She circles all the selves she has ever been, and there is an opening then, a choice about who to be or not to be. It's a very special moment in the trajectory of a person.

Well that's very interesting and Shakespearean, she says. So what you're saying, I think, is this isn't actually about you at all. I'm not dreaming of *you*, as such. Only of myself – the self closest to the one who once loved you, hence your appearance.

Yes, he says. Exactly right, he says.

Well that's bullshit, she says. And now I know you're talking out of your lovely dead arse.

And why is that, he says.

Because all the selves I've ever been have loved and love you still.

She says this while conducting the huge bonfire as if it were an orchestra.

There is music now. Bach, of course. Maria loves Bach.

Andy looks down at his Italian brogues. Talk about well made, he thinks, talk about longevity. He looks back up at Maria. I was afraid you were going to say that, he says. I thought I could make you think otherwise.

Ha, she says. You're still as handsome as ever too aren't you. You haven't aged a bit.

That's how death rolls, he says. It's only the mark of time that ages us, and time has left me alone.

Shall I tell you something else? she says.

Do, he says.

I'm so lost, I don't know who I am or what I'm doing, and I'm completely certain that no one else feels this way. And also, here's another: I feel like I've wasted so much time, and it's too late now for anything real or substantial or brilliantly new. I wish I could just stop this life and start another, do it better this time, make more of time this time.

He is nodding. This is why procrastination is like the hole that keeps on digging itself deeper, he says. It's the distraction that keeps on giving. The later it gets before making your move, before getting on with what you need to do, the harder it is to do anything at all – everything feels pointless, too late. Too much time has passed, you're in too deep, you'll never achieve what you could have if you'd started earlier, so why bother now?

Well exactly, she says. Why bother?

Because you're alive, he says. You could help other people. What happened to your politics?

I'm too depressed, too heavy for all that, she says.

You're not heavy. I bet I could still pick you up, carry you across this beach.

Not heavy in that way, she says. I'm not sure you'll be able to understand this part, Andy, because what I'm talking about here is the weight of time wasted, the knowledge of this, how you sort of end up wearing it, and you grieve for the life unlived.

That I understand, he says.

I'm sorry, she says. How can I be moaning to you about wasted time when yours was cut like a ribbon.

She looks up. In this dream, an orange ribbon flaps about in the air above her head.

He grabs it. This ribbon is real and substantial and brilliantly new, he says. But as an image, it's really not applicable. Ribbons are generally cut when something is ceremonially opened, like a new building. They are not generally cut when something closes.

You're completely right, she says. I wish you had stayed alive to put me right, to right my wrongs. I don't know why I pictured a ribbon just then. Can I have it please?

You want it? he says.

I want it, she says.

He hands it to her. She wraps it around her knuckles.

Oh, she says. It's obvious really, when you think about it.

How is it, he says.

Cut to ribbons, she says. That's why my unconscious produced this image. When you died, my spark was split and torn, remember. Dreams being associative.

And look at you now, he says. You're bright orange, you're the fire and the water, you're anything you want.

Sadly, that is not my truth, she says.

Sadly, it is precisely your truth, he says. Sadly because I can't hang around to see it. Sadly because you don't see it either, and may never.

You're not going already. I won't have it, I won't let you.

And another important thing, he says: collective uncon-scious. Each and every unconscious is connected by something beyond itself. So we are not separate entities. We spark each other off. We spark things off in each other. This is one of the things I've learned while I've been dead. Seren-dipity, coincidence, synchronicity. The way the phone rings, and it's funny, I was just thinking of you. The way a person crosses the mind and then appears in the street. The way you dream of a seemingly random object and see it the next day.

We're hyper aren't we, Maria says, grinning. We're com-pletely hyper. When I get hyper, Jon tells me to calm down, be quiet. He says my hyper moments are hormonal, hysteri-cal, all of those misogynistic words.

I'll be hyper with you, he says. Let's be over and beyond. Let's be hyperactive, hypersonic.

What's hypersonic?

It's when your reach exceeds your grasp. It's when the things you say travel much faster than the speed of sound.

So what would happen if I said *I love you* hypersonically? Or something much dirtier than that, in fact, she says.

And he laughs, and picks her up, and puts her down, then she picks him up, throws him over her shoulder, the whole dead weight of him, the entire live weight of him, and she runs along the beach, faster than she thought she could run, and now they are in the sea, and now they are flames dancing close in deep water, and now they are orange darting fish swimming side by side, and now they are gone.

36

Undressing in public

So tell me again, Belle says. The prognosis. The diagnosis.

So basically, Ruth says, she has post-concussion syndrome and they've repaired her fractured hip, realigned the bone. She'll be on crutches for a while. There'll be physiotherapy, God knows what after that.

Crikey, Belle says.

Yep, Ruth says.

Two women on the beach. Gloves, woolly hats, coffee in paper cups.

Beside them, a small dog is dancing with a giant dog, a quick bouncy terrier and a slow lolloping hound. Are these dogs aware of each other's size? In play, they seem to have the measure of each other. Bottoms in the air, then a pounce and a wrestle and a nibble at the ear. Now they're off again, chasing a curve, Otto pausing to look behind as if to say *are you with me, don't lose me, are you with me, keep up.*

They get on well don't they, Ruth says.

Belle is smiling. She loves watching Stuart, could do this all day. They always look so joyful, she says.

Speaking of joyful, Ruth says. Sydney is definitely concussed. She hates hospitals, I mean *really* hates them, but yesterday she was all jokey and weird and gave me a box of Smarties with a ribbon tied around it.

Belle laughs. Maybe it's the drugs, she says.

Yes maybe, Ruth says. I wish they'd give some to Howard. He's only visited her once since the op, and for ten minutes.

Shit, Belle says. That's pretty bad.

It's complicated, Ruth says.

They have been out walking since seven, walking from dark to light, both of them unable to sleep.

Oh look over there, Belle says, nudging Ruth's elbow.

Sorry?

Her, over there, see?

Ruth turns to look. There is a woman, swaying about. A woman dancing close to the sea.

She does this every day, Belle says.

I wish I was that uninhibited, Ruth says. What's her name?

No idea, Belle says.

She lives here?

Belle nods.

She dances on the beach every day and you don't know her name? Ruth says.

We sort of ignore her, Belle says. Everyone does.

That's awful, Ruth says.

Well it is and it isn't, Belle says. Habits are hard to break, aren't they. Everyone used to think she was strange, dancing in and out of the sea like that, dancing *for* the sea. So they left her to it. And now it's a pattern, you can't break it without force. Maybe she likes the space she is given to dance?

Ruth smiles. She likes Belle. She is open, direct, easy to talk to in a meandering kind of way, a way that makes a conversation feel like a journey, the kind where you take a wrong turn and get lost and end up somewhere you would never have discovered by yourself.

She remembers how she and Sydney used to love driving around on holiday, talking so much in the car they would end up in a random place, and the random places were always the best parts of the trip.

They stroll along the beach, and Belle finds herself wanting to link arms with Ruth, which she doesn't of course, because that would be overfamiliar, intrusive. But for a second she allows herself to lean in, lets the side of her body touch the side of Ruth's. Then she straightens up, strolls on.

Maybe I want a big sister, she thinks. Maybe I want some closeness. Maybe I want to know what it feels like to link arms with someone on the beach who is not my mother.

They are close to the dancer now, can hear her singing.

See, this is what's great about a small town, Ruth says.

What is, Belle says.

In the city, there'd be a big group of people standing around her, filming her on their phones, taking the piss. But not here. There's no privacy in the city.

Oh that happens here, believe me, Belle says. There's no privacy anywhere, just look at this. She unbuttons her coat, pulls it open. Ugh, she says, pointing at the badge pinned to her jumper.

Oh dear, Ruth says.

I know, Belle says. It's new. We only got them yesterday. And now everyone who comes in the shop thinks they're a comedian. *Oh you did a great job of putting my credit card in the machine then, Belle. You did a smashing job of putting my book in that paper bag.*

Surely it's not appropriate, or necessary, for a bookshop? Ruth says.

It gets worse, Belle says. Our book recommendations are going to be rated.

Rated?

Yep.

But everything's subjective, what if people don't like what you recommend?

Oh my God that's exactly what I said. I actually said *everything is subjective.*

Ruth laughs at Belle's excitement. The world's gone mad with all this endless feedback, she says. Next you'll have to say hello to people when they walk in, ask them how they are. I hate that. I hate being asked what else I'm doing today when I'm buying a bloody flapjack. And I'm so polite, I always tell them. Then I feel annoyed with myself.

You should come and tell my boss all that.

Maybe I will.

Will you?

Why not? I can't visit Sydney until this afternoon.

Belle is grinning now. She drinks her coffee, takes a croissant out of its bag and rips it in half. Want some? she says.

Why not, Ruth says.

Within seconds, Stuart and Otto are in front of them, sniffing the floor for flaky pastry, then bottoms flat on the sand, a picture of hope and expectation.

Hello again, boys, Belle says.

They stare at the ocean for a while, eat in silence.

So how do you find it, Ruth says, living here?

I really like it, Belle says.

That's refreshing.

Is it?

Definitely. No one says that about where they live. Especially if it's the place they've always lived in.

It has everything I need really, Belle says. And anyway, if you're really busy I guess it doesn't matter where you live.

Well that depends on whether you enjoy the things you're busy with, Ruth says.

Oh absolutely, Belle says.

Ruth looks at her more closely, this twenty-nine-year-old. Somehow she seems like a much older person, and at the same time, much younger. Belle is curious, maybe ageless, maybe something other than defined by any age. It's hard to put into words, what it feels like to be in her company.

And you're very busy? Ruth says.

Am I busy, Belle says, in a way that means she is really busy, all the time.

And you like that.

I think so. I don't have time not to like it.

Oh you'd know, if you didn't.

So are you then?

What.

Busy, or happy with whatever you're busy with.

Ruth pauses, looks to the sea for clarity about what she has just been asked and how to answer it. I suppose everyone's busy now, she says. As for liking what I do, that's a very big question. And also, I guess we can't like everything we do can we.

Belle is staring at her intensely. It's a myth, I think, to be really honest, that everyone is busy, she says. The papers are always full of articles about how to save time, as if it's the biggest issue affecting everyone. That's rubbish, I think. Loneliness is the real issue. And poverty, obviously. Not lack of spare time. My mum is really lonely so she busies herself, tries to fill the void, you know. There's always a void isn't there, underneath it all. No matter what goes on top of it. That's what I think anyway. And people talk about being busy instead of talking about the void.

They look at each other.

Belle can't tell what's going on in Ruth's mind, she seems deep in thought, and surprised, and maybe cross too.

I'm sorry, that turned into a bit of a rant, Belle says.

Nothing wrong with ranting, Ruth says. Not that I was thinking that.

Belle waits, but there is no explanation. They walk on for a while, further along the beach.

Funny how we're talking about this subject so soon, Ruth thinks. You can spend months, even years, trying to deepen a friendship, to reach a level that makes it feel all right to use words like *loneliness* and *void*.

Jesus it's freezing out here, she says, putting her arm through Belle's. She walks faster now, as if to justify their linked arms, as if she's only trying to hurry her along, move them out of the cold.

They are no longer facing each other. They are closer and further apart. Which makes it easier for Ruth to speak.

Are *you* lonely, Belle? she says. Is that why you keep so busy?

Well, Belle says, as if she has just been asked the lightest of questions, like jam or marmalade, dogs or cats, love or hate Marmite. I came out of the closet yesterday, she says, so I may as well come out again.

Oh, Ruth says. I see.

(She doesn't, not at all.)

I'm asexual, Belle says. I only said it aloud for the first time yesterday. It's all very new. But it's not the same as being lonely or alone.

Seriously? Ruth says.

I've never fancied anyone.

Never?

Nope.

Blimey.

Belle shrugs it off as if it's nothing, so what.

I'm not saying you're a liar, Ruth says, clipping Otto back onto his lead. Or that being asexual isn't perfectly valid. But are you sure?

I think so, Belle says. I don't have the urge to fuck anyone, so I guess the proof's in the pudding.

Ruth laughs. The thing is, she says.

Belle waits with wide eyes. She admires Ruth's wool coat, the dignity of it, the stylish cut.

The thing is, Ruth says.

Hmm.

I don't quite believe it.

How rude, Belle says. She looks cheeky now, younger again.

I'm sorry, Ruth says, but you don't *seem* asexual. You seem like quite a passionate person to me.

What's passion for life got to do with being sexual? Anyway, I'm sure there are millions of celibate people in this world, Belle says.

Celibacy is a choice. You're talking about not having any desire.

Okay, there are millions of people who don't want sex.

Yes, but I bet they did before they didn't. They will have, at some point. What if something's blocking your sex drive, your ability to experience it?

Belle calls Stuart, puts him on the lead. Then she just stands there, shell-shocked by Ruth's response to her self-disclosure, which is so different to how Dexter responded. She feels exposed, as if she has revealed too much, but also too little.

If what you reveal about yourself is not necessarily true –

If what you reveal is just something you are trying on for size –

Well it's uncomfortable, that's what it is. Like undressing

in public. Like trying on new clothes and using another person as a mirror. Like meeting a new version of yourself.

They do say it's easier to talk to a stranger, she says, in an attempt to bring this to a close, to shut down this changing room on the beach.

Want some homework? Ruth says.

Belle's eyes are even wider now. You're such a teacher aren't you, she says.

I think you should fantasise, Ruth says.

I beg your pardon?

Today, at work, during a few quiet moments, just let your mind wander onto anything you like, anything *sexual*, and don't judge it, let it be inappropriate, politically incorrect, whatever. And it can be about *anyone*.

How disgusting, Belle says, with mock disapproval.

Maybe you just haven't found your thing.

My thing?

The thing that floats your boat, Ruth says.

37

Crumpets, a sheepskin coat, a pebble, a poem

Three years ago, Maria started keeping a journal. Carefully, privately, she began to study her existence. During her spare time, when she is not walking or baking or logging silences, she is a conscientious observer of her own pain. Her Book of Many Silences is easier to fill, for silences are everywhere, either manifesting in obvious ways or hiding in the gaps between things – the great unsaid. But the journal describing herself is much harder. Sometimes she has to write twenty pages before even one line feels true.

Which is why she is already on her *eighth* journal.

The notebooks themselves needn't be special, but each one has to meet specific criteria. It must be blue, any shade of blue, and its paper must be plain. No rules to follow, not here, for there has to be a place in a person's life where they can be messy and wild.

And inside this blue notebook, she leaves him.

Inside this blue notebook, she writes the story of how and when.

She breaks her silence in turquoise ink.

Jon, I am leaving, she writes.

Where will you go? Jon says.

We'll make a deal, she says, we'll come to an arrangement. I'll buy a small place, within walking distance of the beach. I'll paint the living room blue, the kitchen yellow. I'll increase my hours, earn more money. But mainly, I'll try to discover who I am when I'm not chasing you.

What do you mean, chasing me? he says.

I'm always busy chasing you for things you'll never give, she says.

She can feel her journal laughing. Oh come on, Maria. You won't do this, you won't say a word of it.

Please don't laugh, she says. I'm using you as a running track, that's all. I'm doing circuits, getting fit, building muscle. Before I run for real. Before I jump.

But why stay? the journal says. Why not leave now, what's stopping you.

Well, thanks to all this writing, I do have an answer to that question, she says. You know how grateful I am for clarity, how much I value it. Blue notebook, you have made me see that I stay *because* of the pain, not despite it. The pain of being married to Jon. I know this pain incredibly well, I've spent hours studying it. Like an artist, I look at its shape, its texture and colour, how it changes with the light, the seasons. Like a scientist, I measure its properties and characteristics, how it expands and contracts, flows freely or solidifies. Like a naturalist, I watch it from a distance in its wild habitat, leaping through the ragged fields of my moods. And the conclusion of my studies is this: I am no longer scared of this pain.

That doesn't explain why you put up with it, the blue notebook says.

Because what scares me is living alone and feeling exactly the same, with no obvious cause. Right now, I know whose hand pushes my head underwater, by not loving me enough or not showing his love, if there is any still inside him. But going under with no one's hand on your head? The thought of that is truly terrifying.

Maria hasn't opened her journal this week, which is unlike her. It sits safely inside her knicker drawer, a place where no one will look. Maria's knickers have been solely her own business for longer than she can remember.

Are you going to the hospital this afternoon? she says, over breakfast.

Maybe this evening, Howard says.

She butters a crumpet, thinks how companionable this is, sitting here with a man who is neutral. He is not invested in this house or this family. He may like her as a person, he may not. Either way it doesn't really matter. She doesn't have to be interesting, chatty, anything. She is an island beside another island. They are blissfully separate. He is distant, remote. And somehow, this feels more like intimacy than any male company she has experienced for years. She is finding it interesting, how someone you are tangled up with can feel like a stranger, how someone you only met this week can make you feel at ease in the world, not only close to them, but closer to everyone else too.

Why don't people talk about this kind of thing in daily life? she thinks. There is only one person who would enjoy discussing this subject, and that's Belle. She would ask probing questions, probably find a TED talk on the subject. And yet Belle thinks she is stupid. How can a woman who moves through the world with such confidence have so little confidence in herself? Maria blames herself for this. Like mother, like daughter, yes?

And while she is on the subject of closeness and distance, she is well aware of how she leans on her daughter too much, leaves an excessive amount of emotion in Belle's personal space, clutters her up. This is something else she has talked through with her journal. It's something else she plans to change, when she is ready.

This thought unearths another. Something she read once, about being ready to act.

She grapples with it, tries to remember.

It was an article about confidence. You don't have to wait until you're confident before doing something scary, the article said. You don't have to be ready, in fact that's the wrong way round. Confidence only comes when you *do* the thing that scares you. It's a by-product of action, not a place from which to act.

It was something like that, she thinks.

Maria and Howard are both deep in thought.

They drink tea, eat buttery crumpets, listen to the radio.

Neither of them is used to doing this with another person.

Howard always eats breakfast alone. Maria is usually so tense over breakfast that her own mind is swamped, or she's chatting to Belle about all the things they plan to do that day.

Would you like to go for a walk around town this morning? she says. I'm not working until this afternoon, I have some errands to run.

Sure, he says. That would be nice.

I'll take you to Belle's bookshop.

Okay, he says. Because what else is he going to do? It's impossible to be here, impossible to leave. Which is the story of his life, of course.

Howard's entire life has been liminal.

In the hallway, beside the gold-framed mirror and one of Jon's paintings of the sea, Maria puts on her sheepskin coat.

Is that heavy to wear? Howard says.

It is actually, but in a good way, she says. And within seconds she has taken it off again, is holding it up behind him, inviting him to step into it. Go on, she says.

So he does.

Now he is standing in the hallway in a coat that fits him perfectly.

Christ, he says.

She looks pleased by his expression. You like it? she says

It's unexpected.

Isn't it.

It's like being held, he says.

She is so moved by this she could almost cry. But she doesn't. She swallows hard. Thinks he hasn't noticed the fragility that passes across her as she speaks in her most rigid voice, the one she presses against the world when it softens her.

Right, shall we start with the beach? she says, holding out her arms, reaching for her coat.

He takes it off, feels naked and small. He thinks she hasn't noticed the fragility that passes across him as he puts on his own inadequate coat, checks its pockets for his wallet and his phone.

She leads him around town.

Unbeknown to her, she is leading a small boy through the streets and onto the beach, where they stroll up and down, then up and down again, as if there is nothing their feet should be doing but walking this stretch of sand.

Unbeknown to him, he is beside a small girl in a giant coat, a girl who wants to be seen, then left to recover from the shock of being seen.

I'll show you my rock, she says. This way, come on.

It's a blustery morning. The air, seawater mist.

Here it is, she says, as they reach the rocky edge. This is my thinking place. Hello my dear, she says, moving the flat of her hand in circles over the rock's body. There is cobalt, rust, amber, silver, charcoal, jade and white, and that's just for starters, the colours go on and on.

A rock on a quiet beach, a thing so faithful and true.

Maria has been coming to this rock for so many years, it feels like it belongs to her. She made a cushion especially, brings it with her each time.

Its cracks are like veins, or maybe roads on a map, the As and the Bs, the beaten tracks and the bumpy lanes, drawn in purple and blue. Other rocks nearby are greener than this one, flecked with lichen. Maria loves these too, but in a different way. They remind her of moss, which she has always admired, its hardiness and rootlessness, the way it carpets the world with tiny threads.

What do you think? she says.

Very nice, he says, but I'll need to sit on it to know for sure.

Do, she says.

He plonks himself down. Pretty good, he says.

Then she says the thing about lichen and moss carpeting the world, and he seems to like that.

She says the thing about cracks on the rock being like roads, and he says yes, I really see that, I have a thing for maps, Sydney calls it my fetish.

It's getting busier on the beach now. There's a man with a metal detector, a group of women jogging, a couple walking a poodle.

Howard and Maria move towards the shoreline. They watch the waves, the water rolling in, close to their feet, then out again.

Maria picks up a pebble and throws it into the sea. Can you do that thing, she says, where the pebble bounces on the water.

Stone skimming, he says. I've never tried.

Shall we? she says.

They collect the flattest stones they can find, try to make them skip across the surface of the sea.

We're officially rubbish at this, Howard says.

We need someone to show us the knack of it, Maria says, while looking down at the one remaining pebble in her hand.

She rubs it with her thumb, likes the feel of its soft chalkiness against her skin.

She wonders how old this pebble is, how long it takes sand and sea to make a surface this smooth.

It's either the whitest of blues or the bluest of whites, she can't decide which.

She puts it in the pocket of her sheepskin coat. Soon, it will be the first object to be placed on her desk. The one she has yet to buy. The one you could almost think of as being made especially for this pebble.

I fancy a second breakfast, she says. I'm so hungry at the moment, nothing seems to touch it. Could you eat anything?

Always happy to try, Howard says, especially if there's a cup of tea involved.

And while Maria eats bacon and eggs, he finds himself, quite accidentally, talking about a woman who died in this town. A woman who was also his wife. He says these things quickly, while eating a biscuit, as if he says them all the time, no problem.

And while he drinks red berry tea, she finds herself taking the baton from his hand and running with it. As she runs, he is still there beside her. It makes her heart beat fast as she speaks. As she talks about a man called Andy.

I know it's not the same, she says, I'm definitely not saying it's the same, but I was engaged to be married, I was just a girl really, I was only nineteen, but I had a future and then I didn't. Don't you think it's weird that our first loves both died? she says.

It probably happens quite a lot, he says, but when people are older. You and I were quite young – you especially. Someone once suggested I join a bereavement group, but I really didn't want to. To be honest, I'd rather read a book of poems about grief.

He watches her reach down under the table, looking for her bag. Just a minute, she says. She puts the bag on her lap, rummages inside it, and plucks two folded sheets of paper from the rubble of her life. Here we are, she says. Poems. I've been carrying these with me for years. Don't tell anyone, but I tore them out of a library book.

You did not.

It's awful I know. It just happened.

Savage, he says.

She likes how that word sounds when he says it, would like him to say it again.

Don't think badly of me, she says, I don't normally go around tearing pages out of library books.

If it helps, I once stole a whole book from a library, he says.

I don't think that's as bad, she says. Because you don't miss what you never knew was there. But imagine taking out a book of poems and finding some pages missing. You'd think those were the most important poems wouldn't you,

you'd be desperate to know why they'd been taken, why someone needed them so much. You'd wonder if you needed them too.

I think we do miss what was never there, he says.

How can we?

I think we sense what's missing, even if we've never known it. It's a senseless kind of longing, I suppose.

Maria wants to give him a book, any old book, and make him read it aloud.

You have a radio voice, she says.

I don't, he says.

You do, honestly. You must have been told that before.

Absolutely not. Anyway, these poems, he says.

Oh yes, she says, glancing down at the pages. I saw myself in these, and I don't see myself very often. So I couldn't risk losing them, obviously. It wasn't until afterwards that I realised I could have just copied them into my notebook. What a terrible person.

Do you see yourself in the mirror? he says.

Sorry?

I just wondered how serious, how literal, this not seeing yourself is. Might you have prosopagnosia?

Might I have what?

Face blindness. Some people can't recognise familiar faces, even their own. I saw a documentary about it.

No, I don't have that. But how interesting, I've never heard of that before. The woman I see in the mirror is someone who resembles me. Does that make any sense?

Yes, he says.

I also see myself inside a gallery sometimes, when I look through the window.

What are you doing in the gallery? he says.

Working, she says. With my sleeves rolled up.

His eyes are half closed but he isn't tired. He is picturing her, the other Maria Norton, at work in a gallery. She senses this and likes it. Now the other Maria exists inside someone else too. And he isn't laughing, he isn't calling it preposterous.

Listen to this line from one of the poems, she says.

Your painting, its sadness, consoled and floored me.
And I realised only then, that for the deepest kind of solace
we must let ourselves be thrown to the ground.

He isn't sure what to say to this. He looks at her for a long time.

She looks at him too, his stubbly face. The sad roughness of him.

Thank you for telling me what happened to your wife, she says, even though they are no longer talking about his wife. I think you must be a very strong person.

He grimaces. Please, he says, I'm really not.

I was so bereft, I think that's why I went with Jon, she says. But you're stronger than me. You're obviously not scared of being alone, from what you said earlier, you know, about not wanting to go on dates.

He thinks about this.

I don't know how to answer that, he says. I mean, my mind is foggy about that subject.

The subject of being alone or not, she says.

The subject of fear, he says.

She looks out of the window, sees the surfers arriving, preparing to enter the water.

Can I say something, she says.

What.

About Sydney.

Hmm.

Well, she was just a child wasn't she.

He nods.

It wasn't her fault, she says.

He tells her how he used to keep a photograph by his bed of Ila holding Sydney when she was a baby. But whenever he looked at it, all he could think was *our girl has torn us apart*.

It was an accident, she says.

I know that, he says.

He has gone deep into his own thoughts now, she can see it. And it clearly isn't comfortable.

I hope you didn't mind me saying that, she says.

He smiles and touches her hand, just for a second. I didn't, he says.

An image flashes through Maria's mind of an angel on a rooftop.

Something has felt different since she spotted her.

Can a person enter one's life from a strange angle, from up high, and alter it?

As they walk towards the bookshop, she tells him about a memoir she plans to buy, one she read about in Saturday's paper. This memoir is by a woman who flourished at the age of sixty, and she herself is fifty-eight, so she thinks it might be good to read this story, inspirational perhaps, and what does he think about this.

I think flourish is a good word, he says.

Isn't it, she says.

To come into one's own, be hearty and healthy and alive.

Exactly, she says. This woman became an activist, but I'd settle for enjoying my days a bit more, feeling like I'm expressing myself.

Things, and people, only flourish in the right environment, he says.

She pictures all the vegetables in Belle's allotment. Then herself, planted in soil. Unusually, this is not a morbid thought. To flourish, to thrive, to blossom, she thinks.

Are you hoping to be one of life's late bloomers, Ms Norton? he says.

Are you, Mr Smith? she says.

They are searching for the memoir.

I'm really sorry, Maria says to Belle. I can't remember who wrote it or what it was called, but I'm sure it had a white cover with red lettering.

Belle is used to this. Last week, a customer asked for a novel with a spindly tree on the front cover. I just know there's a spindly tree, the woman said, with a level of desperation that she had never encountered in any of her customers before, only her authors.

So it's newly published, Belle says.

Definitely, Maria says.

Well that narrows it down a tiny bit.

Oh good, Maria says. What's with the badge?

Belle groans. It's Yvonne's latest big idea. Customers give feedback about our *performance* on the website, then they're entered into a prize draw.

How undignified, Maria says.

Belle kisses her mother on the cheek. Let's find your book, she says.

And while they are looking, the bell rings, the door opens.

It's Yvonne, who has marched up to Belle and is saying something about an upcoming event, how they'll need a venue bigger than the shop. She has just popped in to print off her emails about this.

Howard is busy taking books off the shelf and examining their covers. He is looking for the story of a late bloomer, so he can hand it to a woman he hardly knows. Which is an odd thing to be doing when he should be miles away, working in M&S. It's surprising, even at his age, when he should already know these things, how easy it is to step into someone else's world and forget your own. So this is why people move away, start again, he thinks. He had forgotten this. How there are so many types of distance, all of them connected but quite different. There's the emotional kind: dissociation, distraction, displacement – all those handy D words. There is the passing of time, which is an overrated type of distance if you ask him. And then there is this one, the physical kind, measured in metres and miles.

He is kidding himself, of course. This isn't just any old place, there is no real distance between now and then, here and there. He is standing in the town where his life ended and kept on going, which is a form of madness surely. Up until then, he had believed that madness was for other people, that it visited people who were quite unlike him, those with a predisposition. But madness isn't fussy, rare, extraordinary. Through loss, it comes to us all.

And this week, ever since they arrived, Howard has been so overwhelmed he can't feel a thing.

Dissociation, Mr Smith. It's one of your talents.

Maria relaxes him, even when she is giddy. She is another body beside him, someone to talk to.

He wonders if he will visit Sydney this afternoon or this evening. Or, skip the visit altogether. *Impossible to be here, impossible to leave.* There are things to be said, but he doesn't know if he will ever find the words.

Maria is holding up an illustrated edition of *The Wind in the Willows*, which has been put in the wrong section. Oh I loved this as a child, she says.

My son loved it too, Howard says.

Maria tries to remember the last time she went shopping with a man, and can't. Must have been when they bought their new mattress from John Lewis, which reminded her of Andy and made her cry in the toilets.

Well hello, Maria, a voice says. You don't usually grace us with your presence.

Yvonne, Maria says.

Yvonne looks at Howard, then back at Maria. Are you going to introduce us? the look says.

This is Howard Smith, he and his daughter-in-law are staying with us for a few days, Maria says.

Howard shakes Yvonne's bony fingers.

I see you're in your Del Boy again, Yvonne says to Maria.

Sorry?

Your *Only Fools and Horses* coat.

Oh, Maria says.

Where did you actually get it from? Is it the one used in the TV series? Are you part of some Trotters fan club?

Funny, Maria says.

She remembers finding her coat in a charity shop. It was hanging beneath a sign that said FABULOUS GENTLEMAN'S COAT. She liked not only the coat itself, which was a classic from Nursey in Suffolk, but also how the sign made it sound like it once belonged to a fabulous gentleman. Perhaps some of his fabulousness will rub off on me, she said to Jon, fifteen years ago, back when they used to go into town together on a Saturday, have lunch in one of the cafes looking out to sea.

I bought it locally, Maria says.

Oh yes, where? Yvonne says.

I don't remember.

Must have been a long time ago then.

I tried it on this morning, it feels *amazing*, Howard says.

Yvonne glances down at herself, sensing that something on her person is rucked up, not sitting at the right angle, maybe her skirt or her tights but hopefully not her knickers, hopefully not them, so much harder to adjust in public. She brushes her hands down her woollen skirt, tugs it a little, makes it sit lower on her waist. This adjustment makes her feel better. Better than Maria, that's for sure, in her oversized sheepskin.

Well I'll take your word for that, she says. Can I help you find anything?

Belle has taken care of us, Maria says.

She's a good girl, Yvonne says.

She is, Maria says.

Outside again, after Maria has purchased the late bloomer's memoir, and Howard has bought seven Ordnance Survey maps, they walk quietly for a while, pausing to look in shop windows.

That woman, Maria says.

Which woman?

In the shop. Belle's boss, Yvonne Partridge.

Oh yes, he says.

She's fucking my husband, she says.

He stops walking.

Delightful isn't it, she says, while not quite believing she has said this aloud. But what the hell, she thinks. This is free therapy with a stranger who will soon be long gone, that's what it is. May as well make use of him.

And you're okay with that? he says.

I don't know what I am, she says.

On the pages of her blue notebooks, she thought she knew. She wrote that it was horrible, vulgar. But walking with Howard, saying these words aloud to another person.

I don't know how I feel about it, she says.

And he is shaking his head.

And she is thinking can I, should I? Say a bit more. Tell him how every now and then, there is a different kind of physical betrayal. One that leaves bruises in places that won't be seen. Years can pass before Jon does this again, but still. Her body doesn't forget.

No, she thinks. This is not the place, and Howard Smith is not the person to tell.

Does he know that you know? he says.

Definitely not, she says.

Jesus. I thought this kind of thing only happened on TV.

What, affairs?

No, people being able to keep silent about their partner's affairs. How do you do it? How can you be so calm, so reasonable?

Who said I was calm and reasonable. Anyway, it's complicated, she says. I don't want to sleep with him myself, you see. So –

She doesn't know how to finish this sentence. She sighs. Maybe it works for now, she says. And anyway, it's like that song isn't it.

What song.

'I Can't Make You Love Me'.

The one George Michael sang. That's a really sad song, he says.

I know. I *loved* George Michael.

But Maria.

Yes.

286

How can I put this.

Just say it.

Admittedly, I've only known you for a few days.

Hmm.

But to me, if it's all right to say this, it doesn't seem like you *want* him to love you.

What?

I'm sorry, but.

What.

You don't seem to love him much either.

She stiffens. His words are not the problem, but they are too fast and too soon. She is still adjusting to her own admission, spoken out loud instead of written in the privacy of a notebook.

And you can tell if a person loves another person can you? she says. In a couple of days?

I've crossed a line, I apologise, he says.

He may be a rubbish husband, but he's *my* rubbish husband, my world.

Do you want to live in a rubbish world? Howard says.

Don't we *all* live in a rubbish world? Maria says.

And he can't argue with that.

Not at all.

38

You can either hold it or you can't

Flushed, sweaty, hot under the.

Who turned up the heating?

What will this heat do to all the books?

Especially the books about ice and snow and cruelty and hate.

Imagine those books in a sauna.

Imagine a bookseller in a sauna that's not really a sauna at all, it's just a bookshop.

The bookseller is wearing a thermal vest, a shirt, a cardigan, jeans.

She is doing her homework, set by the teacher.

What kind of teacher tells another woman to fantasise?

A teacher you'd like to know.

Belle's newest realisation, apart from the realisation of her rising heat, is this:

Being told that you don't seem like an asexual person is incredibly powerful.

And here's the thing:

She had expected people to just accept her asexuality, as Dexter did. To say oh well, whatever makes you happy, to fuck or not to fuck. She had expected them to say well, fair enough, you're too busy with the dogs and the pig and the otters and the allotment and your friends from the pub and the authors and the podcasts and the novels and the TED talks and your mother.

And then comes a challenge from a stranger.

You seem like quite a passionate person, she said.

Which, in this context, meant something quite specific.

It meant: *You seem like a person who should be fucking another person.*

Holy macaroni!

What a thing to mean, what a thing to say.

Maybe you haven't found your thing, she said. The thing that floats your boat.

And what's confusing to Belle right now is the creaking and shifting of her boat. She hadn't even realised that she possessed one. It's shocking, and also ridiculous. How those words, spoken by that woman –

But let's not get overexcited.

The boat, it isn't actually floating.

In other words, there is *still* no one in this world she'd like to fuck.

No one she has been able to think of.

Talk about a confession.

But this is not the whole story.

Because the boat, well, it's also no longer *entirely* on the sand.

It has moved, just a little.

It happened on the beach this morning, when Ruth Hansen called her passionate.

Its nose entered the water.

Do boats have noses?

Something happened. With *her*.

So does this mean, she thinks. Does this mean she wants to sleep with *her*?

No, she doesn't.

But she is open to the possibility of a sex object.

To the idea of one appearing, or existing for that matter.

She is restocking shelves, while trying to let her mind wander onto sexual matters.

It's an experiment, she thinks. So calm down, cool off, remove a layer.

That's better.

A bell rings.

She thinks of that song, 'Ring My Bell'.

But it's only a bell above a door.

It's *her*. Troublemaker, boat shifter, dirty little –

Hello again, Ruth says.

Hi, Belle says. My boss isn't here. Well she was, but she left already.

That's a shame. I've just come from the library, it's pretty impressive for a small town. How's your morning been?

Oh you know, Belle says.

Ruth nods. I thought I'd buy Sydney something to read, she says.

Well you're in the right place.

What's the one in the window like, the long poem?

The Early Onset of Love, Belle says.

That's the one.

It's basically political until near the end, when the poet falls in love, then it becomes more like a memoir, structured like a poem. He thinks love is as messed up as the whole of society, just one of many ills.

Sounds awful, Ruth says. Think I'll give that one a miss. Something darkly funny, that's what we like.

We? Belle says. You like the same books?

Well no, Ruth says. Of course not. We like very different books, but we both happen to like dark humour.

I see, Belle says. Do you read the same book at the same time?

There is a long silence.

Silence is like alcohol, you can either hold it or you can't. Belle can't.

I'm sorry, that was a bit of a weird thing to say.

It's fine, don't worry.

I'm a bit woolly-headed, to be honest. Coming down with something maybe. It's probably just a headache. I get them a lot, too much caffeine.

The bell rings again.

It's a man in a long coat, a green dress and black Doc Marten shoes. A man with a beard and a presence that Ruth immediately finds intoxicating, delightful. She watches him walk through the shop towards them.

Belle says hi, I didn't think you were in today.

Dexter takes off his coat. There is a badge pinned to his

dress. Well I am, he says. And I've decided to be defiantly myself in the face of Yvonne's oppression. It's the only way to respond, I think.

And this is you, being yourself? Belle says.

Sometimes, he says. I was sort of inspired by you actually.

Me?

Your openness yesterday.

Oh, she says, trying to ignore Ruth's raised eyebrows, her blatant eavesdropping.

She introduces them. Thinks it's funny how they kiss each other on the cheek instead of shaking hands. Wonders if Ruth is being a bit flirty with Dexter. She's imagining it, surely. Either way, she doesn't like it much.

And now they are both looking at her. Why the expectant looks? she thinks.

Then she gets it. Dexter is waiting for her to comment on his appearance. To say something, anything, about him being defiantly himself.

She doesn't know what to say, needs to think fast so she doesn't offend him. No pressure, she thinks, at high speed, in a nanosecond, in a wordless impression of feeling and thought, a streak of panic, hot hands and face, say something quickly, choose an adjective, for God's sake find a word.

I think you look beautiful, she says.

Beautiful? she thinks.

Yes, she thinks.

Look at him, smiling.

Look at him, in that dress.

She swears she can hear smoke coming from chimneys. Cats prowling across rooftops. A couple's make-up sex from an open window. Sewing machines running across T-shirts. Fish changing course in the sea. The wind changing direction. A giant iron weathervane turning on a rooftop. A woman in a hospital bed, turning over. Her mother's hand curling into a fist. This is hallucination, this is the sound of Dexter in a dress. She hears all the authors she has ever met, asking for gin and tonic. She hears Stuart, her precious wolf-hound, saying I can smell sex on you. Her grandmother before she died, saying Belle your home-grown carrots are the best I have tasted in my entire life. She hears waxy pink flowers opening. She hears people clocking on, clocking off. She hears a watch being fixed, ticking back to life. An intruder setting off a burglar alarm. Owls nesting in hollow trees. The snuffle of a hedgehog in a policewoman's garden. Brush against canvas. Cherry blossom, drifting. The otters, all the otters, gliding through all the rivers. People snoring in the library, the one they kept open by marching with placards, saying WHEN YOU SAVE A LIBRARY, YOU SAVE SOULS.

Why thank you, Dexter says.

39

Power

Jon is working in his studio, trying to finish a commission that was supposed to have been delivered last week. He has demeaned himself, taken on work solely for the money and now wishes he hadn't.

He is painting a portrait of a woman's cat.

Oh dear God is this what I've come to, he thinks, as he looks into the sinister eyes of his unfinished feline, its giant whiskery face taunting him from its canvas, telling him he's an odd-job man now, not a *serious artist*. If word gets around that he paints people's pets. What on earth was he thinking?

He blames Yvonne and her expensive tastes. She wants a night away in a five-star hotel. Tell your wife you're at a painting workshop, she said. I don't need to attend *workshops*, he said. You can say whatever you bloodywell like, she said, as long as you buy us champagne and dinner. He stood naked by her bed. Do you really want all that? Love should be enough, Yvonne. Don't you have everything you need right here? he said, slapping his little belly.

Now he is staring out of the window, thinking of Yvonne

and how sometimes he hates her. And yet he knows he's also obsessed. *Properly* obsessed. There's no denying this now. How can this have happened? he thinks. She is obnoxious. She makes him feel like a disappointment. Still, he can't stop wanting her. Even when he has planned to end things he finds himself backtracking, begging. It's undignified behaviour for a man like him. A man who is usually in charge of himself and his lovers. He is shrinking, he is the shrinking man, all thanks to Yvonne.

Shrinking artist more like, he thinks, at he turns back to the cat, the one that has slowed down his days, made him too aware of the clock.

He sits at his desk, picks up his iPad, checks his emails. Then he flicks to his artist page on Twitter, posts a quote by another painter. Jon collects things that other people have said about art and posts one every day.

He googles *garden studios*, flicks from site to site, researching how much it would cost to have a shed built in the garden. He has been considering this for some time, a way to get out of the house, have more privacy. Maria hates the idea, calls it decadent and unnecessary. You already have a room with a sea view to work in, what more do you want? she says.

Now he checks the news: cultural, global, national, local, always in that order. He swigs brandy from the bottle he keeps in his desk, moves from story to story.

Oh, he says aloud. Will you look at this.

It's a photo of that woman, Sydney Smith. Lying in the

dark outside the second-hand toyshop. Sprawled and twisted on the ground.

He zooms in, then out again. Wonders who took this picture. It definitely wasn't Maria. And she would never have let someone else take it, not while she was there.

Which means someone took it *before* she arrived.

Which means, she wasn't the first one there.

So her theory about a *special connection*, all that talk of *serendipity*.

It was absolute bullshit.

You're full of shit, Maria.

In his hands, power.

He can feel his body relaxing, his shoulders dropping.

He sighs, loudly. Or maybe it's not a sigh. More a moan of pleasure.

Now he stands up, walks over to the unfinished canvas.

Oh pussycat, he says, poking his tongue into his cheek in the way he always does when he senses a way to win a fight.

He stands with his legs wide apart, his back arched, his stomach pushed out, staring at the cat.

He picks up a paintbrush, adds a tiny speck of paint to the cat's nose.

40

Accidental reverie

Belle is in the Black Hole, drinking cider with Dexter. They have never been to the pub together before. They are having a special meeting to discuss the issue of having been pitted against each other in a feedback competition.

I think we might need to talk this through, discuss how we're going to deal with it, Belle said this afternoon. We could always go to the pub?

Why not, he said.

And now they are beside an open fire, on blue velvet seats.

So one response I thought of, Dexter says, is we refuse to play the game. We could recommend really bad books, try to get terrible feedback.

Oh that's good, Belle says.

We can turn it on its head, see who's the most rubbish bookseller.

I like it, she says, while wondering if he knows that this dress brings out the colour of his eyes.

There is an urge to place her hand on his leg. Specifically, his thigh.

It makes her sit still, as still as humanly possible.

Keep your hands to yourself, she thinks.

+

Maria and Howard are on the yellow sofa in the kitchen, drinking their second bottle of wine and talking about death. Since this morning's revelations on the beach, death is all they have been able to think about.

While she was at work this afternoon, removing the plaque from people's teeth, Maria was remembering how she used to sit in the corner of Andy's bedroom after he died, head on her knees, hands on her head, as if she were waiting for a second bomb to drop.

Earlier this evening, while he was sitting beside Sydney's bed, failing to apologise for his coldness over the past few days, Howard was busy thinking up questions to ask Maria.

How long were you with Andy? he says.

How long before you were then with Jon? he says.

So what was she like, your Ila? Maria says. I like that you met while trying to guess the weight of a ferret.

Ila was political too, he says, but quietly, you know? Not in the way your Andy was.

Your Ila.

Your Andy.

Do you know what's strange? Howard says. I really did assume that I'd meet someone else a few years after she died. That's what usually happens, isn't it? I thought Sydney and Jason would have another mum. But it hasn't worked out like that. I genuinely haven't wanted anyone in the way I wanted her. I'm seventy this summer, I'll have been mainly by myself for thirty-seven years. Can you imagine living with someone after all that time? What's the point? But the strange thing, Maria, is how vivid she still seems. The older I get, the less I seem to remember day-to-day stuff and the more I remember her. It's as if she's getting closer. And do you think, well –

Do I think what? she says.

Do you think it's because I'm getting closer to death, and therefore her? Does that sound crazy?

No, and yes, she says.

Is it memory then? Is this what happens to memory as the brain ages?

I think it's because you've given up.

On what?

She smiles, just for a second, then looks down at the floor.

Did I say something wrong? he says.

Not at all, she says, turning to face him. But that thing you just said: *what's the point.*

Hmm.

That's what brings her closer.

He thinks about this, doesn't get it.

We're pretty hopeless, both of us, she says.

Speak for yourself, he says.

Without hope, all we have is nostalgia, she says.

Very profound, he says.

I read it in a novel from the fifties. I love those melancholy novels.

So do you agree with that, he says, do you think nostalgia is a kind of hopelessness.

Maybe, she says.

Maria has never thought of herself as a person who has opinions about things like hope and nostalgia. She isn't sure where these words are coming from, or who is saying them.

Howard refills their glasses. I guess I'm a nostalgic old fool then, he says.

She tells him that she thinks she's quite drunk.

She tells him about the dreams she's been having lately, how they seem more real than her waking moments, and this is making everything seem more unreal than usual, especially herself. In one of these dreams, she says, I was telling Andy how I'm grieving for *life unlived*.

Must be something in the air, or maybe the water, he says. My dreams keep waking me up. I'm so tired from all this dreaming.

You do look a bit knackered, she says.

Thanks very much, he says.

+

Anyway, Belle says, can I ask you something?

Okay, Dexter says.

Do you mind everyone looking at you?

Who's looking? he says.

Only *everyone*, she says.

It's true. The whispers, the nudges, the why's he wearing a bleedin' dress?

I'm trying not to think about it, he says.

Sorry, she says. So you don't usually go out in a dress then.

I have done, but only for a walk along the coastal path. I've never worn one to the pub.

So why now? she says.

Because you invited me, he says.

+

Maria is by the sink, filling the kettle, about to make herbal tea.

Howard is still on the sofa.

They are listening to the radio. The presenter is saying something about parasites, how one species will live and feed on another. Someone is saying that a human being often plays host to hundreds of different species of parasite at any given time. To which Maria says *gross*.

I feel really itchy now, Howard says.

Me too, Maria says, washing her hands.

Now someone is describing the evolutionary role of parasites, how they move and travel and adapt.

It's as if these people are here, in the kitchen, speaking only to them.

Oh, Maria says, leaning against the counter. That's interesting isn't it.

Howard hasn't listened to a radio programme in such a relaxed way with another person since Sydney and Jason left home. Music yes, plenty of music, mainly with Ruth, but that's not the same thing, that's him choosing a record, sharing it with her, putting it on to entertain her. This is accidental reverie. It's lounging around in a kitchen, tuning in and tuning out, listening to whatever comes on. He had no idea that another person would enjoy doing this. That it would be enough for them.

He leans back into the saggy cushion and listens.

What kind of tea? Maria says. How about lemon and ginger? Or echinacea and raspberry?

Actually, he says, why don't we pop to the pub for last orders? Is there a good pub nearby?

Really? she says.

I spend my whole life sitting at home drinking herbal tea, he says.

Saddo, she says, and winks.

Maria hasn't winked for years. Affectionate teasing doesn't come easily to her, no matter how drunk she is. She looks like she is trying to show a child how to wink.

Howard laughs.

You really want to go to the pub? she says.

If you'd like to, he says. But can I make a strange request?

I don't know, can you? she says.

Can I wear your sheepskin coat?

She finds this hilarious and overly exciting.

She doesn't get out much, have friends round.

They are fifty-eight and sixty-nine.

They are fifteen.

They are wearing each other's coats.

She has forgotten to tell Jon they are going out.

They are walking through the dark streets.

They are stepping into the Black Hole.

Oh look, Maria says. It's my lovely daughter.

They walk over to where Belle and Dexter are sitting.

Dexter stands up, kisses Maria on the cheek. He offers to buy them a drink, says would you like to join us?

Oh no, Belle thinks. Can't they sit somewhere else?

Goodness, Maria says, taking in Dexter's appearance. Look at you.

Belle holds her breath.

What a *smashing* dress, Maria says. Are you transgender, dear?

No, he says. If I were, I'd probably have got rid of the beard.

That's a bit presumptuous, she says. Why shouldn't you identify as a woman *and* have a beard? Because actually, what *is* a woman? I would love a beard. To be able to let your facial hair grow when you feel like changing how you look. Amazing.

Dexter doesn't know what to say.

Mum, are you drunk? Belle says, mainly to redirect the flow of words away from Dexter. She doesn't recognise her mother, or the coat she is wearing. Whose coat is that? she says.

It's mine, Howard says.

Why have you swapped coats?

Why shouldn't I wear a man's coat? Maria says.

Genderqueer, Howard says.

Yes exactly, Dexter says, triumphantly. Because he is

triumphantly genderqueer, that's what he is, but usually only at home, never in the Black Hole.

Do you know, Maria says, I've always thought it was silly how only women wear dresses and skirts, especially when men have all that tackle, don't they? Your tackle must get so hot and sweaty in trousers. Much better to wear something more breathable, like a skirt.

Mother, Belle says, wishing they would all sit down, stop drawing attention to themselves; wishing her mother hadn't used the word *tackle*.

I try to avoid synthetic fibres, Howard says.

Who is this wonderful man? Dexter thinks.

I don't think we've met, he says, holding out his hand. I'm Dexter.

Howard Smith, nice to meet you. I tried to grow a beard like yours once, but it was so wispy and thin. How do you achieve such fullness?

I condition it with coconut oil.

Do you really, Howard says. He wants to reach out and touch this beard, give it a good squeeze, feel it contract and expand in his hand, go flat then fluffy.

Dexter nods. Can I get you both a drink? he says, for the second time.

Then he is at the bar, ordering two glasses of wine, two ciders. Everyone inside the Black Hole has watched him walk across the room, apart from Maria and Howard, who are too busy telling Belle what an interesting colleague she has.

You on your way to a fancy dress party? the barmaid says, as she pours the wine.

Dexter braces himself, tries to hold on to the buzz of just now, the unexpected warmth, the way Howard said *gender-queer*, so matter-of-fact.

No, I just sometimes wear dresses, he says.

You have a nice figure, the barmaid says, as she jigs about to the music, does a little dance with her chin, as if this is the only part of her body that is allowed to dance.

She's being sarcastic, he thinks.

Thank you, he says.

I'd have to go back to Slimming World for a year to get in that, she says. Where'd you buy it?

Hobbs, he says. But the outlet store, not the one in town.

She nods quietly to herself while pulling a pint of cider. I never think to go there, she says. It's so hard to know where to buy clothes these days. I hate clothes shopping don't you?

Depends if I'm buying jeans or dresses. Different challenges, obviously, he says.

I'm sure, she says. Well if you ever need a second opinion, Dexter, I'm happy to come with you.

Are you being serious? he says.

'Course, she says. But can I give you a piece of advice?

Go on.

I'd take that badge off. It's a bit freaky to be honest.

That's what she calls freaky, he thinks. Not the combination of my long beard and my dress. But the little badge, the one that says PLEASE LET ME KNOW HOW I DID TODAY.

Would you like some pork scratchings? she says. Monster Munch, custard creams?

Go on then, he says.

All three? she says.

Why not, he says.

+

Things have become unusually boisterous in Maria's kitchen.

Belle and Dexter are making toast for five. Maria and Howard are drunkenly playing ball with Stuart and Otto. And Ruth is by herself on the sofa, back from taking the dogs for a long walk, thinking blimey, what's got into everyone tonight. She says yes to a whisky, because this is not the place to be sober right now. She texts Sydney: *Are you asleep yet, love? Thinking of you xxx*

There is no sign of Jon, who must be able to hear them. To their house guests, it's as if he doesn't live here. But not to Maria, who can feel his presence, all the time.

Sydney texts back: *Hi sweets, noisy in here tonight, woman opposite is loopy on meds, doing a lot of groaning. Love you xXx*

They gather around the table for toast, tea, whisky.

Stuart keeps raising his nose in the air like a wolf in the woods, about to howl the place down.

Maria takes a block of Cheddar out of the fridge, cuts it into cubes, searches through drawers for the unopened tube of cocktail sticks that she remembers buying years ago.

In this moment, cocktail sticks seem immensely important.

Belle goes upstairs, and comes back down with her signed photograph of David Essex and a book about otters. See, she says to Dexter. I really do possess these things, I wasn't making it up.

You certainly are one of a kind, he says.

Also, she says, I hated that stupid book you liked, *The Early Onset of Love*, I thought it was totally pretentious.

Oh really, he says.

Yes. And I'd rather eat my own vegetables than pay silly money in a restaurant.

Well, he says, seeing as we're playing *this* game, I would rather spend all evening trying to read the most obscure novel than see some inane movie at the cinema.

Oh would you. Well *I* would rather walk next-door's pig than watch TV.

I would rather be alone than get my heart ripped out and trampled on.

Oh, Belle says. Goodness, she says.

What are they doing? Howard whispers.

I have no idea, Maria whispers back. Some kind of modern mating ritual, maybe.

Howard shrugs. The youth of today, he says.

Yes, Jon can hear them. He is furious. This infernal noise, these strangers in his house. It's impossible to work tonight, and he needs to work, to finish this bloody cat.

He puts down his paintbrush, walks over to his desk and sits by the window, where he swipes around his iPad.

It's still there, of course it is, because nothing ever disappears online. The photo of Sydney Smith. On the local news site there's a follow-up story, probing deeper into the fact that someone took the photo and didn't stick around, and what this means, what it says, whether it's a symptom of a sick society. Everyone's a reporter now, everyone's a journalist, but what about personal responsibility?

The photo has provided three news angles: what the tourist looked like after falling, how the tourist was abandoned, and how this moment is symbolic, voyeuristic, please discuss, post a comment.

Since Jon saw the photo, it has stayed with him like a joke he wants to tell, a punchline he wants to deliver. And he has been delaying the gratification, waiting for Maria's guests to go to bed so he can be alone with her when he tells her. But so what if they're all here, he thinks now. Isn't it *better* this way?

He gets up, walks downstairs.

As he enters his own kitchen, it's like being late for a party that he wasn't invited to.

Well fuck you all, he thinks, as he marches in, stands the iPad on the table in front of them.

+

The door opens, making the dogs jump to their feet.

What's going on in here? Jon says.

We're a little tipsy, Maria says. Did you finish your pussy?

He scowls at the sound of laughter, steps past the dogs,

pushes a plate of half-eaten toast aside to make room for his iPad.

What are you doing? Maria says.

I have something you might want to see, he says.

And they all peer at the screen, apart from Ruth, who can't see from the sofa.

Maria looks at Howard, then back at the iPad.

Of all the silences she has experienced, this one says the most. But she doesn't notice or observe it.

What is this, Howard says.

I'm afraid it's your daughter, Jon says.

And why do you have this photo, Maria says.

I don't, Jon says. It's online. It's on the news.

What? Howard says, feeling Ruth's hand on his shoulder as she peers at the screen.

Someone took this picture, then left her there, Jon says.

Now Belle and Dexter are looking too, and Ruth has turned pale, and Stuart is sniffing the air again, inhaling the shift in atmosphere, the violent change of weather.

I'm sorry, Maria, Jon says. But you weren't the one to find her. Someone else was there first. So all that stuff about what it meant, about a special connection, was nonsense I'm afraid. I thought you deserved to know.

Maria's eyes are closed. She can see blocks of colour: saffron, black, tangerine. Tears sting her eyes. Jon has stung her, yet again. But *this* is something else.

She stands up, shoves the wooden chair away from her, stares at her husband.

There's no need to cry, he says.

Oh according to you, there's never any need, she says.

Ruth has taken the iPad over to the sofa. She is hunched over it, touching the screen, touching Sydney. My poor darling, she says, too shocked to cry, too sickened.

Now Howard is on his feet too. Why do you look so pleased? he says.

I'm not *pleased*, Jon says.

That's my daughter.

I know that, Jon says. I was just –

You were just *what*.

I was simply pointing out –

Jon pauses. Waits. Considers his words.

Howard takes a step towards him. How would you feel if I showed you a photo of *your* daughter injured on the ground, left for dead? he says.

Belle doesn't jump about on buildings, Jon says.

I beg your pardon?

I'm just saying, if you mess about on rooftops, it sort of serves you right doesn't it. Honestly, what did she expect at her age, I doubt she has the same strength that she used to, that's all I'm saying, it's probably what everyone's saying. What is she trying to prove?

How dare you, Howard says. My daughter has always done this, ever since she was a girl. She trains for hours every day. She doesn't *mess about on rooftops*, she knows what she's doing. This is who she is.

Look, Jon says. I think we've –

And do you think it's kind to put this photo in front of us? In front of me and Ruth? It's heartbreaking, Howard says.

No longer waiting for scraps of toast under the table, Otto runs over to Ruth. She picks him up, wraps her arms around him. There is something between her and the world now, a warm body, eyes looking into her eyes.

Dexter is eating toast for comfort. He hates conflict. Who took the photo? he says.

No one knows, Jon says. That's the thing. It was sent anonymously to the paper.

Whoever it was should be arrested, Dexter says.

I agree, Belle says.

You can't arrest a person for doing nothing, Jon says.

Actually you can, Dexter says. Did you hear about that woman who fell into the sea, and the man she was with, he was drunk or something, he just stood there, watched her drown. He was convicted of manslaughter by gross negligence.

Sydney isn't *dead*, Jon says.

Ruth shivers. She zooms further in to the photo.

Same kind of situation though isn't it, Belle says. This person didn't call for help, it's so neglectful.

Howard pours whisky into a glass, takes it over to Ruth. He lifts Otto from her arms and sits beside her.

The families are divided now.

Jon has divided them.

Belle is staring at her mother. That look on her face, what is it? she thinks.

How happy you looked just then, Maria says.

What? Jon says.

You looked so happy when you walked into the room.

I didn't look *happy*.

The thought of taking something away from me, it gave you such pleasure didn't it.

Maria, these people are all here because you believe you found her.

No, Jon, they're here because I invited them to stay, because I want them to be here, I want to spend time with people who are not you, to look after people *who are not you*.

Excuse me?

She shakes her head. I will no longer excuse you, she says. You and that revolting Yvonne deserve each other.

Yvonne? Belle says.

Maria turns to face her daughter. I'm really sorry, darling, but your father is fucking her. Has been for ages.

Oh. My. God, Belle says.

That's *disgusting*, Dexter says.

Is this true, Dad? Belle says. It's not true, is it?

Of course it's not, Jon shouts.

You're lying, Belle says.

Do you know what, I'm past caring, Maria says. Your face tonight, that look on your face. I really am past caring. I'm leaving you, Jon. *I'm leaving you.*

That line from her notebook. The one she had written over and over again, like a girl serving out a school punishment.

Don't be ridiculous, Maria. Yvonne is nothing. She's just –

Just what?

I feel sick, Belle says. I actually think I'm going to be sick. Can I please sleep on your sofa tonight? she says to Dexter.

He stands up, brushes the crumbs off his dress, holds out his hand. Come on, he says.

Why are you wearing a *dress*? Jon says.

Leave him alone, Belle says.

Dexter has balls, Maria says. Under that dress, he has bigger balls than you'll ever have.

The room falls silent again.

Dexter bites his lip, tries to remain serious, feels flattered and exposed.

I'm leaving you, Maria says. I want you to buy me out of this house. And until then, I want you to go to Yvonne's. Starting right now.

Buy you out of the house? Jon says. His laugh is full of spit.

Over the past year, Maria has taken supplements to clear her foggy mind. She has had blood tests to check for thyroid inactivity and deficiencies, all of which were normal, perfectly healthy. So why this fogginess? she kept saying. Why this lethargy? And maybe it's just adrenaline, maybe it's just the wine. Either way, her mind is clear.

Absolutely not, Jon says.

Yes, she says.

I don't want to go to Yvonne's.

Tough shit.

This is my house, I work here, he says.

You don't work here. You piss about, you feel sorry for yourself, get drunk and produce paintings that look like painting by numbers.

He gasps.

Sorry, she says, but it's the truth.

And this is what makes him turn and leave the room.

This is what makes him pull clothes from a drawer and push them into a holdall and go to Yvonne's.

Not the fact that his wife wants to end their marriage.

Not the fact that she told him to get out.

Not the hideous gang in his kitchen.

But the comment about his art.

Painting by numbers.

Maria knows how to hit him where it hurts.

And now he is reeling.

He is staggering through the streets.

He hurts so much he can barely walk.

And whose legs are these, whose arms?

They are the limbs of an amateur, a dilettante, a dabbler.

Jon has lived by one rule: if you do something long enough, eventually you become good at it. 10,000 hours, isn't that what they say, isn't that how long it takes to be good? There's no such thing as innate talent, only practice practice practice.

This is what he believes.

It's the lie he has lived by.

And Maria, all this time, has known what's true and what isn't.

He never expected that from his wife.

41

*And he is rubbing her feet, and they are
listening to the radio*

In bed that night, he listens to the sound of her going up and
down the stairs every couple of hours. She is unsettled,
understandably so. Who would sleep soundly after an evening like that? Or a whole life like that, in fact. The death of
Andy and then, as she told Howard yesterday morning on
the beach, that moment of looking at her new husband and
feeling terrified of what she felt and didn't feel. But you live
with what you have chosen, Maria said, and better this devil
than a wonderful man, stepping into my world once again
and leaving my world once again. You don't survive that
twice, she said.

Based on what evidence, he thinks now, as he adjusts the
pillow, tries to get comfortable.

He is also unable to sleep.

Jon is no longer in the house, and his absence has gener-
ated what feels like electricity.

You can hear it, the hum, the charge.

And those footsteps going up and down.

There is no stillness to the middle of this night.

But is it really that, he thinks. Or is it in fact *this*:

Maria Norton has revealed herself to be a woman who interests him very much.

The small act of listening to the radio with her.

How much he liked it.

The other women, the ones who were not Ila, the few he had slept with before it all came to nothing and he came to expect nothing. If being with those women brought moments of joy, it was only the joy of being distracted from his own heaviness, or of hoping this empty kind of pleasure would deepen into something else. But walking with Maria, listening as she told him about her beloved rock on the beach, as she read lines from a torn-out poem, watching her get drunk and loud, sitting with her in the kitchen discussing parasites, yes parasites of all things.

He dreams of her while he is awake. In his dream they are on a sofa, wide and soft and pale blue, and she is lying with her legs across him, her reading glasses on top of her head, and he is rubbing her feet, and they are listening to the radio.

He jumps out of bed, puts a jumper over his pyjamas, goes downstairs.

She is in the kitchen, on the sofa with Stuart. Such an amusing sight, this enormous hound snuggled up to and almost covering his owner.

Can you actually breathe under there? he says.

It's comforting, she says. He's so warm, and he smells really good.

Really?

317

He smells of Weetabix and lambswool.

I take it you can't sleep, he says.

No, she says.

He notices how she has tucked her pyjamas into her socks. Can I make you some tea? he says.

Yes please. As you can see, I can't really move.

No problem. I think I can remember where you keep it.

Cupboard on the far right, she says.

He boils the kettle. Rinses two cups. Empties a bag of dried fruit into the little blue teapot, switches on the radio, turns the volume down low.

I'm sorry, he says.

Why are you sorry?

I'm sorry things are so difficult for you.

Well, she says, what can you do.

Hmm, he says.

I was just thinking, before you came down, that all I want is to be on my own. I never thought I'd hear myself say that, she says, kissing Stuart on the head.

Obviously you'll take your boy, he says.

Obviously. And Belle if she wants to come.

He makes the tea, puts it on a tray.

I want a small place, she says, so I don't have to do much cleaning. And I want to put a framed photo of Andy somewhere. Because I never did that. I never got to walk past him, to say stupid things to his photo, to cry by myself.

Howard thinks about this, wonders if it's healthy.

Pot, kettle, he thinks. Honestly, who am I.

She is making plans already. He expected her to be in

shock, unable to think, too daunted by the prospect of dismantling a life. And maybe she is. Maybe this *is* Maria shocked and daunted.

He reminds himself that he doesn't know her, not really.

As soon as it's light outside, and while Howard and Ruth are asleep in their beds, Maria takes Stuart for a walk.

You're such a good boy, she says, touching his head.

On the beach, she removes her walking boots and socks, leaves them by the railing, rolls up her trousers and sets off towards the sea.

She wades in, the water is so cold.

Stuart is up close, staring quizzically at her feet.

It's all right, boy, she says.

She lifts her arms above her head, takes a deep breath in.

She imagines that this ocean contains the sorrow of every person, all the sorrow in the world.

She imagines a girl and a boy losing their mother.

A husband losing his wife.

She is standing knee-deep in other people's pain.

It's a relief. It softens her, makes it easier to move.

And when she turns round, she sees a woman further along the beach, also by herself.

She is dancing.

Maria steps out of the water, walks over to this woman.

Good morning, Maria says.

Good morning, Kate says.

42

This girl, this boy

And before they leave, he goes there.

Because someone has to.

He walks through town, towards the coastal path.

The view from up here is still beautiful, and it takes his breath, shocks him.

He expected the beauty to have gone, been destroyed.

He steps across the grass to the clifftop, to the exact spot where it happened.

It is awful. And yet somehow, not as awful as he imagined it would be.

The scene unfolding in front of him is no more vivid here than from his armchair, his sofa, his bed.

Hands deep in his pockets, he watches a family.

A man and a woman in their early thirties, with a boy and a girl.

The man and woman are deep in conversation.

The boy is walking just behind them, looking at the sea.

Out in front, the girl swirls and spins. They take no notice, they are clearly used to this, must see it all the time.

But today she is on a clifftop. The sun is in her eyes. The sea flickers with dappled light. This girl doesn't look at the landscape because she *is* the landscape, she is part of nature, just another wild thing, like the circling seabirds, the breeze, the sky. And she is unencumbered by thought or caution as she cartwheels and jumps into everything that is beautiful, that's what it feels like to be this girl right now.

Her mother begins to run. She is instinct, she is love, she is nothing else.

She reaches down. She can see her daughter on the ledge but it's way too far.

Beside her, father and son do not move.

And so she jumps. But she is not made for such things. This woman has many strengths, but physical agility is not one of them.

She lands badly, temple on slate.

There is a pool of blood by the girl's feet. Her white and green plimsolls, turning pink.

And she bleeds and she bleeds.

Men in bright uniforms, eventually arrive.

The man looks down at his wife and daughter. He is terror, he is shame, he is nothing else.

This shame will never leave him.

Shame on you, Howard Smith. You did absolutely nothing.

At her funeral, he reads notes scribbled on flashcards, makes a shoddy kind of speech.

Afterwards, he doesn't remember doing this. Doesn't

understand how he managed to speak fluently, sensibly, in front of a crowd. Not the garbled nonsense of pain.

Today, he has brought a bunch of flowers, because this is what people do.

Yellow roses.

He throws the flowers down onto the ledge.

Thinks what was the point of that.

He should have come here years ago, that's what's on his mind. And why didn't he, what was wrong with him.

He has neglected to do so many things.

As he turns round, his back to the sea, he remembers the needle-felted hare from his dream.

Were you never a boy, Mr Smith? it said.

And here on the grass, he is stock-still as he sees himself.

The years before Ila, the years before Sydney and Jason.

It's the story his children have never heard, the story of their father as a boy.

This boy would climb anything he could climb.

This boy would run and jump, always believing he could make it from here to there.

You worry me sick, his mother used to say,

to his grazed elbows, his muddy shorts,

his grass-stained knees.

43

Curious information

And when she is strong enough, when it feels like the right time, there is a lecture, one that Ila Smith would have been proud of were she alive to hear it, were she standing in her daughter's kitchen, watching her hop about on crutches as she tries to help with the stir-fry, the one Ruth is making without paying full attention, because this lecture has been a long time coming, she has practised and rehearsed it and wants to get it right.

I don't want to do this any more, Ruth is saying. I just don't. I never see you. You're always training or recovering from training. To everyone else, you're this amazing visual spectacle. But to me, you're barely visible.

She came up with these lines while staying with Maria, typed them into her phone, saved them for later.

And you could've died, Sydney. This time you really could have died.

I've explained, Sydney says. It was being in *that place*.

I know, but you're always in pain of some kind, always exhausted.

True, Sydney says.

And the thing is, Ruth says, while chopping vegetables. The thing is, other couples have a cup of tea in bed together in the mornings, are you aware of that? They don't all get up at dawn and go running.

Right, Sydney says.

And you just sort of accept the way a person is, you think it's fixed and unchangeable, but to be honest, I don't think the way you are is necessarily *who* you are.

Well this isn't really an issue any more is it, Sydney says.

Oh it will be, as soon as you're back on your feet again.

That's very optimistic.

Is it?

Anyway, I know what you're trying to say, Sydney says.

What am I trying to say.

You want to leave.

Ruth stops chopping, holds up the knife. What? Where did that come from?

Don't you?

I don't want to leave, you idiot. This is my life.

Seriously?

Yes. Why on earth do you think I want to leave?

I've been expecting it. For ages, actually.

Well that's news to me. Why didn't you say something?

It's not that easy.

Of course it is.

So you haven't been thinking of leaving, Sydney says. I mean, you haven't considered it.

No, I really haven't. You drive me insane, you can be

infuriating, and sometimes I wish I'd fallen in love with someone else instead, but no.

What curious information, Sydney thinks.

So what do you want? she says.

I want to *see* you, Ruth says. No need to look at me like I'm crazy. You and your father, you're as bad as each other, she says.

What do you mean?

You both have one foot in, one foot out. And I'm sick of it. None of us is getting any younger. And I've spoken to Jason about all this, he agrees with me.

Jason?

Yes.

I didn't know you spoke to Jason.

We spoke a lot when you were in hospital.

Oh.

Look, I want you to imagine something, Ruth says. Imagine what would happen if you took all the energy you put into freerunning and put it into work and our relationship. Imagine the characters, the books. Imagine how much we could finally do together. We could have a *normal* life.

Sydney takes the soy sauce out of the fridge, hands it to Ruth.

There is a possibility, she thinks, that Ruth has just asked her to imagine a place that she would eventually have arrived at by herself, in her own way, via her own convoluted route of mishaps and wrong turnings. And maybe, right now, considering how she has felt since the fall and returning home, her mind and body are already busy with the task of coming to this place, or at least testing it out – a new kind of normal. But now it has been forced upon her: *go there*. Which is only one way of looking at it, of course. Another: *join me*. And another: *I still want you*. She feels wanted and rejected at the same time.

Take some time to think this over, Ruth says. Then we'll talk again.

Sydney doesn't know what this means. There is only haziness now, neither good nor bad.

Then the sound of barking, coming from the back garden.

She hops over to the window, flicks on the outside light.

Otto is bouncing up and down the lawn like a rabbit, chasing Helen, the neighbour's cat. When he realises he can't possibly reach her, that her physical prowess is beyond him, he bounces about some more while barking continuously, as if to express his outrage, panic and failure, the fact of how he couldn't catch her, even in his most outlandish dreams.

Sydney watches Helen land on the roof of the garden shed in one glorious move.

Such effortless grace, she thinks, her nose touching the glass. Such strength and precision.

She watches Helen jump from the shed to the fence.

Watches her walk all the way along it as steadily as if she were walking on the ground.

Helen doesn't even glance at Otto. His protests can't touch her poise, her balance.

Now she crouches and steels herself before leaping high into the branches of a tree.

So capable, so light on her feet, Sydney thinks.

So autonomous and free.

44

The night we kissed in the park

He floats on his back in the floodlit pool, wonders what's taking her so long.

Which door are you behind, Ila?

The water feels colder than usual tonight, the floodlights dimmer, the sky more black than inky blue.

He swims up and down to warm himself up, then back to the edge, where he leans over the side, his chin resting on his arms, his arms resting on a mosaic tile, as he waits.

He sinks back down into the water, goes right under, comes back up. He peeks over the edge of the pool.

Who are you hiding from, Howard? There is no one inside these circles but you.

The circular swimming pool. The circle of mosaic tiles, blue and white. Then the yellow path, the orange mosaic tiles. And the steps leading up to an outer circle of changing booths. Ila's steps.

She is slow to join him tonight. He is impatient.

Ila, he calls. I'm here, I'm waiting.

He hears her voice behind him.

Hello my love, she says.

He spins round, confused. She is standing at the other side of the pool, all polka dot and smile.

Where has she come from? She always opens one of those pastel-coloured doors, always steps out of a changing booth.

He wonders what now, will he go to her or will she come to him, and what difference it makes, if any.

He sets off fast, swims towards her, underwater. He surfaces in the centre, the halfway point, neither here nor there, with or without her.

Her face, like an unopened letter.

He can't bear it, how beautiful she is and was and is.

Or how a good feeling is never a good feeling by itself. Even the most perfect moment contains a sadness, a loss.

Do you remember the night we kissed in the park? he says. That was the most perfect moment of my life.

Of course I remember, she says, stepping down into the water.

Why are you taking the steps? he says. You always dive over my head and you pause in mid-air and I look at you.

I don't know, she says. So what's with all the reminiscing. Don't I even get a hello?

Hello, Ila, he says, and kisses her.

Why that moment of all moments, she says.

The night we kissed in the park? he says.

Yes.

We'd been to the pub, do you remember. We were walking to the bus stop when you dragged me through that little opening in the hedge.

I seem to remember you pushing me against a tree, she says.

I think it was you who pushed me, he says.

Maybe, she says, smiling.

We hadn't moved in together yet, he says. We had everything ahead of us.

That's right, she says.

And they are silent for a moment. Treading water.

In the weekend paper they have a Q&A, he says. One of the questions is what was the best kiss of your life. Well that was mine. Every Saturday morning when I read the paper, I think of that kiss in the park.

That makes me sad, Howard, she says.

Don't be silly, he says. Anyway, that evening you were early. I walked into the pub and you were already there. You were sitting at a table, drinking cider and reading a book. I've tried so hard to remember the book.

Emily Dickinson, she says.

Really? I thought it was a crime novel.

No, it was definitely Emily Dickinson.

Well now I know, he says. We talked about children that night, how we both wanted children. I kept telling myself not to stare, not to be so intense. But the way you looked in that black jumper, the way it slipped off your shoulders.

It was raining, she says. It was February.

It was January, he says. It was freezing cold.

Talking of cold, she says, this water could be warmer.

I know, someone's taken their eye off the ball. I'll have a word when I leave.

Good, she says. Shall we swim?

And instead of the usual diameter or radius, she wants to swim the circumference. He follows her lead, swims behind her.

Warmer now? he says, as they float on their backs, star-shaped.

Much, she says.

Ila, he says. Did we ever –

What?

Did we disappoint each other? Did we argue, get bored?

Of course we did.

I can't access that, he says. And it's really unhelpful.

Access? she says. What a strange word. It makes me think of files on a computer.

You never used a computer.

I roll with the times.

Never a truer word spoken, he says.

She is looking at him now, looking down at the shifting shape of his body underwater.

I see you have new bathers, she says.

I do.

Navy blue, very sensible. I liked your red ones best.

I think I'm a bit old for bright red swimming shorts.

Since when?

His face turns serious. There's so much to talk about, he says.

I know, darling.

Sydney was in the hospital, he says.

She pushes her fringe back from her eyes, says I know, did you think I wouldn't go?

You were there? he says.

Of course, she says.

He glances down at the geometric drawings beneath their feet.

Oh, he says.

The photo you took of her, the one with Ruth and Maria, that was nice, she says.

How have you seen it? Have you been snooping around the house?

I like to look at what's on your noticeboard, she says.

So you didn't mind going there? he says. I mean, back to where you –

I go there a lot, she says, always have. She touches Howard's chin, lifts it back up, forces him to look her in the eye. I'm proud of you, she says.

Don't, he says.

And for what it's worth, I like Maria.

Maria? What's she got to do with anything?

I'm just saying I like her.

She's just a friend. Not even that really.

Well that's a shame, Ila says.

Howard doesn't want to talk about Maria any more. He doesn't like how this feels.

Anyway, he says, splashing her.

Hey, she says, splashing him back.

She disappears for a few seconds, then her legs shoot out of the water, perfectly straight. She is doing a handstand.

Show-off, he says to her legs, which are moving apart, making a V.

She is back now, and pleased with herself.

Still got it, she says.

She looks happier and younger.

Funny how an underwater handstand can take years off a person, he thinks.

And he splashes her again.

Then he grabs her, pulls her close.

Do you remember the night we kissed in the park? he says.

We had everything ahead of us, she says.

45

His truth, or something of it

A parcel arrives in the post, a long cardboard tube.

Howard pulls the plastic caps off both ends, holds the tube in front of his face and peers into it as if it were a telescope.

All he can see through the tube is his hallway. He shakes it about until a large cylinder of rolled-up paper begins to slide out, with a smaller one inside it.

Dear Howard,

I hope this letter finds you well. I think of you often, and wonder how you all are.

I'm writing because I wanted to send you something. I've been going to art classes, and I've finally plucked up the courage to send you one of my paintings. I hope you won't mind, and also, that you won't hate it! When you look at it, please be gentle and bear in mind I'm only a beginner.

It's so much fun, painting people. I'm in the middle of a portrait of Belle and Stuart, which I'm doing at Belle's allotment. We've bought a little camping stove,

*so we can make tea while she tends to the vegetables
and I paint.*

*I did a self-portrait too, which was surprising. In
this painting I'm a mechanic in overalls, covered in oil.
I'm tinkering with an engine, taking it apart, cleaning it
up. I'm not sure why really, but I think that maybe I'm
the mechanic and the engine.*

*Howard, I also wanted to say how sorry I am that I
haven't been in touch for a while. I needed to take
some time. I do hope you'll understand why.*

*I've just finished decorating the spare room in my
cottage. It's starting to feel like home now. If you'd like
to come and stay sometime you'd be very welcome, if
you can face coming back here again.*

*Well, I'd better stop now. I'm meeting Belle and
Dexter soon, to do the weirdest thing – they persuaded
me to join their Pilates class, and we do it in the sea, on
those stand-up paddleboard things. You should come
and watch, it'll make you laugh. I'm rubbish, but
Dexter is even worse.*

Call me if you'd like to, but no pressure.

With love,

Maria Norton

*PS I have a new radio, very hi-tech, I think you'd
like it. When I listen to it at night, I often wonder if
you are listening too.*

He smiles at how she has written her full name.

The painting sits beside him on the stairs. He unrolls it,
holds it flat on his lap.

He stares at the picture for a long time.

The man looking back at him is smiling. He looks tired. He has silver stubble and sad eyes, but this is not all. It's as if someone has just told him a joke, someone he likes very much, and the moment has almost passed but it's still here, reflected in this man's face. There is affection, silliness, the passing of time.

Somehow, without knowing Howard back then, Maria has captured something of his youth.

He squints, tries to work out what he means by this exactly. It's not that she has made him look younger, not at all.

Then he understands. This painting reminds him of old photographs, taken when he was young. It's as simple and complicated as that.

He knows this man and doesn't, remembers him and doesn't.

We always think it's other people we miss, rather than ourselves.

But Howard has missed this man.

He puts the painting down. It springs back into a cylinder.

He sits at the foot of the stairs, facing his front door.

The thought of another person, no of *her*, standing in front of a canvas for hours and hours, to find his likeness, to catch his truth, or something of it.

To catch *him*.

He thought she had forgotten all about him.

He leans forward, slow motion, curls into a boy, hugs his knees to his chest.

He imagines Maria asking if he liked the painting, and him saying I did thank you, I liked it very much.

And now he is on his fect.

He picks up the letter, reads it again from the start.

Newport Community
Learning & Libraries

AUTHOR'S NOTE

The St Ives in this book is a St Ives of the author's imagination. While it was inspired by St Ives in Cornwall, and based loosely upon it, the setting in this novel is fictitious.

DO NOT
FEED
THE BEAR

BONUS MATERIAL

A letter from Stuart the Irish wolfhound, followed by a Q&A
with Stuart and Otto

A letter from Rachel Elliott to the woman who became
Sydney Smith

A list of books that inspired the novel

Reading group topics

A letter from . . . Stuart the Irish wolfhound

Well I never, how strange life is.

One minute you're napping on a sofa, dreaming of long empty beaches, then you wake to the most curious thing. An author in your living room. In *Maria's* living room. The author of *Do Not Feed the Bear*, a novel I recently appeared in.

Hello again Stuart, Rachel Elliott said.

I could smell oranges, the colour blue.

She put her arms around me and hugged me for a long time. Then she stroked my head and looked into my eyes.

I have a favour to ask, she said.

Being a dog, I am always more likely to say yes than no. Dogs are affirmative creatures, we say *yes* to life, *yes* to play, *yes* to chasing the breeze on a windy day. But I am one of the cleverest, so I bartered. How will you make it worth my while? I said. For I could be out walking with Belle, up at the allotment with Maria, or simply sniffing the wonders of the world, all the leaves and rivers and songs, all the books and moments of kindness.

Rachel Elliott's offer was impossible to refuse. In return for a Q&A about *Do Not Feed the Bear*, she is taking me on holiday! Anywhere you like, she said.

I have chosen Dungeness. I have always wanted to visit Derek Jarman's garden.

Also, I have one condition, I said. Otto does the Q&A with me.

It's a deal, Rachel said.

See you in Dungeness, dear reader.

With a wolfhound's love and soulful optimism,

Stuart xx

Q&A

Stuart: Otto, you're here! How wonderful.

Otto: I am I am! I love you I love you.

S: Soppy old thing. How have you been? Steady on now, you'll bring down the ornaments.

O: I've been good I've been good! Tell me some marvellous things, go on.

S: (Please bear with us – Otto likes me to tell him marvellous things, it's something we do when we get together.) All right, here's a quick list: my humans are superstars, the sea smells amazing, Maria has been baking me home-made biscuits, utterly delicious, and did I tell you I have a new walking pal? Dexter from the bookshop. He likes to take me to the forest, says the air is so pure, he stands and listens to the trees, says it puts him in touch with his own wildness. On these walks we are two old romantics, human and hound.

O: I want to come to the forest!

S: I'll see what I can do, little man. Right, we'd better get to work.

O: Shall we begin by eating a salmon biscuit?

S: Work first, *then* we can eat. Ask me a question, go on.

O: All right. Why did Rachel choose to have a dog, namely you, speaking as a narrator?

S: Excellent choice of question, you're *such* a good boy. Well, dogs are the perfect narrators. We can smell a change of mood, a shift in the atmosphere. We are always watching, always listening. My superb skills in *Do Not Feed the Bear* are a magical extension of a dog's ordinary attentiveness. We smell it like it is. Life, I mean. So doesn't it make perfect sense to have a dog *telling* it like it is? All the loss in the air, the sadness emanating from human beings, not to mention the constant low-level panic and the effort it takes them to pretend it isn't there. The stench of human emotion, Otto. If only humans were more like dogs. If they could rise each day with nothing more in their hearts than the desire to love and eat and run, to worship the natural world and take regular naps.

O: Woof!

S: And, of course, there's the fact that Rachel is besotted with a miniature schnauzer called Henry. Like me, he has a soft grey head. But he has your size and stature. In fact, you are partly him.

O: Partly him? I thought I was just myself, like you are?

S: There are so many aspects to all of us, little man. Our author is obsessed with this too, as well as that dog.

O: Does this idea feed into the book?

S: Yes, in different ways. None of the characters are fixed, identity is a shifting thing. Take Dexter for example, who feels that gender is fluid, performative, socially constructed. And most of the characters are in flux, they find themselves disrupted.

O: Disrupted?

S: That's the word Rachel used. They have their ideas about themselves disrupted, all the narratives that run in a person's mind, often covertly, about who they are and what their lives should be like. A bit of disruption can be immensely helpful, and different people draw out different aspects of each other, but anything can disrupt: a person, a beach, a forest, an artwork, a dog. This is something Rachel loves to explore in fiction – the question of what makes change happen.

O: What *does* make change happen?

S: Well in this book, the big shifts begin when humans meet other humans who are deeply interested in them. The impact of this should never be underestimated. Look at Maria and Howard, they seem to understand each other, they have both experienced the loss of a great love, never quite realised how much they needed to talk about this in detail, but not just with anyone. They have been a bit frozen, or stuck. But in each other's company, they start to experience new, and maybe old, versions of themselves.

O: Woof woof!

S: Otto, focus. People often talk about the importance of location and place in novels. But relationships are also environments, which shape how we thrive or fail. As Howard says: *Things, and people, only flourish in the right environment.* And one of the joys of writing, Rachel says, is placing characters in new environments and seeing what happens. I remember her getting really excited about the idea of putting Sydney in front of a Mark Rothko painting, placing Belle and Ruth together on a beach, Howard and Maria in a cafe.

O: You make it sound like a game.

S: It's good to be playful in all areas of life, little man. But what we're talking about here, if we really strip it down, is making something of value from suffering.

346

O: Are we?

S: Yes. When it comes to human beings there's always conflict, trouble, a problem. And for Rachel, writing is a kind of listening, it's about tuning in to a person's experience, bringing some tenderness to it, trying to find the beauty or the humour. This is why kintsugi is mentioned. Do you remember that Ruth goes to kintsugi classes?

O: Of course. Our kitchen is full of old pots that she mended, their cracks painted gold, all part of their charm, Ruth says.

S: Exactly, and Ruth hasn't repaired those pots in a typical way, by trying to hide the cracks, she has carefully preserved the breakages, made them a feature of these objects. Rachel had been thinking about the method of kintsugi in written form – how you might depict, or paint, a person's breakages and hurts. She was working all the time with fault lines. Also, when Sydney's graphic memoir is complete, it will be a precious object, one that honours someone she has lost, brings her grief and guilt out into the open, and which contains a rupture that will always be part of her. This has much in common with the philosophy of kintsugi, because Sydney is making a wonderful piece of art from a place of fracture. Humans *are* their flaws and brokenness, their suffering and mistakes – so much of life is unresolved – but they are encouraged to hide these things, be ashamed of them, cover them up, move on. There's something freeing about the idea of honouring the mess.

O: I *love* mess.

S: Now is not the time to play, Otto. Put that toy rabbit down, we have a job to finish. Next question.

O: Okay, here's a good one. You used the word *honouring* just now. I heard Rachel use that word too, while talking about this book. Something about honouring the dead. How can a novel do that?

S: Good memory, curly boy. In this book the dead have a real presence, they are not just remembered. They are here, walking and talking, but they are not ghosts. This is because Rachel wanted to honour the fact that people who have died remain part of those who loved them; they have an ongoing impact on the living, there's an ongoing bond. Humans do not move on from grief, nor should they be expected to. Instead, in *Do Not Feed the Bear,* the characters keep going, put one foot in front of the other, try to rebuild their lives, which is a very different thing to moving on.

O: It's weird really, all this talk of sadness, and yet some parts of the book are very light-hearted, they made me laugh. Do you find your tail wagging when a person laughs? I do.

S: Always, it's involuntary, laughter is contagious. And humour is really important to Rachel. To be honest, I find her rather silly. But this is why her writing blends the tragic with the comic. Life is quite absurd, she says. And dark humour just seems to naturally evolve from the most difficult moments, it's a way of getting through. It's also one of life's joys – to laugh, see the funny side, not take yourself too seriously.

O: Should we say something about *how* Rachel writes? Practically, I mean.

S: Well, on a laptop, dear boy, preferably in the morning, that's her best time. Or she makes marks on paper in pencil. Current favourite pencil: a Palomino Blackwing Pearl.

O: There were so many diagrams, I found it very odd.

S: All those waves, circles, dots and lines all over the page. I liked them.

O: She also played Max Richter on repeat, I thought it would never stop.

S: Don't forget all the Dusty Springfield, Kate Bush and Leonard Cohen. She had a whole playlist of songs didn't she, music that suited each character, music for each scene, and as it grew the playlist became a world to step into – *our* world. Rachel and I agree that music is full of different textures and shapes, tastes and smells.

O: I was delighted when she bought those massive headphones.

S: Were you? I missed the music. I think I might love Kate Bush in a very intense way. Maria took me to see a choir the other day, they sang 'Running Up That Hill', I swear my hairs were all standing on end.

O: Sydney and Ruth have never taken *me* to see a choir. I've been to the cinema though, our local one has dog-friendly showings.

S: What were we talking about?

O: How Rachel wrote this book.

S: Oh yes. Well, there was a lot of walking, wasn't there. And for a while she became fixated with St Ives at night, all those late evening walks through the streets. Henry loved it. They took photos of a working artists' studio and gallery, all lit up at night. It was like looking at a theatre set and trying to imagine the play. There was something about the light in there, the fullness of an empty place, the work paused yet still going on.

O: I remember those photos, and the ones of Porthmeor Studios.

S: I really loved the painting she had on the desktop of her computer while writing this novel. It was called *The Blue Studio* by Wilhelmina Barns-Graham, who apparently was known as Willie. It was of an artist's studio overlooking the beach, the waves visible through the window.

O: I've got a friend called Willie. He's a Petit Basset Griffon Vendéen.

S: *Anyway*, writing is a visual process for Rachel. By the end, the room she wrote in was such a lovely mess, she was always printing out pictures: abstract paintings by Mark Rothko, sculptures and sketches by Barbara Hepworth, all those drawings of Henry Moore's hands, the photos of Cornish rocks. Oh, and that pesky postcard of a cat leaping through the air. But my favourites were by Dee Nickerson, all those beautiful paintings of people and dogs out in nature, walking on beaches, deep in thought or conversation – I could look at them all day. Maria has one in her bedroom now, I'll show you in a sec.

O: You've forgotten to mention all the photos of Irish wolfhounds and fox terriers. Now *those* were marvellous things.

S: Happy days, little man.

O: Happy days, Stuart.

A letter to . . . The woman who became
Sydney Smith

I was in London when I saw you.

In the hazy distance of a warm afternoon you were soft and quick and blue.

I was walking along the South Bank, not far from the Royal Festival Hall. There were many people walking, their feet on pathways, pacing sensibly through areas designated safe for human beings.

But not you.

You seemed to embody the season itself, all the new life, all the springing.

I watched you jump onto a wall, leap across to another wall, then down onto a railing.

It seemed impossible, more animal than human, pure instinct.

Then you were back on the wall, running along it.

You were artful, creative. You were strong and graceful and precise. A soft fragile body, dancing with the hard lines of a city.

I was in awe of how confident you were, how unselfconscious. It takes courage to believe that you can make it from here to there, again and again – to risk falling. You were something to admire, something to hold on to. You forged your own path, saw springboards where others saw obstacles.

Then, for a moment, you stopped. You looked down and noticed me watching. You held up your thumb, so I did the same.

We were two strangers on a Saturday afternoon, saying *I see you*, saying *yes*.

Whatever it was we were saying yes to, I took it home with me that day. And time passed, and I forgot all about you. Or so it seemed.

Until I went to St Ives. It was winter, the days were quiet and the weather was wild. I stood on Porthmeor Beach, enjoying the cold salty air, and the sense I just have on a windy beach that I am somehow letting go, somehow being reset.

I turned to face the Tate gallery. And there you were. Up on the roof, all dressed in blue.

It was *you*.

Only it wasn't.

I saw her wherever I went that week. She was running along the beaches, up on the roof of the cinema, the shops, even the fishermen's cottages.

She was shouting from the rooftops, shouting the odds, seeing if she was in with a shout of making me follow. Sydney Smith, the embodiment of a process you had begun.

Sydney's emerging story led me high and low, and I followed her gladly, but the starting point was you. The person who gave me a sign that said *everything is all right* on a springtime afternoon.

We can never know the effect we have on other people's lives.

You were a seed, a beginning, a gift. *Thank you.*

Maybe one day you'll walk into a bookshop and stumble upon this novel. Stranger things have happened.

With immense gratitude,

Rachel Elliott

Books that inspired this novel

These are a few of the books that spoke loudly, or quietly, to *Do Not Feed the Bear*:

Alison Bechdel, *Fun Home*

Alison Bechdel, *Are You My Mother?*

Chris Ware, *Building Stories*

Alexandra Horowitz, *Inside of a Dog*

Wendell Berry, *The Peace of Wild Things*

Anne Carson, *Autobiography of Red*

Mary Oliver, *House of Light*

John Berger, *Confabulations*

Matthew Gale & Chris Stephens, *Barbara Hepworth*

National Gallery of Art, Washington, *Mark Rothko*

Deborah Levy, *Hot Milk*

AM Homes, *Music for Torching*

Alfred Hayes, *In Love*

Patricia Highsmith, *Carol*

Reading group topics

1. When Sydney goes to St Ives, we can understand why she lies to Howard about where she is going, but why does she also lie to Ruth?

2. Time, memory, and how we experience the past are central themes of this book. In chapter 5 the author has written: *Time is an excellent example of a circle.* What do you think she means by this?

3. Why do you think Maria becomes fixated with Sydney, and invites Howard and Ruth, two complete strangers, to stay in her house?

4. Some people would have known that Ila was dead before they began reading the book. Others only found out in chapter 8. Do you think knowing a plot detail like this spoils the story, or makes little difference?

5. Howard feels that people are expected to move on from their grief, to 'get over it' in a certain amount of time. He feels judged for still loving and missing Ila, and isolated by this. Do you think he is right? Are we able to talk openly enough about death and bereavement, or are they still taboo subjects? Do we allow each other to express our grief in the way we might need to?

6. Maria and Jon are obviously unsuited and the marriage is an unhappy one for many reasons. Why do you think Maria chose Jon, and why did the relationship last so long?

7. Belle is sensible, mature, highly responsible. Yet every now and then, while out with Stuart, she shoplifts. Why do you think she does this?

8. In his relationship with Ruth, Howard has found a father-daughter relationship that feels simple and straightforward. Ruth has found an adoring father figure. Do you think this happens at the expense of Sydney's relationship with them both?

9. There are two lido scenes in this book, chapters 5 and 44. They are similar but have crucial differences. What do you feel these differences express?

10. Belle doesn't pay much attention to other people's opinions of her. So why does she listen to Ruth when this complete stranger questions whether she is really asexual?

11. One thing the author wanted to explore in this novel is the nature of family dynamics. The dynamic between Sydney and Howard is particularly complex. Towards the end of the book we discover that when he was a child, Howard was just like Sydney, always running and jumping. Yet when Sydney fell, it wasn't him who instinctively jumped to save her, it was Ila. Do you think the distance between Sydney and Howard is partly caused by his own guilt over this, and why has he never told her what he was like as a boy?

12. When Ruth tells Sydney she wants her to stop freerunning, Sydney's response is complicated. She feels wanted, because this plea pulls her close, and also rejected, because it fails to accept her as she is. How do you see this panning out? Do you think Sydney and Ruth will stay together?

You are invited to join us behind the scenes at Tinder Press

TINDER
PRESS

To meet our authors, browse our books
and discover exclusive content on our
blog visit us at

www.tinderpress.co.uk

For the latest news and views from the team
Follow us on Twitter

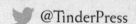 @TinderPress